BROAD

AWAKENING

By the Author

Underwater Vibes

Broad Awakening

Visit us at www.boldstrokesbooks.com

BROAD
AWAKENING

by

Mickey Brent

2018

ISBN 13: 978-1-63555-270-6

This Trade Paperback Original Is Published By
Bold Strokes Books, Inc.
P.O. Box 249
Valley Falls, NY 12185

First Edition: October 2018

CREDITS
Editors: Victoria Villasenor and Barbara Ann Wright
Production Design: Stacia Seaman
Cover Design by Melody Pond

Acknowledgments

This book would not have been possible without the encouragement of my family, friends, students, and writing buddies. You know who you are! Many thanks to my editor, Victoria Villasenor, whose explicit expertise on the craft of writing—and great humor—helped make this book what it is today. Thanks to Barbara Ann Wright for swift and efficient copy editing, Stacia Seaman for production design, and Melody Pond for the terrific book cover. I am especially grateful to Radclyffe, Sandy, Cindy, Carsen, Ruth, and my colleagues at Bold Strokes Books who are always working with incredible dedication and professionalism during the publishing process. Lastly, to my readers, thank you for choosing *Broad Awakening*. I hope you enjoy this fun and amorous sequel to *Underwater Vibes*.

To C, my family, and friends.
Your encouragement makes me want to keep on writing.

CHAPTER ONE

R ain fell in sheets over Hélène Dupont's face, licking her glasses in smeary streams as she pedaled aimlessly through the slick streets of Brussels. Like a dizzy mermaid, she made her way through rows of drenched cars, not caring about a thing. Not herself. And certainly not *her*. *I'm ruining my life.* She dragged her toe through a puddle. The midafternoon droplets slamming against her glasses reminded her of the day before, when she and Sylvie, her private swimming coach, had escaped to the Belgian coast for a secret dip in the ocean. The adventure had been on a whim, *une folie*; Hélène had let down her guard, allowing herself to be swept off her feet, literally, with waves crashing down on their half-naked bodies, their noses filled with the sea air's salty spray.

As Hélène pedaled furiously, she remembered how roused her heart had been, pounding hard under her wet T-shirt when Sylvie, the sexy Greek goddess, first wrapped her muscular arms around Hélène, sealing their embrace like sweet honey. Then, with the sun's rays highlighting Sylvie's glistening body, she had cupped Hélène's face in her hands and kissed her tenderly on the lips.

"I adore you too," Hélène had whispered, before taking a deep breath and kissing Sylvie back. The sensation of their hot, mingling tongues had made Hélène's heart pound even harder. Within seconds, their awkwardness had turned to tenderness, which blossomed into real passion.

Hélène shuddered at the all-too-fresh memory as she raced

her bike down the glossy, cobblestoned street. *What's wrong with me?* She searched the sky, but the response she was waiting for— some sort of explanation, anything at all—showed no signs of manifesting. So she wiped the sweat from her brow and pedaled on, feeling increasingly anxious. *How could this have happened? I'm forty years old. I'm married. And she's a woman...* She shook her head to clear her thoughts, causing droplets to leak from her helmet into her eyes. *What kind of straight woman kisses a woman? God knows I'm not the lesbian type. I must be bloody insane!*

Hélène rode down an empty street until she spotted a large pine tree. With a defeated sigh, she discarded her bike and plopped herself beneath the tree. Raindrops trickled onto her shoulders and helmet through the thick branches above; she shrugged them off. Seizing the tops of her waterlogged socks, she squeezed the cotton until water oozed into her boots. The chill of moisture flooding over her ankles made her giddy. *Je suis folle.* She snorted and did it again. *I must be nuts.*

Suddenly, streaks of lightning flashed across the dark clouds. Hélène ducked her head between her knees and squeezed her legs. Despite the hardness of her helmet, she had high hopes she'd attract an electrical shock. *Maybe this will crush the pain.* The squeezing reminded her of crushing lemons as a kid—making fresh lemonade with her grandma's old metallic lemon press.

After a few more thigh squeezes, Hélène admitted defeat. She wasn't a lemon, and the fruits of her efforts smarted her ears. Hot tears mingled with chilly raindrops slid down her cheeks. She gritted her teeth, trying to block the intensifying beat of her heart, synced to the rhythm of her sobs, like ancient African drums before an ambush.

She was so soaked she hadn't noticed she was sitting smack in a mud puddle. As her pants soaked in the pungent brown liquid around her, she experienced a sensory revelation: her chosen spot was probably where dogs congregated during their daily constitutionals. Forming tight fists, she glared upward. She had always wondered what it was like to hit rock bottom.

Now she knew.

"Is this a midlife crisis or what?" Hélène glared at the menacing sky. Yanking off her steamy lenses, she squinted at the mass of blurry clouds.

"*Alors*, is it?" The response—a rumble of thunder, followed by a crack of lightning—confirmed her supposition. She took a deep breath. *I can deal with this.*

But inside, it hurt too much. *Who am I kidding? I can't deal with this right now. Why can't I just rid my mind and body of all feeling and go numb? Why can't I turn myself into a tree...or a flower? Why can't everyone just leave me alone?*

She glanced at the glistening leaves swaying in the wind. *The bushes are waving at me. Is it the storm that's wreaking havoc? Or me? How open-minded am I anyway?* She squinted at the fuzzy yellow heads poking through the puddle her derrière was soaking in.

"You nasty little critters!" she shrieked, groping at the daisies. With their stems between her fingers, she ripped the flowers from their muddy roots. "You've no right to live in this beastly world."

She shook the stems, draining them of vitality. When the feeble beings wilted in her palms, she felt better instantly. This sadistic act numbed her pain—at least for the time being.

Flinging the lifeless flowers over her shoulder, Hélène suppressed a cocky smile. *So now I know what it feels like to be a murderer*, she thought. *What dreadful thing will happen next?*

Just then, she heard a shriek. *Mon Dieu, those blossoms were still alive!*

Hélène cringed with horror.

"Are you completely mad?" erupted a shrill voice behind her. Hélène swiveled around, displacing her buttocks firmly planted in the mud. The voice came from an elderly woman leaning diagonally on a wooden cane, two paces behind her. Apparently, the muddy blooms had torpedoed her oversized, floppy pink hat, which now lay over the woman's soiled rain boots, exposing a mound of gray hair bunched atop her head. A few lifeless, green stalks trailed down the front of her powdery pink rain jacket. With her jaw set, the elderly woman's light blue eyes were aflame.

"*Désolée, Madame.* I didn't mean to hit you," mumbled Hélène, looking away from the offending flowers.

The old woman seemed to detect suffering in Hélène's feeble voice; she locked eyes with Hélène and stated matter-of-factly, "You're experiencing quite a nasty day, *n'est-ce-pas, ma chérie?*" Hélène nodded while lifting her chin as a rush of tears flooded her eyes. *How does she know how much I'm suffering? It's like she can read my soul.*

"Follow me." The elderly woman in powdery pink rain gear extended a withered, bony hand and, to Hélène's bewilderment, swiftly pulled Hélène to her feet.

Following the elderly stranger like an obedient pooch, Hélène pushed her bike in silence, except for the simultaneous squish, squish, squish of their rain boots mingled with the plop, plop, plop of a puddle-piercing cane. Muddy droplets cascaded off the old woman's floppy pink hat as the rain relentlessly spat down on them.

After two blocks, the old woman stopped in front of a tiny brick house. It was quaint, with pale-pink awnings, and was graced with a small yet lush garden bursting with greenery: pines, palms, bamboos, bushes, hanging plants, and rows upon rows of pink and yellow roses. A wrought iron bench sat strategically in the midst of the lawn, facing the flower bed. Hélène drew an appreciative breath. On sunny days, so rare in Belgium, this miniature garden would likely be a delight for the elderly woman to spend her leisurely afternoons.

"*Entrez.*" She opened the front door with an old iron key. She settled herself on a metallic bench inside the entryway, slid off her pink boots, and motioned for Hélène to do the same. She hung Hélène's dripping coat on a wooden peg next to hers.

"Tea." It was more of an order than a question.

Hélène nodded. It wasn't a habit of hers to enter a stranger's house—even less likely since she didn't know her name—but this elderly woman didn't seem like a dangerous breed. Quite the contrary. She seemed to draw Hélène toward her like a magic wand. Hélène glanced one more time at the delicate garden before the old woman shut the front door. *Anyone who can care so lovingly for a garden like that must have a generous heart.*

When they entered her tiny kitchen, the woman put a thick towel on a wicker chair for Hélène to sit on and gave her a smaller pink one to wrap her wet hair in. Humming a pleasant tune as if she were alone, she swiftly lit a match. Soon, her iron kettle was boiling. Hélène simply sat on the muddy towel, soaking in the peace that reigned in the homey kitchen.

Still humming, she prepared a tray with a steaming pot of tea; two pink, earthenware mugs; a pot of honey; and two silver spoons and motioned for her guest to follow her with the tray. Hélène acquiesced, glad to not have to think about anything on her own.

"*S'il vous plaît*, set it there." The woman motioned to an old coffee table before she lowered herself into her chair. She handed Hélène another soft towel. They sat in a dim, yet cozy room decorated with a womanly touch. On the table, a dainty metallic lamp separated them. When the woman flicked the lamp switch, a soothing light warmed the room.

Hélène first noticed the outdated, flower-papered wall, then a couch draped with a hand-knitted bedspread and round, pastel pillows. Above the couch was a small corner window with half-closed violet curtains overlooking the street. Hélène felt the coziness of the room as she wrapped her fingers around her hot mug of tea. Her mood lifted. *This is so quaint and so unexpected. What would it be like to live in a place like this? To be as old as her living alone?*

Abruptly, the elderly woman stopped humming. "Hilde."

Hélène's eyes darted back to her hostess and focused on the gray bun perched atop her head. Smiling politely, she cleared her throat. "Almost. It's Hélène."

"*Non*, I'm Hilde." The elderly woman nodded with a gentle smile. "*Enchantée.*"

Hélène blushed at her mistake. "Nice to meet you too. I'm Hélène."

They sat facing each other for a few quiet moments, sipping their herbal tea with honey. Instead of feeling awkward, Hélène noticed how at ease she felt in this elderly woman's house, in this barely lit, tiny room. She wrinkled her nose. Here she was, sitting with muddy, soggy pants on the woman's thick towel, with her wet hair piled atop her head. *She doesn't seem to care that I'm probably ruining her chair. It's like I'm in a movie. Some sort of bizarre documentary.* She hugged her earthenware mug to her chest. She should've been at work. But she didn't care.

I wonder why I don't care? As she glanced around the room again, a tingle shot up her neck. *I have the strangest feeling I should be here.* Her hands went to her cheeks. At last, they were warm.

"Having one heck of a nasty day, weren't you, *ma chérie?*"

Hélène nodded, still conscious of the tingle.

"No more worries. Hilde is here to help you." The older woman's face crinkled into a grin. "Have you ever met a psychic?"

"A psychic?" Hélène stared at the woman sitting across from her to see if she was joking. *She seems serious. Where did this come from?* Hélène was taken aback but not entirely surprised. *She has a slight accent. Must be Flemish. With a name like Hilde...* She scratched her chin. *Maybe I didn't hear her right. I hope she's—*

"You heard me all right."

With this, Hélène leaned way back in her chair. Her neck was tingling again. *Can she really read my thoughts?*

"Yes, I can." Hilde nodded so hard, her gray bun nearly toppled over. Then her wrinkled lips formed a genuine smile. "Welcome to my humble abode, *ma chérie*. Ours wasn't a chance meeting."

Hélène gulped. "It wasn't?" She glanced at her forearm. The tiny blond hairs stood upright.

"*Mais non.* You were in a most tormented state when I found you, *n'est-ce pas?*"

"I've had better days."

Hilde nodded again, with her light blue eyes piercing Hélène's.

"You certainly have. You were at rock bottom." She paused. "You were in so deep, you were even contemplating murd—"

"No, I wasn't!" Hélène jumped up so fast her towel upset the tea tray. Hilde's bony hand shot out to steady it.

"Sit down, *chérie*. You're just upset. I'm here to help." Hilde's tone was soothing. "Besides, it's raining cats and dogs outside. You don't want to go out in that."

Hélène glanced out the small corner window. Sure enough, rain was hammering the glass like a mob of angry protesters with sticks. She settled back in her chair with an apologetic grimace. "I'm sorry. It's just...I'm not used to going to strangers' houses for tea." Her shaking hand tucked a few loose strands of wet hair behind her ear.

"Of course you're not. But I'm not a stranger." Leaning forward, Hilde peered deeply at her.

The motherly warmth radiating from the elderly woman's soul had a soothing effect on Hélène. Her shoulders relaxed. *She's probably somebody's grandma anyway. What harm can she possibly do?*

Smiling timidly at her hostess, Hélène snuck another discreet peek around the dimly lit room. Dozens of religious icons of various persuasions adorned the faded, flowery walls. Hélène saw Buddhist, Christian, Hindu, Jewish, and Islamic symbols. Even though she wasn't familiar with all the others, it was clear that Hilde was some sort of spiritual connoisseur.

Hélène felt the tingle return. *Maybe she's just a quack. In any case, she sure is different from most grandmas.* She downed her lukewarm tea.

"So, what do you want to know?" asked her hostess solemnly.

Hélène nearly choked. "About me?"

"About you."

Is she pulling my leg? Hélène's nostrils flared in defiance. *Let's see how far she's going to take this.* "Are you trying to tell me you know things about me that I don't even know?"

Hilde retorted with a measured answer. "Let's see...How open-minded are you?"

That's ironic. Hélène set down her empty cup. *I've been wondering the same thing lately.* "Not very. Until now." *What do I have to lose anyway?*

Before she could stop herself, she blurted, "So, if you really are a psychic, Hilde, tell me something interesting about my future."

The elderly woman closed her eyes. "I will need a few moments of silence to connect."

Hélène sat patiently, listening to Hilde's deep breathing, which sounded more like a throaty rattle than a series of breaths. Through the diffused light of the tiny table lamp, she studied the crinkles at the corners of Hilde's eyes and the deep creases in her pale cheeks. Her lips, faintly lined at their upper edges, were still well defined and generous. *She must've been stunning when she was younger.*

With nothing else to think about, Hélène's palms soon grew sweaty with nervousness. *I wonder where she's connecting to?* Empty seconds ticked louder in Hélène's mind.

Just when Hélène was about to bolt from the table, Hilde's eyes popped open.

She began to speak in a clipped, direct fashion, which accentuated her Flemish accent. "I see light. Then I see darkness. Then I see light." As she spoke, the lamplight between them flickered.

Mon Dieu! A shiver raced down Hélène's spine. She opened her mouth to say something, but Hilde put her finger to her lips and uttered a forceful *shh.* She continued speaking as if this flickering light were a normal occurrence—as normal as spreading butter on toast. "I see an angry man. A very angry man."

Despite the warmth in the room, Hélène shivered. *She's right about that. How does she know Marc?*

"He is yelling. There is a lot of fighting. I see a young boy. They leave. Never to return."

A young boy? They leave? Hélène gulped. "Excuse me, but what young boy? Who is he?"

Hilde squinted at her. "You tell me."

I don't know any young boy. Marc doesn't want any kids. He's made that quite clear. "I don't know," stammered Hélène, fighting the sudden tightness in her chest. "I don't have a son."

Hilde closed her eyes again—causing Hélène's chest to nearly explode with impatience—until the elderly woman's lids popped up. "Your brother," she declared gravely.

Quoi? I got all worked up over nothing. Hélène stifled a laugh. *This is a bunch of crap.* "I don't have a brother."

"Yes, you do."

Hélène studied Hilde's wrinkled face. The lamplight flickered again. Hélène's knees jumped. *Enfin, she's serious. But how could I? When Papa...* Hilde's words resonated in her mind, prompting her to consider other possibilities. *Mon Dieu. That angry man must be Papa. Do I have a brother?*

Hélène crossed her arms defensively. "Where is he? How old is he? What's his name?"

"It seems that he's your older brother. You were born to protect him," stated Hilde matter-of-factly.

Hélène clenched her fists. *So, I have a brother and a father who might be alive? Why didn't Maman tell me this?* She felt the anger rising in her throat. "Tell me. Where did they go?"

Hilde closed her eyes to contemplate the question.

"I see light. Then I see darkness. Then I see light." Once again, the lamplight between the two women flickered. Hélène gripped her chair, fearing the obscure secrets about her life that would soon roll off this psychic lady's tongue.

Hilde leaned forward. "You were a Catholic nun in a former life."

Hélène instantly relaxed, chuckling at the idea. A vivid image popped into her head. There she stood, every night at bedtime in her decades-old, trusty flannel nightgown laced with a scratchy neckline, yawning before Marc, her husband.

So that explains why I've never been very excited about sex.

"Let's see," continued Hilde, ignoring Hélène's suppressed chuckle. "It was during the time of St. Francis. You were an extremely studious, very religious nun."

"That's exciting and all, but let's get back to this life, *d'accord*?" Hélène knew she was being rude, but she couldn't help herself. "Where are my brother and father?"

"Patience, *ma petite*. I'll see what I can find out." Hilde placed her pale hand over Hélène's tapping fingers. After a minute, she began: "I see a tall, dark person." The crinkles in her mouth lifted. "He is most attractive, with lots of passion in his eyes. He is athletic, with a muscular body and a prominent nose. He is reaching out for you, Hélène."

Hélène's heart started beating faster. She wiped her clammy hands on her pants.

"You are in a bright living room with wide windows across the wall. It's an apartment on an upper floor with trees outside. You are sitting on the sofa. There's a cat at your feet, watching you. You are waiting for a drink…A cocktail. Music is playing; there's a large bookshelf full of interesting literature, and several photos are on the wall."

Hélène tried to imagine the apartment. Everything seemed foreign to her, especially the photos. She raked her mind. *Who do I know who has photos on their wall?*

"He is approaching the sofa. He hands you a cocktail and sits down next to you."

Hélène felt the sweat break out behind her neck.

"He looks into your eyes. He has a most attractive face."

"No mustache, right?" asked Hélène, conjuring up Marc's face. *He's so proud of that dreadful thing. Too bad he's the only one on Earth who finds it attractive.*

Hilde closed her eyes again. Then she shook her head. "*Non.* No trace of a mustache. But he has a strong nose, with dark, glistening eyes."

Hélène sighed with relief. *I knew it wasn't Marc. She's talking about my brother.* Feelings of joy flooded her heart. *I've got a brother. I can't believe I have an older brother.*

Suddenly, Hilde stiffened. "Wait. *Mon Dieu!* He is putting his lips on yours."

My brother? Hélène's heart jumped. *This is insane!* "Who the heck is he?"

Hilde sucked her breath through her dentures, creating a high-pitched whistle. "I'm not sure how to tell you this, *ma petite*, but this dark, handsome person kissing you is actually..."

Hélène watched Hilde's expression as her voice trailed off, and a flash of unease swept over her wrinkly face. She shifted in her chair. *What's she seeing?*

Hilde's eyes popped open. She pursed her lips as her gaze fell on Hélène's silver wedding band.

What's wrong? Wringing her hands, Hélène asked, "Who is it?"

"A woman."

After her impromptu visit with the peculiar old woman, Hélène found herself once again squinting through water-streaked glasses while zigzagging through torrents of unyielding rain.

At last, she threw open her front door, flooding the hall with muddy rainwater as she squeezed Chaussette, her trusty pet, to her chest. The black-and-white cat meowed loudly.

"*Salut, mon lapin!* Sorry I'm a bit soggy." Hélène planted a sloppy kiss on her kitty's head. Hoisting the petite animal under her armpit like a load of chopped wood, Hélène hobbled up the stairs toward the bathroom, leaving mucky bootprints in her wake.

"*Voilà!* This should do the trick," exclaimed Hélène, facing the large, porcelain tub and turning on the bath water. She sat on the edge of the tub and yanked off her muddy boots. Next, she removed her wet woolen socks. *This is better.* Perched on the cool porcelain like a curious rabbit, she sniffed at the sterile bathroom walls. Sure enough, it was the same bathroom she had shared with Marc for twenty years. But today, it seemed different. More spacious. Less sterile. The tiny hairs stood up on her neck. *I feel different too.*

Her eye caught a bottle of cheap bubble bath a colleague had given her for her birthday years before. "Let's throw in some of this." She hadn't found a good occasion to use the bubble bath—until now. Chortling with unexpected feelings of liberation, she held up the blue bottle, which was shaped like a curvaceous, nude woman.

If I'm hitting a midlife crisis, a bubble bath seems like a brilliant way to start!

This thought seemed even more out of character since she had never considered herself a bath-taking kind of gal. Hot water soaks characterized a glorious waste of time, water, and money. Her best friends, Cecile and Mathilde, had given up trying to convince her that baths would do wonders to soothe her nerves and boost her self-care habits. Yet she consistently ignored their advice, considering baths just another excuse to promote a hedonistic lifestyle. Even though she was a scientific translator by profession, she had written a savory report for one of her translation courses entitled: "Bubble baths: the epitome of frivolous behavior."

Hélène had always proudly avoided all forms of self-indulgence with two exceptions: Chaussette, her cuddly cat, and her weekly drug: fresh-cut flowers.

But this afternoon was not normal. She had just learned deep secrets about her family from a psychic. *I need to let this information soak in. Might as well do it in style.*

With a naughty grin, Hélène brought the curvaceous, nude female filled with blue bubble bath liquid to her mouth. After uncorking the bottle with her teeth, she pointed the woman's blue buttocks in the air. "Bottoms up!"

She dumped the contents of the entire bottle into the tub. Then she switched on the radio. Mozart's "Overture from The Marriage of Figaro" swept into the bathroom.

"Be right back," she informed her cat before racing down the stairs. Seconds later, she returned out-of-breath with an ice-cold beer. While Chaussette sat watching on the edge of the bathtub, Hélène flung her soaked garments at the steamy mirror.

Hélène giggled when lightning flashed through the skylight while sheets of rain pounded on the curved window; Mozart's composition—with its swiftly changing moods—blended with the forces of nature to create the perfect setting for her clandestine afternoon soak.

Covered in tufts of steam, Hélène eased her limbs into the bathtub. Within seconds, an army of bubbles attacked her curvaceous body. Her feet, perched on the edge of the porcelain tub, escaped the scalding water. With her toes wiggling in delight, she reached for the cool beer. Grasping the bottle like a thirsty baby, she brought the suds to her mouth. Yeasty beer smells filled her nostrils.

"Santé!" she exclaimed, cocking back her head as the fizzy brew slid down her throat. Grinning, she lifted Marc's one-liter bottle and took another hefty swig.

A few minutes later, she contemplated her soggy clothes littering the floor. Her tidy bathroom had become a stage, which was most uncanny, for Hélène didn't even like the theater. She had never understood how grown people could pay good money to watch other grown people parade around in costumes, pretending they were someone else. And here she was turning into a drama queen in her own house. *Bizarre.* How did she get here? Why on earth was she taking the lead in this quirky, melodramatic play?

To figure it all out, Hélène took another long gulp of beer and, bottle lodged between her lips, slid her body under the soapsuds. She remained underwater for a few seconds, watching tiny bubbles float up. As soon as her lungs could no longer take it, she spat out a stream of foamy water and sat up.

"Come to *Maman.*" She extended her arms to Chaussette. But the cat—paws gripping the tub's edge—refused to budge.

"Are you afraid of me, *bébé?*" asked Hélène with a feigned pout.

Wide-eyed, Chaussette twitched her whiskers.

"Eh bien, I don't blame you." Hélène took another sip. "You know I never do this…Guzzling Papa's beer, playing hooky in the tub. *Tiens,* this stuff ain't half-bad. Wanna try?"

Hélène stuck the bottle under Chaussette's nose. The cat sniffed, then licked the tip of the bottle. She wiggled her furry head and sneezed.

"Not your cup of tea? *Tant pis!* Too bad, more for me." Hélène polished off the amber liquid with a grin.

When the bathwater became lukewarm and the suds turned thin, Hélène frowned at her pale, puckered fingers. *I'm bored.* She spotted a pink sponge. *Might as well do something constructive.* She began scrubbing her soft skin. Once she reached her chest, however, she released the sponge. Leaning back, she blew air kisses at the tips of her nipples floating between the tiny bubbles.

That beer is working wonders! The alcohol had miraculously stifled the raging storm outside while numbing the chaos tormenting her mind. "*Ploup...ploup...ploup.* Down you go!" She poked the pink tips of her nipples. But the little buttons refused to drown. Each time they resurfaced, she poked them down. When they came up for the fifth time, she slurred, "*Attention...C'est* JAWS!" Roaring like an infant, she splashed water at her breasts. Then she changed tactics: instead of poking, she pinched a nipple. Pain mixed with pleasure swept through Hélène's body. She pinched the other nipple, then caressed it in little round movements. Instantly, her entire body was aroused. Her erect nipples transformed into tiny antennas. Hélène had never realized how sensual her body could become by simply caressing her breasts—something she had never dreamed of doing, since, of course, she was married. Marital sex was her only option—or so she had thought. And it wasn't something she even liked. Not in the slightest.

Ever since she had been an adolescent, Hélène had concluded that her body was different from others'. She was convinced that when God created her, he had forgotten to equip her with the necessary components of a sexual being. When she listened to her friends' experiences, her machinery seemed to be lacking an essential part. *So, I function in safety mode. At least I still function,* she had rationalized. *Why try to fix something when it still works?* She had never admitted to her friends that she had never felt anything even remotely close to an orgasm. Ever since her wedding day, she had feigned satisfaction with her sex life with Marc. It was easy; she had already convinced herself of this fantasy. But who was she really kidding?

It was embarrassing to admit, but she had never even been slightly curious—and certainly not envious—of women who took pleasure in describing their erotic escapades and erogenous sensations. That kind of discourse had always bored Hélène. Besides, "masturbation is a sin," her Catholic teachers had always insisted. And she had believed their repertoire of stale theories—until now. Feeling the buzz in her head, she studied her erect, pink nipples.

I wonder. Do nuns ever take baths?

She lay shivering in the tepid water, contemplating the idea. Her thoughts returned to her unexpected afternoon visit with Hilde.

So, I was a super pious Sister. That's bizarre. I've never felt compelled to go to church. At least, not in this life. Maman always said that... The tiny hairs on Hélène's submerged arms bristled at the thought of her deceased mother. *Why didn't Maman tell me I had an older brother? And a father who's alive? If this is true, where are they? And what about Hilde's last words? That kiss?* Hélène gulped. *With a woman?*

She caught her breath as her gaze fell on the empty bottle of bubble bath. She studied the nude woman's sensual glass curves. Hélène's mind drifted back to the wet, passionate kisses with Sylvie the night before as the two swam in the ocean waves. She licked her tender lips, relieved at how the beer buzz seemed to numb her guilt. At the same time, she felt new stirrings erupting from down below, but she would have to pursue further erotic aquatic explorations some other time. After such an odd afternoon—with her mind marinating in a full liter of beer and Chaussette staring down at her with inquisitive eyes—Hélène was too pooped to party.

CHAPTER TWO

The familiar sounds of screeching gravel woke Hélène with a start. When she realized it was Marc's latest Ferrari stopping a mere half centimeter from the garage door, like every evening, she felt her usual sensation of dread. She cringed, knowing that when her husband entered the house, like clockwork, he would drop his heavy sports bag, slip off his sneakers, and fumble with the wall switch until the lights came on. She imagined him sniffing the air to detect signs of dinner, then checking his watch impatiently. She knew he would sigh, then cross the hall and burst into the kitchen.

"Hélène?"

She heard him holler into the dark kitchen. *He's so impatient. Only a matter of seconds now.* She shut her eyes tight as she heard him racing up the stairs three at a time. When he flung open the door to their bedroom, she tried not to jump.

He gasped, "*Quoi?*" and switched on the light.

This is kind of fun. Hélène imagined the scene as if she were watching her life on a movie screen: Her husband runs into the room to find an oblong lump protruding from under the bedcovers. He sees her curled up like a cat, sound asleep, the edges of her lips lifted in a smile. A black-and-white bundle of fur lays on the pillow next to her blond head.

A groggy thought seeped into her mind. *Hope he's in a good mood today.*

"*Mon Dieu!* What the heck is wrong with you?" Marc shook

her shoulder. The bundle of fur flew off the pillow, scrambling under their matrimonial bed.

Hélène's smile faded as she struggled to open her eyes; despite her efforts, her lids made it only halfway up. And when she tried to lift her head, it felt waterlogged. Swiftly, it dropped back onto the pillow.

"Mmm…" she mumbled, squinting at Marc. But as soon as she recognized his scowl, she squeezed her lids shut.

"Hélène, what the hell?"

She jacked up one eyelid while straining to perceive the tiniest hint of empathy from her husband. As usual, his hard eyes and gruff voice betrayed his most valued interests. She knew he cared more about his empty stomach than her health. Still groggy, she licked her teeth to buy some time. When she did this, her parched tongue, dislodged from the roof of her mouth, made an abrupt clicking noise.

Marc crossed his arms. "Answer me. What the hell is going on?"

What happened this afternoon? Hélène wondered, panicking. *Enfin…I remember biking in a thunderstorm, soaking in a puddle, Mozart, a bubble bath, beer, and nipp—*

Stifling a grin, she turned to avoid Marc's face, growing redder by the minute.

"Hélène!" he bellowed in her ear. "What the…Explain yourself."

Hélène winced into her pillow. Confusion took over as she searched for a plausible answer. She had always prided herself on her honesty—a quality she admired in others. And up to now, she had always told Marc the truth.

But today was different. As her mind slipped back to the afternoon's events and especially those of yesterday, when she was at the beach with Sylvie, warning flares shot up. *I'll just skirt some of the details.* Besides, her head was spinning. At this point, she wasn't even sure if this was all really happening. *Maybe I'm still in a dream?*

She squinted again at Marc to see if he was real. Without her glasses, his face was fuzzy, but she could still feel his beady eyes boring into hers, hardening with rage. How she hated the way his beak-like nose flared when he got upset. He was the falcon; she was the prey.

He's real, all right. So now what?

In a burst of inspiration, Hélène nestled her nostrils in the crease of her elbow and took a whiff. Her skin—soft and squeaky clean as a baby's—smelled like cheap bubblegum. She stifled a snort of triumph. That was all she needed to explain her story.

"I wasn't feeling well, so...I took a bath and went to bed." Now fully awake, Hélène sat up. The covers fell away from her bare chest. "*Mince!*" She yanked them over her breasts.

"*M'enfin*, you're naked!" gasped Marc.

"Glad you noticed, *chéri.*" Hélène winked.

"What the..."

"I'm not used to taking baths, you know, and the bath water made me so hot, I—"

"Never mind," said Marc. "So, now that you're feeling better and you've had your little nap, it's dinner time." He thrust Hélène's bathrobe at her.

"Actually, I was thinking..." she began. "Why don't we go out tonight?" But as soon as she asked, she grimaced.

"You just said you were sick."

"Hmm. Guess it's my lucky day. I'm fine now."

Marc's eyes narrowed. "You know I can't stand eating out. Reminds me of all those business trips, remember? How sick I was of—"

"*S'il te plaît?* Just this once? We never go out. Besides, I'd be happy to pay for—"

"You know it has nothing to do with money. We're not going out." Marc pulled his sweat jacket over his head and stormed toward the bathroom. "Conversation's over."

Hélène watched his lanky silhouette in the doorway as he flung the jacket away. *Voilà.* She clicked her tongue. *On the floor. When is he going to learn?*

"What the...*Attends*, did you have one of my beers?"

His surprise made her laugh. "*Ouais.* It was pretty good, too. But Chaussette didn't care for it, *n'est-ce pas, chérie?*" She caressed her kitty's little chin.

Marc marched over to the bed with the empty bottle. "Since when do you drink beer?"

"*Eh bien...*" Hélène's eyes lit up. "Since today." Her cheeks flushed at a naughty idea. "*Tiens,* why don't you join me? It's kind of chilly under here." Hoisting up the covers, she flashed her husband a preview of her recently refurbished, fully naked body. At last—after dieting and working out like a maniac—she was proud to share the fruit of her efforts with someone. *And the logical choice would be my husband,* she reasoned with her hangover-induced buzz, rather than her heart. They hadn't been sexually romantic in a long time, which was fine with her. Because of the feelings Sylvie had awakened in her, she knew deep down she deserved more than being treated like a mere appendage. Yet she still had an intense desire to be wanted.

Her mind flashed back to Sylvie's gorgeous face. When they had finally separated at the pool after an unforgettable afternoon at the beach, her heart had ached with longing. Only yesterday, she couldn't wait to see Sylvie again so she could kiss her sensuous lips, taste her tongue again, touch her silky dark hair, be squeezed by her strong, swimmer's arms, and spend the rest of her life with her.

Yet today, she had woken with a heavy heart, filled with terrible guilt and regret. She was afraid to contact Sylvie. To make things worse, now she was literally throwing herself at her husband. What had happened to her in only twenty-four hours? She felt nauseous.

Grabbing the covers and pulling them against herself, Hélène rolled over. She squeezed her legs to her chest to lock in the warmth instinctively rising between her thighs.

Then she realized the gravity of her situation: she was lying naked before her husband, and she'd just made an offer.

Guess I better get this over with. She turned around to face him. To her relief, Marc gawked at her as if she were a wild ape in the zoo. Finally, he shook his head. "Some other time. I'm starving.

Viens. You're going to catch pneumonia like that." She almost laughed when he held up her bathrobe again and ordered, "Put this on."

Hélène waited until the shower was running before she slipped out of the sheets. Then she tiptoed over to an ancient oak closet, pulled on a fresh pair of black jeans and a white T-shirt, and reached for one of her worn sweaters. As she fingered the heavy wool, a knot formed in her throat. She brought the sweater to her nose. *This thing's got to be thirty years old.* Its roughness tickled her upper lip; its worn wool smelled of old rain and Chaussette. Her eyes watered with emotions from the past—all those times she had worn that sweater and thought she was happy. Feelings of sadness were somehow woven into the gray yarn, piercing her soul.

The knot in her throat swelled. She felt an urge to let out a wild animal cry from the recesses of her belly. Instead, she sniffled. *Forget the past.* She thrust the old sweater back into the drawer and stood before her closet, contemplating what to wear. She settled on a brand new, cherry-colored sweater. Donning the soft, fuzzy garment, she smiled at her reflection in the mirror. *This stretchy material does wonders to my breasts. Quite uplifting.*

Just as Hélène made her way toward the stairs, Marc, wrapped in a fluffy beige towel, intercepted her. "What's with the sweater? And aren't those new glasses?"

Unable to meet his disapproving stare, Hélène's eyes lingered on her husband's bare chest. She opened her mouth to speak, but Marc held up his hand. "Shh." He hissed through his teeth, glaring at her breasts. "I get it. New diet. New clothes. New glasses. Why don't you shop for a new husband while you're at it?"

He stomped away, and the bedroom door slammed behind him. Standing in the darkness above the stairs, Hélène listened to the creaking floorboards as Marc returned to bed. She hated how fragile and self-conscious she felt around his absurd reactions. *No matter what I say or do, he always has the last word. Why does he always have to win?*

It was so convenient to push him out of her thoughts. His irrational behavior turned him into a real pig. Hélène had relied on her natural defense mechanism for years: just close her eyes and shut him out. How many years had she been doing this? She felt her neck muscles tighten. *Maybe Ceci's right. My head's been buried in the sand. Denial is certainly more convenient than reality.* She contemplated the thought as she reached toward the wall switch. When the light flickered on, she felt a nudge at her ankles.

"*Oh là là!*" she gasped. "*Chaussette, ma chérie,* you startled me!" She scooped up the cat. "*Désolée, bébé.* Papa's in another foul mood."

As they headed down the stairs, Marc's final comment chipped at her heart. Instead of stifling her anger, as she normally would—today was anything but normal—she turned to face the bedroom door.

This should get him. Revenge had never been her forte, but he had gone too far this time.

"*Alors,* Chaussette," she hollered up the stairs. "Got any ideas where I can go shopping for a new husband? Where can I find a nice, decent man?" Listening for a reaction, she pulled Chaussette closer to her chest, comforted by the kitty's tiny heart pounding against her own.

The floorboards creaked. Hélène stiffened. The doorknob turned, and she heard a click as the bedroom door locked. Sighing with relief, Hélène nuzzled the base of Chaussette's neck. The warm, fuzzy fur smelled so familiar. *This cat is my only family*, she realized. "Looks like we're spending the night on the couch, *bébé.*"

CHAPTER THREE

A rare ray of Belgian sunshine trickled through the living room window, warming Hélène's face. She felt it sweep tenderly over her eyes, nose, and cheeks, finally lingering on her lips, rousing them until they parted. Her eyelids fluttered as her subconscious mind coasted. As Mozart's "Requiem" cascaded through the room, torrents of rain pounded the skylight. She could no longer contain herself. Her lips parted, and she emitted a silent scream as her body succumbed to an avalanche of feelings, unleashing years—decades—of pent-up tension. Oh, this feels good. *When the avalanche subsided at last, she squeezed her eyes to savor the vestiges of pleasure. The opera softened as the raindrops subsided. She inhaled deeply. Wild tenderness. Her spent body trembled, bathing in the explosion's aftermath.*

Hélène stretched as the late morning sunlight filtered into the room. Then reality hit. "*Mince!*" she exclaimed, wincing at the pinch in her back. Their sofa was sagging over its springs—not the best option for a good night's sleep. Chaussette, napping on Hélène's stomach, woke with a start. Purring heavily, she rubbed her furry face against Hélène's cheek until she sat up and scratched the kitty's chin. With her other hand, she groped under the sofa cushions. "*Ah non*, not again. Where are they?"

When she got on all fours, her nose a centimeter from the floor, blood rushed to her throbbing head—a nasty reminder of the alcohol she had imbibed the day before. To make matters worse, her nostrils balked at the carpet stench. *Génial—stale beer and dirty socks.* She held her breath to block the foul odors as she scrambled around the sofa, sweeping her hand like a windshield wiper to find her glasses. After scouring the area, she sat on her heels, squinting at the blurry room.

"Great way to start the day." Hélène shrugged. "I give up." Chaussette hopped off the sofa and began sniffing one of her shoes under the table.

"*Eh bien, voilà!*" Hélène thrust her hand inside the shoe. "Such a smart *minou.* What would I do without you?" She donned her glasses and hugged her pet. "You've certainly earned your breakfast."

Moments later, Hélène sat at the kitchen table, scribbling in her diary. With a sigh, she set down her pen to sip her herbal mint tea. "Want to hear this?"

As usual, Chaussette started purring.

"*D'accord.* Remember, this is just between you and me…so shh!" She began reading the day's entry:

I thought about things all night long. He can be so mean when he wants to. I even had to sleep on the sofa, which is really lumpy. It was awful. I don't even want to think about yesterday with the psychic and what happened with Sylvie the day before. I don't feel like seeing her, but I'd better get it over with. We've got to talk. But something about her really disturbs me. Not only is it messing up my mind, but it's messing up my relationship with Marc…

Hélène's voice rose as she read her husband's name. Just then, she heard footsteps on the stairs. Chaussette performed a flying leap while Hélène stuffed her diary in her backpack with her bathing suit and ran into the garage, not bothering to change out of the clothes she'd slept in. "*Désolée, bébé,* Maman has to go swimming now."

❖

She should be here any minute, thought Hélène, smiling at her figure in the mirror. The black stripes on her teal swimsuit made her silhouette seem thinner. She had never had any muscles before— even as a kid. Her flesh had formed one smooth blob, which had grown thicker throughout the years. She had always hidden her body so nobody could see it. Not even herself—until now.

With her excess pounds gone, Hélène looked and felt years younger, despite her dreadful night on the couch. Her body felt stronger. She looked at her chest. *Fuller and firmer. Let's see about here.* She grabbed her buttocks. *Less fleshy. More compact.* She grinned. Then her eyes went to her face. *The glasses are a huge improvement. But this is horrendous.* She wet her hands under the faucet and slicked her hair back. *I'm not such a disaster after all.*

For once, Hélène felt good, really good. In fact, she felt so good that she forgot where she was. Reaching her arms high into the air, she began dancing on the tips of her toes. Just as she was performing a double pirouette, she heard clapping. Her heels dropped with a thud.

"You seem ready to roll." Sylvie quickly kissed her on the cheek.

"I guess so…" Hélène stammered, pulling away. But it was too late. Sylvie's soft skin—and distinctive scent—had already grabbed her senses. Her body remembered their passionate kisses at the beach the other night and felt weak all of a sudden.

Sylvie flashed Hélène a grin. "So, I guess you made it home all right?" She tugged the string to her sweatpants.

Hélène caught her breath as Sylvie removed her pants, revealing her smooth, muscular thighs. Shedding her sweat jacket, Sylvie pulled her T-shirt over her head. Masses of black curls tumbled onto her broad shoulders. A few untamed strands settled between her breasts, propped up firmly by her swimsuit.

Despite the locker room's damp chill, Hélène felt her cheeks boiling. Her gaze remained riveted to Sylvie's body. She cleared her throat. "That's a nice suit. *Enfin*, I just love yellow."

"Me too." Sylvie grinned. "In case you haven't noticed, nearly everything I own is yellow: my car, my apartment, my cat—"

Even your nipples, thought Hélène, eyeing the erect pair in Sylvie's Lycra suit. "Excuse me." Hélène raced toward the nearest bathroom stall. She plopped herself on the toilet seat. *Why do I always feel like such an idiot around her?* The answer came instantly. *Because I'm always acting like an idiot around her. Mais pourquoi?* Another answer cropped up: *Because I've never been exposed to such raw beauty, and certainly not on a daily basis. Nor on a touching basis. I've never even looked at women before. Consciously, anyway...*

Hélène's heart pounded as images of Sylvie's body flashed before her. *Now I see what men are talking about*, she realized, squeezing her clammy thighs together. Just then, a light knock, followed by Sylvie's sexy voice, penetrated the stall.

Hélène froze. She looked up at the ceiling, wondering what to do next.

"*Alors*... You all right in there?" asked Sylvie.

"I'll be right out." Hélène tiptoed out of the stall, trying not to draw attention to herself.

Sylvie, in a white bathrobe, stood next to the sink, patiently waiting.

Hélène thrust her hands into the cold faucet water, hoping it would calm her nerves and other body parts. Sylvie's dark eyes were staring at her in the mirror.

"Listen, I'm sorry about the beach. I'm not quite sure what happened—"

"*Ne t'inquiète pas.* Forget about it." Sylvie draped her arm over Hélène's shoulders. "It's freezing in here. Let's go work out before we catch frostbite."

If she only knew, thought Hélène, wiping the sweat off her brow.

❖

Once they were waist-deep in the cool water, Sylvie handed Hélène a kickboard. When Hélène reached for it, their fingers touched. But this time, Sylvie noticed that Hélène didn't pull her fingers away. They looked at each other for a moment that seemed way too long. *This is awkward. Really awkward. She's married. What have I done? Why do I always let my impulses take over? Such a great way to get hurt...Again.*

Finally, she broke the silence. "I asked my boss about Saturday lessons. It's no problem. We can start this Saturday, if you want. Did you talk to your husband?"

Hélène shook her head. "Didn't have a chance. I wanted to, but..." She sighed. "I might as well tell you. Communication's not the best between us right now."

"*Vraiment?*" Sylvie felt her heart leap. "I'm sorry to hear that." Sylvie felt guilty as soon as the words left her mouth. *Am I? Not really.* Her mind went back to the softness of their first kiss, the warmth of their bodies pressed together, holding each other as the ocean waves licked their bodies. She could almost taste the salt in the air and Hélène's sweet breath.

Then, with a jolt, her thoughts returned to the present.

"We used to be so close." Hélène's expression was sad and distant. "But lately I've been realizing just how different we are. We're exact opposites."

Sylvie looked closer at Hélène. Judging from her disheveled appearance and the dark circles under her eyes, she had weathered a rough night. *Mon Dieu, I hope he's not violent with her.* She remembered the scene he made at the flower market the day they met, a few months before. He had acted like a complete idiot. She was glad Hélène was confiding in her. She looked as if she was suffering. *That's the last thing she needs. I'd love to knock that jerk around.* She leaned closer. "How so?"

"I don't know. You see who I am." Hélène swept her hand over her body. "I'm just your average woman. I like the usual: cats, cooking, literature, poetry, nice flowers, pretty music. Guess you could say I'm *romantique.*"

"There's nothing wrong with that." Sylvie hardly considered Hélène "average," but she wasn't about to say so and make things awkward again.

"Not at all. In fact, when we first met, *eh bien,* we could talk about these things. Marc was interested in them. We used to have these long, fascinating conversations. We'd pull all-nighters in the library. We were really young, just students, but we had all these amazing things to say to each other. It was stimulating. *He* was stimulating." Hélène's eyes began to glow. "And was he romantic." She glanced forlornly at the other end of the pool. "But that was twenty years ago. And now, all he does is work out at the gym, watch sports on TV, sketch race cars, guzzle beer, and..." Hélène's eyes hardened as her voice trailed off.

"*Continue.*" Sylvie gently tapped Hélène's fingers on the kickboard.

"It wouldn't be so bad, except..."

Sylvie gulped. *Here it comes.* "What?"

"He completely ignores me at the dinner table."

Sylvie made an effort to keep from laughing. *I thought she'd say "He smacks me black and blue every night at bedtime" or "He threatens me with knives in the staircase." What a relief.*

"That's terrible." She grabbed another kickboard. "*Viens...* Let's at least pretend we're here for a swimming lesson."

Hélène followed the white foam bubbling in Sylvie's wake.

"*Un, deux, trois...*" Sylvie repeated as Hélène, grasping her board tightly, imitated her moves. Finally, Hélène caught up with her. Side by side, they propelled their bodies forward.

Sylvie was just getting used to kicking beside Hélène when she heard her gasping for air after their second lap. "Are you all right?" she asked, touching her board.

"Hanging in there." Hélène nodded. "And sorry for blabbing." She grimaced. "I know we're here to swim, not gossip. And I rarely confide in people, especially about Marc. I'm not quite sure why I keep telling you these things." As she kicked, she took a deep mouthful of air.

Sylvie looked at her with concern. *I'd like to know that myself. The least I can do is bolster her confidence.* "I wouldn't worry about him. People change, you know. It's inevitable." Sylvie smiled warmly, trying not to show the disappointment she felt at the distance between them today. She'd hoped for something...else after their time together in the ocean. But it was her own fault; she knew better than to want what she couldn't have. Just then, as Hélène thrust her ankles furiously, halfway down the pool, she lost control of her board, and her body rubbed against Sylvie's.

Sylvie felt a tingling at her thigh where their bodies briefly touched. *Mince. Wonder if she noticed that?* She veered to the side. *I sure did.* She felt increasingly uncomfortable as warm sensations spread over her body.

Over the splashing, Hélène hollered, "What about you? You never talk about yourself."

"*Ah bon?*" *Darn. I was hoping she wouldn't get around to this.* To appear casual about a sticky subject, Sylvie grinned broadly when they reached the deep end. "So, what do you want to know?" she asked, treading water.

Hélène pinched her lips while seemingly trying to keep her head above water.

"So, what do you want to know?" Sylvie repeated, camouflaging her anxiety with a confident tone. She hated these kinds of questions.

"How about the truth?" blurted Hélène.

What? Sylvie was so surprised, she stopped treading and began to sink. It wasn't until her chin dipped under the surface of the water that her legs kicked in. At once, her body rose, flashing her muscular chest. "What do you mean *the truth?*"

"You know, the truth about your love story."

I can't believe she's asking me this! Sylvie looked away. "What are you talking about?"

Hélène grabbed her board and whispered, "You know, the love of your life."

What nerve... Sylvie gave a nervous laugh and shot a sideways glance at Hélène. *How does she know about Lydia?* Sylvie forced a grin. "Now that's a good one. What love story?"

Hélène looked serious. "I'll give you a hint."

Sylvie's back muscles tightened. "*D'accord*, shoot."

"Do the words 'eternally yours' mean anything to you?"

Sylvie hesitated. *What the heck is she talking about? I never said that to Lydia.* Her fingertips dug into her Styrofoam board. She shook her head. "Not really. *Pourquoi?*"

"How about Theodorós. Ring a bell?"

"What did you just say?"

"I said 'ring a bell?'"

"*Non*, I think you said a name. In Greek."

"I did. Theodorós."

"Théodoros." Sylvie corrected her pronunciation. "How do you know that name?"

"You know who I'm talking about."

"It's an old Greek name. So old, *en fait*, that nobody uses it any more. In my country, it's as rare and obsolete as our ruins."

Hélène narrowed her eyes. "You sure?"

"*Bien sûr.*" Sylvie nodded. "Wait, I take that back. I think a couple of famous Greek athletes were named after..." She gave Hélène a puzzled look. "But what's that name got to do with me?" asked Sylvie, releasing the grip on her board. She knew that Hélène's legs must be aching. New swimmers often got fatigued while treading in the water, beating their legs to stay afloat. Sylvie was also tired of beating—in the water and around the bush. It annoyed her, the way Hélène seemed to be playing games with her, trying to pull worms out of her nose, so to speak, to get to the truth.

Her thoughts kept seeping back to the day they met a few months before, at an outdoor Saturday market in Brussels. Their brief encounter at the flower stand had made a deep impression on Sylvie. By accident, she had dropped her silver Greece keychain on the ground. Hélène had found it and taken it with her to the local market café to meet her obnoxious husband.

Her precious silver keychain was in the form of a fish with the word "Greece" etched into it. The timeworn silver fish had *To my dearest Joanna, with all my love forever. Théodoros* engraved in Greek on the back.

Sylvie remembered every moment of the scene at the outdoor café when she saw Hélène with her keychain as if it were happening again. Hélène's flushed cheeks, wild hair, and sparkling blue eyes had mesmerized her. She'd been attracted to her instantly, and the feeling hadn't gone away.

Sylvie's thoughts returned to the present; she glimpsed Hélène's red face as she furiously beat her legs in the pool.

Hélène raised her voice. "*Enfin*, Sylvie. You know very well who I'm talking—"

"*Non.*" Sylvie shook her head. "If I did, I'd tell you. I promise." *And why does it matter to her so much? This is supposed to be a swimming lesson, not an interrogation into my private life. Belgians can get so complicated sometimes.*

Sylvie tried to calm her nerves by breathing slowly as she pedaled her legs. A few awkward moments ticked by.

At last, Hélène said, "Just think for a minute. Isn't there anyone who—"

Sylvie gave in. She clearly wasn't going to let it go. "Well, if you're talking about my grandpa—"

"Who? Your grandpa?" Hélène snickered. "Don't try to tell me he's the love of your life—"

"He certainly was Yaya's. Yaya is my grandma. And in a sense, he was mine too. I've always admired him."

"*Tiens*, how sweet," Hélène replied. "But the truth is—"

"The truth is, we're here to swim. *Non?*" Sylvie said, exasperated. "And if you want to exchange life stories someday, that's fine. We'll go have a cup of coffee and..." *Time is really running out. And we're getting nowhere with this swimming lesson.* She glanced at the clock. "*Ah, dommage.* Too bad, it looks like our lesson's over." Relief and disappointment swept through her. She was glad to be away from the personal questions, but it meant cutting off her time with Hélène, which was both a blessing and a curse right now.

Before Hélène could react, Sylvie began kicking toward the shallow end.

"*Attends!*" shouted Hélène, struggling to keep up. Halfway to the end, Sylvie slowed down.

Hélène grabbed her board. "Promise?"

"Promise what?" *Why should I promise her anything?* She watched Hélène gulp for air.

"That we'll go for a coffee?"

Startled, Sylvie stopped swimming. *"Bien sûr.* But after what happened at the beach, I thought—"

"Forget that ever happened. Today's a new day." She shivered when Hélène placed her hand over hers. "Right. So it is." Sylvie resumed kicking, harder this time. "Keep your legs straight and point your toes. And try not to splash too much."

As their legs thrashed next to each other in the water, a single thought kept racing through Sylvie's mind: *Now we're going out for coffee? What in the heck am I doing? I can't get involved with a married woman again. And certainly not my student.* Then she remembered their passionate kisses in the ocean, sending a bolt of electricity up her spine. Maybe she didn't have to get involved. Maybe they could just be friends. She looked at Hélène's face, beautiful even in exertion, and knew she was deceiving herself.

When Sylvie strolled out of a shower stall wearing crisp white jeans, black sneakers, and a tight, dark-brown V-neck sweater that made her feel sexy, she noticed Hélène wincing at the mirror while blowing her hair dry. Sylvie mentally rehashed their conversation in the pool. *What does she want from me?* Before she could stop herself, she flashed Hélène a boyish grin and moved beside her in front of the mirror.

She could feel Hélène's gaze in the mirror as she added gel to her slick, wet hair with her strong, nimble fingers. She loved the feeling of cool gel oozing through her wavy locks.

All of a sudden, Hélène's face flushed. Rising hastily, she averted her eyes from Sylvie's amused gaze.

"Thanks for the lesson. See you tomorrow."

But Sylvie had other ideas, even though she knew full well they weren't good ones. *Where does she think she's going? She wants the truth and promises from me, and then runs off like a rabbit.* Placing her hand on Hélène's shoulder, she spoke in a deep, throaty voice. "*Attends.* Don't go yet."

"*Désolée,* but I'm in a hurry. I need to get a blood test before work."

"Weren't we going to get a coffee?" Sylvie grinned, pressing her fingers into Hélène's arm. "There's a café around the corner. It's not healthy to go off without breakfast, *tu sais.*"

"But I've got to go on an empty stom—"

"Why don't you do your blood test another day? Say you're on your period or something." Sylvie cracked a prize-winning smile, knowing very well that Hélène didn't have a choice. Like it or not, they were on their way to sip coffee together.

The café was old-fashioned and typically *Bruxellois.* Folksy Flemish music was blaring from an ancient jukebox in the corner. Two workmen in light-blue uniforms were hovering at the counter, sipping their thick coffee and smoking Belgian cigarettes. As soon as Hélène and Sylvie settled into a ruby-red corner booth, the workmen interrupted their conversation to stare.

Hélène felt as if someone had just flipped back the pages of time at least a century. Easing herself into the worn vinyl booth, she strategically placed her elbows on the wooden table to block the two pairs of eyes at the counter. Nobody else was in the café, rendering the atmosphere more than intimate. Hélène felt apprehensive nestled together in a booth that for some reason felt far more intimate than it should. She tried to act naturally but couldn't help avoiding Sylvie's gorgeous eyes. She had tried to get out of this coffee date for that very reason. She was afraid of what she would say to Sylvie in such close quarters. But Sylvie's white teeth and full lips were so perfect, so enchanting. Her heart fluttered. *How can I refuse this?* She was unable to concoct a valid reason why she shouldn't sip coffee right now with this gorgeous Greek goddess with glistening wet hair.

"You win. I'll go another day," she had promptly responded, accepting the look of triumph in Sylvie's dark eyes.

While Hélène had struggled to keep up with Sylvie's long strides toward the café, she had tried to ignore her raging emotions. As her boots slid over the uneven cobblestones, she had focused on the soft, early rays of sunshine reflecting off their shiny surface. The bouncy rays lifted her heart; the tight knot in her throat had melted, releasing a refreshing breath of dewy, morning air.

Today's a new day after all, she had decided, swinging her arms toward the sky. She'd been thinking about what she had learned from Hilde, the psychic, and although she'd been tempted to go back and see if she could get more answers, she wasn't sure if she believed the old woman. Perhaps she just wanted to know she wasn't truly alone in the world. Either way, she'd been putting it off. As they made their way to the café, she'd considered mentioning it to Sylvie to see what she thought.

But now, sitting across from her and finding a distinct lack of words, she wondered if she'd given in to the invitation for coffee too easily. She was trying to act naturally, but it was impossible with Sylvie's gorgeous eyes right in front of her.

To her relief, a thin, weathered waitress strode out of a back room to take their order. She quickly came back with two steaming coffees and a basket of buttery croissants. Famished after their workout in the pool, Sylvie and Hélène attacked the pile of flaky pastries.

Between bites, Sylvie broke the silence.

"We don't have much time, so here goes," she whispered. "Remember you asked me about the love of my life?"

Hélène's eyebrows shot up. *Wow. I can't believe she just said that.* She glanced over at the workmen. Then her eyes darted back to Sylvie's. *Dark. Forbidden. Luscious.* They seemed almost edible, like chocolate.

"I don't have a boyfriend."

Hélène caught her breath.

Sylvie pushed a strand of hair behind her ear. "I've wanted to tell you this for a while, but I didn't want to shock you. *Tu vois*, I'm not—"

"I know. You're not Sylvie." Hélène smirked, wanting to lighten the mood, to delay the seriousness in Sylvie's expression.

"*Quoi?*" Sylvie's eyes bulged.

"You're not Sylvie. You're Joanna."

Sylvie shook her head slowly. Staring into Hélène's eyes, she whispered, "I really don't get you, Hélène. I have no idea what you're talking about half the time." Then she downed her coffee.

Hélène's mouth twitched as she tried not to frown. The comment stung, especially since Marc didn't seem to get her either. She brought her fingernail to her lips and was about to take a bite when she remembered she had given up that habit. Just then, Sylvie's eyes lit up.

"Now I get what you were talking about in the pool!" Sylvie raised her hands. Giggling, she dangled her keychain before Hélène's eyes so she could see the Greek words engraved on the back. "*Dis-moi*, Hélène. Since when do you read Greek?"

Hélène's lips twitched, this time in a mini smile. "I don't. But remember the waiter at the café, near the market? He does."

Sylvie laughed. "That explains it. But that guy needs new glasses."

Hélène gave her a puzzled look.

"See this? That's a date. It says 'nineteen-hundred and thirty-two.' You might have already guessed, but I wasn't even born then." Sylvie's voice softened. "*M'enfin*, my mama wasn't even born."

"*Alors*, you're not Joanna?" Helene smiled, glad the mood had lifted.

"Of course not! And there's no Théodoros in my life, unless you mean Grandpa, who gave this to Yaya, my grandma, for their engagement. She passed it on to me when he died."

Laughing, Hélène looked at the café's colorless wall. "*Mon Dieu.* I'm such an idiot!"

"*Non*, you're not." Sylvie placed her hand on Hélène's.

"So, there's no Théodoros courting you?" asked Hélène, trying to ignore the pulsating sensations of Sylvie's warm hand on hers.

"Not that I know of."

Before she could change her mind, Hélène added, "Can I ask you another question?"

"Shoot away. At least *we're* having fun," Sylvie glanced at the counter. "Which is more than I can say for those—"

"If you don't have a boyfriend, then maybe you have a—"

Now it was Sylvie's turn to gaze at the wall. "Girlfriend?"

"*Oui,*" replied Hélène. The word felt heavy, as if it sat on the table between them.

"Nope." Sylvie's expression grew serious.

Mince alors, thought Hélène. *That was dumb of me. I'm not ready for this conversation.*

"But you're on the right track." Leaning forward, she whispered, "I'm waiting for the right person, even if it takes years. I'm sick of going out with women who aren't good for me." Then she winked.

Before Hélène could react, she heard a snort from across the café. The two workmen and the wiry waitress seemed to be relishing their private conversation. Apparently, Sylvie's wink was icing on the cake. She turned her attention back to Sylvie. "*Mais…*What kind of women aren't good for you?" she asked in a shaky voice.

"You know, the usual. Straight, married women."

Hélène nearly choked on her coffee. "Women like me, you mean."

"*Oui.* No offense, *bien sûr.*" Sylvie flashed her a quick smile. "It's just that…I just keep getting hurt."

This wasn't the answer Hélène was expecting. She jumped up. "So, why in the heck did you drag me in here?" she hissed, throwing down her napkin.

"*Attends,* you've got it all wrong." Sylvie stood up. "I was hoping we could be friends. Especially after what happened at the beach. Please sit down, Hélène." She pleaded with her eyes. "*S'il te plaît.*"

Reluctantly, Hélène obeyed. She tried sipping her coffee again, but now it tasted like burnt sawdust. Her hand trembled as she lowered her cup, nearly spilling its contents.

Sylvie's eyes were glistening. "Just let me explain, *d'accord?*" she whispered. "You're different, Hélène. I feel so at ease with you."

Hélène tried to keep her attention on her coffee cup, but she could hardly see through the mist in her eyes as conflicting thoughts overwhelmed her. *I'm the one who's married, after all. This shouldn't affect me. Why am I tearing up?* She tried to block the irrational emotions flooding her soul.

Sylvie leaned forward. "I know I can trust you. We can be great friends. *Tu vois,* you're not the type to take advantage of me. Just to see 'what it's like,' like other straight women I've come across. Especially recently. It's really refreshing, believe me."

Recently? Especially recently? Hélène felt her heart twisting. *Who else has she been kissing lately?* After an uncomfortable pause, she spoke tenderly. "I'd never do that to you. I could never hurt you like that, Sylvie. I don't play games. I'd never..." Then, unexpectedly, her voice cracked. She turned her head in a vain attempt to shield herself from those tender brown eyes and soft, round lips.

Why is she doing this to me? I know it's not fair to expect anything more from her. But I would've hoped that... Hélène clenched her fists. Suddenly, it became clear what she needed to do. The question was: whose hair should she yank out first? *I know she hasn't done anything wrong. Why am I being so emotional right now? Why am I'm losing control like this?*

"*Qu'est-ce qui se passe?* Are you okay?" Sylvie placed a hand on Hélène's shaking shoulder. Ever so gently, she removed the arm shielding her face. But something in Hélène's eyes made her quickly motion for the bill.

"Anything else, *Mesdames?*" the waitress drawled in a thick *Bruxellois* accent, batting her fake lashes at Sylvie.

"*Non, merci.* We're in a hurry," Sylvie replied, slapping a five-euro bill onto the table.

She reached for Hélène's arm as they left the café just as Hélène burst into tears. Sylvie pulled a tissue from her pocket and wiped her wet cheeks.

"Hélène..."

Hélène lifted her chin. She didn't even care that her eyes were dripping with emotion. Their faces drew close. *I know I shouldn't be reacting this way, but I just can't help it. Mon Dieu, she's irresistible. I can't keep myself away from her. She's like a wild animal, drawing me in for the kill.*

Just when their lips were about to touch, Sylvie whispered, "You're married."

Abruptly, Hélène pulled her head back. "*Comment?*" she gasped.

"I said, you're married." Sylvie sighed with a resigned smile.

It took a second for Hélène to regain her composure. She brought her hand to her burning cheeks. "*Exactement.* I'm married... and straight. But does that really matter? I thought maybe..." She struggled to come up with a good argument. *We need to be together. I don't care how, or why. C'est trop fort. Our feelings are too strong to ignore.* She'd just promised she wouldn't hurt Sylvie. She wouldn't play the games other women had played with her. But here she was, begging for a chance at something she didn't understand.

Sylvie took a step back. "You should take some time and think—"

"I've already thought about it. *A lot.* If you only knew!" Hélène pulled Sylvie toward her. She felt a fierce magnetic force as the energy between their bodies surged through her entire being. Their sudden intimacy, blended with the scent of chlorine, gave her head a spin.

To her surprise, Sylvie pushed her away. "Then *I'm* the one who has to think about it."

Hélène felt as if she were going to vomit as she ran toward her bike. *What the heck is wrong with her? She's a monster. She's a tease...*

"*Je suis désolée*, Hélène!" Sylvie called after her. "I had no idea you felt this way. I'm so sorry!"

When Hélène rode past Sylvie, bitter words flew from her tongue. "You're right! I'm straight *and* married. Of *course* I'm not your type!" Gesticulating wildly, she nearly fell off her bike.

I'm such an idiot! She passed the two workmen and waitress hovering at the café entrance, watching their every move. *Who cares about them? Who cares what the world thinks about us? Wait... There is no us.* Hélène circled back to Sylvie, hissing, "Just forget it!" and pedaled away as fast as she could. At the end of the street, she looked over her shoulder and shouted, "And now that I think of it, you're not *my type* either!"

Sylvie simply shook her head and turned away.

Helene rode blindly home, hating how conflicting emotions and irrational desires kept swirling in her path.

❖

After several awkward, interminable swimming lessons, Sylvie was relieved to allow nature to bring a sense of normalcy back to her life, especially after their disastrous coffee escapade. Each morning, as soon as they were clothed and dry, she led Hélène outside the pool building. With childlike wonder, she delighted in the colorful birds flitting from tree to tree, sharing secret messages as they chirped across the tender grass. Like a pair of birds on a branch, she and Hélène sat perched on the brick wall, soaking up the poetic atmosphere for a few precious minutes.

Today, after the warmth of the steamy locker room, she winced at the sharpness of her breath. Gradually, her lungs acclimated to the early morning chill. Looking down, she noticed her legs were wide open. *That's rather butchy*, she mused. *Wonder if Hélène cares how androgynous I am? She didn't seem to at the café or when we were kissing in the ocean. What made her come back to our lessons anyway?* She swept her wavy hair from her face and decided to ignore the question. It didn't really matter why, just that she had.

Just then, a bluebird flew by. "Sure is exquisite out here," she said, breaking the silence.

"Sure is," replied Hélène, swinging her legs. Then she cleared her throat. "*Alors*...You always go out to eat?"

"Sort of. I eat breakfast at home, but it's just so much easier to go out than to try to fix something edible. I'm not the greatest cook and—"

"*Vraiment?* I *love* to cook."

Sylvie raised her eyebrows. "That's great. I admire people who have the patience to—"

"I'd love to make you dinner sometime," blurted Hélène. Then she bit her lip.

The invitation caught Sylvie off guard, especially after Hélène's severe reaction at the café. She was certain they would never do anything together after that. *Except sit on the wall and admire the birds, like this. I'm not quite sure what she wants from me.* She peered cautiously at her to see if she was joking.

The sincerity lurking in Hélène's blue eyes took her by surprise. Before Sylvie knew it, the words slipped off her lips. "I'd like that." Then she had an alarming thought. She saw herself dining with Hélène and her brute of a husband. *Much less appetizing.* "But I'm not sure your husband would—"

"What does *he* have to do with it?"

"*Alors,* for one, you live with him. *Segundo*, you tell me you always eat at home, just the two of you, and I don't want to interrupt your—"

"There's nothing to interrupt, believe me." Hélène chuckled. "Besides, we wouldn't go to my place. I'll come to yours. Didn't you say you had a cat?"

Sylvie's eyes rested on the soft, golden highlights—a gift from the early sun—shining in Hélène's hair. "*Eh bien...*" She gulped. "My place?" She hadn't thought of that. Even though her skin began to cool—a usual red flag indicating possible danger—her mind argued. *What harm could it do?* "*D'accord.* But on one condition— I'm cooking."

Hélène laughed. "Come on, you already told me you're a disaster in the kitchen. Why should we both suffer when I *love* to create my own homemade meals?"

"Because it's a Greek rule. Or a family tradition. Whatever. I don't care how things work in Belgium because when Greeks invite guests to dinner, our guests don't work. It's normal." Sylvie drew in a breath. "So, if you come to my place, you're not lifting a finger, *chère amie.*"

"That's fine, in theory, and I'm all for respecting cultural traditions." Hélène nodded. "But you don't understand. You'll be punishing me if you don't let me cook. I truly enjoy it, and I'd love the chance to make you dinner. To thank you for all you've done for me." Hélène grinned. "Besides, it'll be fun."

Sylvie squinted at her. *Fun?* Just then, a shadow from a low cloud swept over Hélène's face, emphasizing its paleness. *She seems so sad lately. It's not such a big deal, and if it would cheer her up...* She tapped her fingers on her knees, deliberating what to do.

"Just consider it a cooking lesson," Hélène continued. "That way you'll learn—"

"Okay, you've convinced me. But I'm paying for the groceries."

Hélène wagged her finger. "*Ah non!* You invited me to lunch."

"*Non,* I didn't. You—"

"This is such a waste of time," said Hélène, climbing down from the wall.

She always walks away when she doesn't get her way. Sylvie held her back. "Okay, you win."

Grinning, Hélène settled back on the wall. "Super. I knew you'd come around."

"It's not fair. You know my weakness," Sylvie protested, rubbing her stomach. "My appetite."

"By the way, Marc's not around this weekend. He's going to London."

Sylvie noticed the guilty look in Hélène's eyes. *Interesting timing. He goes away, and she decides to ask me to dinner.* "Really?"

"It's unusual, actually. He never travels for work anymore."

Sylvie flashed what she hoped was a sympathetic smile. "That's too bad."

"It is?" Hélène looked surprised.

"I mean, for you."

Hélène's eyes opened wide. "What's that supposed to mean?"

"*Non,* I mean, for him...So, he won't be in Brussels this weekend?" Sylvie felt tension rising up her neck as she fumbled with the right words. *Where is this conversation going? Am I dancing too close to the flames? If her husband is out of town, Hélène might be tempted to stay over. And I might be tempted to let her. We're attracted to each other, and I've fallen for married, straight women before. And I've been badly burned.*

Hélène shook her head. "I'm all alone with Chaussette."

"Who?"

Hélène giggled. "Chaussette's my cat."

"Nice name. I assume his paws are white, like socks?"

"*Bien sûr.* Just like yours." Hélène aimed her boot at the white socks under Sylvie's jeans. "And it's a *her,*" she added, teasing Sylvie's ankle with the tip of her boot.

Sylvie felt a tingle race up her leg. "*Stop!*" She pulled her leg away, pretending like it hurt, just to gain a bit of distance.

"Sorry," said Hélène. Her grin said otherwise.

Sylvie couldn't help thinking about Hélène's roving toes during their recent lunch at her favorite Greek restaurant before their inevitable swim in the ocean. After they had ingested glassfuls of retsina wine, Hélène's legs had strayed in her direction, making Sylvie ache in places totally inappropriate in public. Blushing at the memory, Sylvie jumped down from the wall. "Mine's a girl too. Her name's Marigold."

"Mmm. I love marigolds. *Mais c'est bizarre,* I've never seen a yellow cat before."

"*M'enfin,* she's not yellow! Remember those plants we bought at the flower stand the day we first met? Those plants with tiny flowers? She's more that color."

Hélène flashed a stunned expression. "You remember what I bought that day?"

"How could I forget? I lost my keychain, remember? And we both bought the same plant." Sylvie sensed Hélène's struggle to suppress a smile. *That was the day we first met. Guess I made an impression.* Suddenly feeling giddy, Sylvie yanked an orange flower from the grass and handed it to Hélène. "She's this color. Anyway, I live in Forest. Rue des Pépins. How about Saturday at eight?"

"How gallant of you." Hélène sniffed the flower's syrupy scent. "Eight's fine. But remember, I'm cooking."

Sylvie whistled through her teeth. "How could I forget?"

"You do like vegetarian food, *n'est-ce pas?*" asked Hélène, dangling the flower before Sylvie's nose.

"I think I've tried it before. But don't worry. As you might have noticed, I'm not exactly a picky eater."

CHAPTER FOUR

All afternoon, Hélène struggled to concentrate at work, but her mind kept slipping back to her conversation with Sylvie. To settle her nerves, she downed multiple cups of herbal tea. At last, in a quasi-trance, she focused on the golden threads of honey dripping into her cup...

Until she spotted *him*. Her nerves jumped when she realized how much she hated having him stare at her all day long. It was bad enough at home. With a swift flick of the wrist, she stuffed Marc's picture into her drawer. She winked at Chaussette's picture. "Much better, *n'est-ce pas, ma chérie?*"

Then the phone rang. "Translation department, Hélène Dupont speaking."

"*Bonjour, Madame Dupont.* I'm sorry to disturb you, but since I didn't hear from you the other day, and I see you didn't—"

"Dr. Duprès! *Je suis désolée*, I completely forgot. How embarrassing! I don't know where my mind's been these past few days."

"Don't worry, we all forget things now and then. But please, get your blood tested as soon as possible."

The sense of urgency in Dr. Duprès's voice shook Hélène from her daze. "*Bien sûr, Docteur.* I'll do it tomorrow, I promise."

"*Très bien.* Call me in a few days. I should have your results by then."

"*Merci, Docteur.* And I'm really sorry—" Before Hélène could finish, the line went dead. *I'm losing it.* She cradled her head in her hands. Just then, a strong, sweet smell entered her nostrils. She opened her eyes to the orange flower before her nose. She had placed the flower that Sylvie gave her in a glass, and after the morning bike ride, it had popped back to life. But now, it seemed to be playing tricks on her. Just like her mind. *Why did I insist on cooking dinner for her? What was I thinking?*

"Stop teasing me!" She grabbed the flower by its neck and—like a farmer ripping feathers from a duck—mercilessly plucked its petals. *I must be going crazy*, she decided, blocking her ears to shut out the petals' screams of anguish.

❖

The next morning, Hélène rode straight to the hospital after her swimming lesson. Trying to ignore emerging hunger pangs, she examined the items on her blood test. She remembered how shocked she had been when Dr. Duprès had first explained her immediate health risks after she had collapsed at work.

"Hélène, your blood test results were far from optimal. In fact, I'm not at all surprised you fainted. I don't want to shock you, but you must absolutely change your diet."

The words had hit Hélène hard. She felt like a coil unwinding—a pair of gray eyes loomed before her as the room started spinning. She tried to focus on Dr. Duprès, but the doctor's voice became distant.

"…an increased risk of cardiovascular disease, which could lead to heart attacks or even strokes."

The garbled voice droned on.

Heart attacks? Strokes? Hélène had shaken her head to clear the fuzziness. "*Attendez!* That's impossible, I'm only forty…"

"These are real risks." Dr. Duprès had pointed to the test results. "Iron deficiency…high blood pressure, sugar, and cholesterol levels…"

That was when she had started preparing nutritious meals at home, taking private swimming lessons with Sylvie, and biking to work every day. Now she was going to find out if all her efforts to become healthier were working or not. At least the dizziness had stopped, and her allergies seemed to be clearing up. She examined the items on her blood test again. *Mince, look at all these.* She glanced around the empty waiting room, then ticked off a dozen more items to be analyzed. She chewed on her lip. *Better safe than sorry.*

Just as she was stashing her pen, a chunky nurse with thick glasses and buckteeth entered the room. Hélène first noticed the yellowness of her horse teeth, then the sweat stains under her armpits. *This is going to be fun.*

Nurse Horse took Hélène's blood test form. "Follow me, *s'il vous plaît*," she barked. Next, she sat Hélène in a chair and with short, thick fingers rolled up her sleeve. Hélène cringed at the dozen test tubes ready to soak up her blood.

"This might hurt a bit, so take a big breath. When you exhale, try to think of something pleasant. It will help you relax."

"I'll try." Hélène eyed Nurse Horse's large, shiny pin that announced: "Smile, you're on Candid Camera!" Hélène leaned back in her chair, closed her eyes, and exhaled deeply. Images of Chaussette licking her cheek came to mind. She giggled until the nurse poked a fat needle into her arm. *Yikes!* After the painful prick, she squinted at the needle poking out of her vein, then at the blood squirting into the first tube.

Gasping, she shut her eyes again.

"Shh. It will be all right. Remember, try to think of something pleasant." Nurse Horse clamped her hand over the needle while studying Hélène's face through her thick glasses.

Hélène shuddered at the nurse's hot breath caressing her clammy cheeks. Squeezing her eyes even harder, Hélène tried to conjure up something pleasant instead of the needle ravaging her arm. She had never liked the idea of needles, not even ones for knitting. And this one was sucking up her blood like a vampire. At last, a more sensual scene emerged in her mind:

Sylvie is standing next to her, waist-deep in the swimming pool. Hélène is staring at her long, wavy hair and androgynous features, realizing how stunning she looks in her wet bathing suit. The sight of her smooth, powerful body makes Hélène tingle all over.

As Hélène's body shuddered, her eyes popped open. They fell on Nurse Horse, who was busy filling test tubes. She was taking so much blood that Hélène felt her lips pucker. *Bet my face resembles a dried fig right now. What's coming next?* Goose bumps erupted on her arms.

Nurse Horse leaned her corpulent body toward her and held up the fat needle, still oozing with blood. Hélène's nostrils—crushed between a pair of torpedo-shaped breasts—inhaled curious odors emanating from the nurse. *Mon Dieu!* Hélène instantly fainted.

She woke abruptly as Nurse Horse slapped her cheeks. "Feeling all right, *ma petite?*" she inquired, prying Hélène's eyes open with her stubby fingers.

Blood loss had jarred Hélène's brain into slow motion, giving her plenty of time to distinguish a potent blend of polyester uniform and stale deodorant. Gagging, she forced her eyelids open. Everything around her was blurry.

A full minute passed. Finally, Hélène's eyes adjusted to her surroundings. Nurse Horse's name tag loomed in front of her. When she read "SYLVIE," she nearly fainted again. Groggily, she watched Nurse Horse waddle out of the room only to return with a jelly donut and a tiny paper cup of orange juice.

The sun was still high as Hélène pedaled home from work. Its rays warmed her skin and her mood. She was feeling much stronger after her dreadful blood test that morning. To take advantage of this unusually fine evening, she headed toward Cinquantenaire Park. Under a clump of pine trees, she spotted a dozen individuals clad in white uniforms and multicolored belts. They were doing spectacular kicks and air chops. *Looks like karate.* Then she gasped. A woman who looked just like Sylvie was surrounded by several burly guys ready to attack her. Hélène felt a tingle race up her neck when the woman crouched, thrusting her hands in the air. She looked gorgeous in the crisp, white uniform that favored her dark, olive complexion. Even though she was in a crouched position, Hélène noticed a sliver of black cotton wrapped tightly around a waist so small, it could only be Sylvie's. Her dark hair was swept back tightly in a ponytail.

It's got to be her. Hélène jumped off her bike to approach the group. All the other uniform-clad athletes were men. Suddenly, three of the biggest ones—all black belts—yelled "Hiya!" in unison and attacked the woman. Hélène covered her eyes while trying to block the sounds of six feet and hands coming at the woman from all angles. After a few agonizing seconds, Hélène peeked through her fingers. To her surprise, the woman was knocking off her opponents like an expert bowler wiping out pins.

It's her! Hélène beamed. *"Salut!"* she called out timidly. But Sylvie was too busy pulling her attackers up from the grass to notice her waving at her from behind a tree.

Hélène gulped when she saw more black belts creeping up on Sylvie from behind. *Probably not the best time to distract her,* she concluded, picking up her bike. *And what other hobbies does she have hidden up her sleeve?* Instead of heading home, Hélène turned at the next light. *I think I'll buy myself a book about karate.* As she passed the spot where she'd run into Hilde the day she'd hit rock bottom, she briefly contemplated changing direction. *I'd like to clarify some things with Hilde.* But something inside told her to wait. *Not yet.* The problem was, Helene didn't have anyone else to ask. Without family, she had to take the old woman's word for it, and that seemed too out of the ordinary. *Or maybe it's too scary.*

She shook off the thoughts that were haunting her and headed to the bookstore.

❖

"Marc?" Hélène followed the heavy snores to the lounge chair in their garden. Side-stepping his beer bottle, she kneeled down and sniffed her husband's breath. *What's he still doing here?* She cleared her throat. "I thought your flight was this afternoon."

Marc sat up and rubbed his eyes. His tousled hair sprang out in all directions. "*Comment?*" He scratched his head.

"You must have missed your flight," Hélène sighed. "I knew I shouldn't have gone to the—"

"I didn't...I'm taking a later one. I was waiting for you, to say good-bye."

What weird bug bit him? Hélène placed her hand on his forehead. "How considerate. You must have a fever."

Marc brushed her hand away. "What did you expect me to do, just take off without saying good-bye?"

"Actually..."

"Come on, *chérie*. I'm not that bad, am I?"

Hélène looked into her husband's eyes. *This isn't at all like him.*

He seemed to take her lack of reply as an accusation. "Can't I even say good-bye to my beloved wife? I'm going to miss you."

"Now I *know* there's something wrong with you. You never say things like that!"

Hélène's head started to spin. That donut clearly hadn't been enough to keep her upright after all the tubes of blood she had filled at the hospital. She teetered and fell into Marc's lap. Now a centimeter from his face, she scanned his features to make sure he was really her husband. *It may look like him, but it sure doesn't sound like him.* At least not for the past two decades.

Marc brushed her hair from her eyes. "Where did you say you went again, *mon lapin?*"

Hélène took a deep breath. "Nowhere. Just the bookstore."

"*Bien sûr.*" Marc's voice grew gruff. A look of contempt crossed his face. "For more dictionaries, I suppose?"

Hélène studied the hard lines around his jaw and waited for his favorite line.

"Just what we need...more junk upstairs."

Even before he said it, she felt instant relief. *It's him all right.*

It was true. She had gone to buy a karate book but ended up in the poetry section, as usual. After perusing all the books whose titles she knew by heart, she had finally settled on one she had never seen before—a rare volume on floral poetry, translated from Greek. As soon as she rode into the driveway, the idea had come to her. Lately, she got her best ideas while biking. *I'll give it to Sylvie. It's a perfect gift. Besides, I can't just show up at her place empty-handed.* The fact that she was bringing dinner didn't count.

Hélène was so busy thinking of Sylvie, she didn't notice Marc looking at his watch. Only when he pulled her face to his and asked, "Anyone in there?" did she realize where she was, and with whom.

She stood up abruptly. "You'd better scoot, or you'll be having supper with Chaussette and me."

Marc didn't need any nudging. He pecked her on the forehead and rushed into the house. "I'll call you from London, *d'accord*? Be a good girl and behave yourself!"

The front door slammed.

What's he trying to say with that "Be a good girl and behave yourself?" line? I should have replied, "Be a good boy." Hélène smirked. *I can't imagine him as a girl.*

Then she frowned. *But I can imagine him* with *a girl...*

She settled in the lounge chair to force the distressing thought from her head, ignoring the fact that she'd been desiring a girl herself—that was different. "*Un...deux...trois,*" she counted, breathing deeply; the fresh oxygen relaxed her muscles as her body sank into the chair's plastic grooves.

After a quiet moment, she turned to her cat. "*Alors,* what do you think, Chaussette? A weekend just for you and me!" She drew her knees to her chest and rocked side to side. *Free from all constraints.* She grinned. It had been so long since she felt this way.

Chaussette jumped from a bush and landed on Hélène's stomach. "You big tiger!" The cat brushed her whiskers against her face. "Trying to tell me something?" She placed her ear on the kitty's neck where the purring was most intense. "You're right," she said, pressing her ear closer to absorb the vibrations of feline pleasure. *If I could purr, this would be the moment*, she mused, contemplating her weekend plans. She rubbed Chaussette's soft neck. "Party time, *bébé!*"

CHAPTER FIVE

The next morning, Hélène woke with a fuzzy sensation against her head. "Chaussette! You know that's Papa's pillow! He'd strangle you if he were here." She tried to push her cat away, but Chaussette wouldn't budge. All Hélène got was a look of defiance. Then it hit her. "You're right. What he doesn't know can't hurt him." Feeling naughty, she squeezed the cat against her nightgown.

"I don't know about you, but I'm starved. Time for a nice, healthy breakfast before the market opens." The idea of food got Chaussette off the pillow. The cat crisscrossed in front of Hélène's slippered feet, meowing in agreement all the way down the stairs.

A few minutes later, Hélène sat in her garden in a floppy straw hat and huge plastic sunglasses, cheerfully devouring muesli with chopped banana, fresh organic fruit, orange juice, and herbal tea. Hunched in the grass next to her tapping toes, Chaussette gobbled up her own *light menu* kibble.

Then the phone rang. Reluctantly, Hélène sauntered into the living room. "Marc?" she garbled into the receiver as she chewed.

"Why would I be Marc?" a feminine voice asked. "It's Saturday morning. Isn't he with you?"

Hélène crunched a mouthful of cereal. "Hi, Cecile. As a matter of fact, he isn't. He—"

"*Ah*, Hélène. I'm so proud of you!" Cecile's high-pitched voice hurt Hélène's ears. "So, you finally kicked him out! What did I tell you? As a woman, you have to stand up for yourself. Nobody else will do it for you. What a jerk he's been to you all these years!"

"Don't get so excited, Ceci. He's just on a business trip to London."

Cecile loudly slurped a drink. "Right. So he says."

"Well, he *is*. He left last night and—"

"I thought he didn't travel for work anymore."

"He doesn't. I mean, he didn't. This is an exception."

"An exception? I doubt it..."

Hélène could tell this was going to be a long one. Conversations with Cecile lasted hours, and when she got onto the subject of Marc and the way he treated Hélène, there was no stopping her. She pushed aside her half-eaten breakfast and settled in her lawn chair outside.

"How long's he gone for?"

"Just the weekend," replied Hélène, opening up her bathrobe. Chaussette took this as an invitation; she hopped up on her T-shirt and settled between Hélène's breasts.

"*Ah bon.* So, tell me, who does business on weekends?"

"Well..." Hélène shut her eyes to consider the question. *Let me see. Hairdressers?*

"About car engines?" Cecile's voice rose a notch. "I hate to say it, but this trip smells fishy. *Ma chérie*, wake up and smell the marigolds!"

Marigolds? Hélène's thoughts flashed back to her recent conversation with Sylvie. She sat up abruptly, forcing Chaussette off her chest. "What do marigolds have to do with this?"

"*Ah*, Hélène. You can be so naïve. You know what I mean. Wake up and smell the coffee!"

Hélène heard Cecile take a deep drag on her cigarillo. "You really think you can trust him?"

"*Quelle question!* Marc would never do anything behind my back. He's not the type." She thought of the niggle of worry she'd felt the night before when thinking about him with another woman and shoved it aside.

"*D'accord.* If he's not doing anything, then why didn't he take you with him?"

Hélène began fiddling with her fruit. "Guess he didn't think of it?"

"Did you go through his clothes like I said?"

"*Ouais*, I did. No lipstick and only Chaussette's hairs on his jacket. I trust him, Cecile, that's all I can say." Hélène picked up a banana and began carving doodles in its skin with her fingernail. "Besides, wouldn't I know if he were cheating? After all, I *am* his wife."

"Not necessarily. Spouses don't always see everything going on around them."

At that precise moment, Hélène made a face as Chaussette started humping one of Marc's old sports shoes on the grass. She answered, "I guess you're right, but—"

"A woman can never be too cautious. Look what happened to me." Cecile gave a feminine cough. "What about his pockets?"

"Just a few sketches of race cars, engines…And a torso."

"A what?"

"You know, a torso." Hélène's finger began caressing the grooves on the banana. "A self-portrait, I'm sure. You know how Marc worships his muscles. Even though they're smaller than mine." *I hate how he stands in front of the mirror every day, staring at his puny biceps.*

Cecile hissed into the receiver. "That's gross."

"I don't have the heart to tell him how ridiculous it is. At least he's not sketching other women." Hélène pushed the banana aside and grasped two oranges. As she contemplated the thought of her husband drawing naked women, she arranged the fruit in front of her. They looked like a pair of boobs.

"I guess you've got a point there."

"Don't worry, Ceci. I know my husband. He's so predictable. All he ever does is go to the office and lift weights with the guys at the gym. He never even *looks* at other women."

"Maybe that's the problem," retorted Cecile. "What if he's gay?"

"*Mon Dieu*, Ceci. Sipping too many daiquiris again?" She heard Cecile sputter. "*C'est ridicule.* Marc's just away for the weekend. There's nothing more to it. And for once, I get to be alone and just relax. I'm actually enjoying it. Besides, I've got plans for tonight."

"I *knew* it! You can't hide things from me, Hélène. You've got a guy lurking around. I can *smell* him from here!"

Hélène thrust the receiver from her ear as her friend began hacking.

"You've got to stop smoking those nasty cigarillos. That's what you're smelling."

"Just on Saturdays, *ma chérie*," Cecile said with a dry cough.

"*Alors*, who's the lucky guy?"

"*M'enfin!* Just because your libido's so—"

Cecile chuckled. "I'll take that as a compliment, *merci*. So, do I know him?"

"What the heck? I'm just going to a girlfriend's place for dinner."

"*Ah*, come on," Cecile whined.

Hélène began peeling the banana. "You know me, Ceci. I'm not the cheating type. I'm the old-fashioned kind of wife." She raised her butcher's knife. "Quiet, decent, and…" Furiously, she chopped up the banana. "Harmless." She slid the pieces into her half-eaten bowl of muesli.

Cecile sighed. "You're too decent for your own good, Hel. Take some advice from me: live it up! We're not getting any younger, *tu sais*. Our body clocks are ticking," she whispered into the receiver.

"I can hear yours ticking all the way over here! Why don't you dump your friend tonight, and let's go out just the two of us? We'll go hunk hunting."

Hélène frowned. "You know what, Cecile? You really should grow up one of these days. Besides, I can't cancel my dinner tonight."

"Okay, you win. She can come along if she's not too ugly. We don't want to attract flies, you know."

Hélène glanced at the two orange halves propped on her plate like firm breasts. A fly landed on the tip of one. "How thoughtful of you, Cecile. Maybe another time." She shooed away the fly.

"Don't tell me you'd rather spend your Saturday night sipping tea with some lousy girlfriend, instead of fishing for a…" She sneezed into the receiver.

"Bless you! I bet you're wearing that teensy pink bikini of yours and sipping frozen daiquiris. Am I right? Be careful, Ceci, we're in Brussels, not Florida. It's too cold to be sitting out there half naked." Hélène shook her head when her best friend tried to deny it. "Let's talk about this on Monday, *d'accord?*" *Hunk hunting is the last thing I feel like doing tonight.*

CHAPTER SIX

S till chewing the last of her mushy muesli, Hélène lay down on the lawn chair, adjusted her sunglasses, and pulled her floppy hat over her eyes. *I'll just relax while I digest my breakfast.* Within seconds, her eyelids closed, and her mind drifted back to her recent adventure with Sylvie at the coast, a moment she kept replaying as the days flew past.

Sylvie was grinning. "What does it look like? We're going swimming."

"Out there?" Hélène gulped at the waves crashing in the distance.

Sylvie grabbed her hand and broke into a run. "Whatever... *On y va!*" she yelled, pulling Hélène over the hot sand. Once they reached the water, she dropped her hand and dove into the ocean. She resurfaced like a dolphin.

Hélène pouted as she tiptoed into the cool ocean with her arms suspended in the air. "It's freezing!" She clenched her teeth and advanced one centimeter at a time. As soon as the water reached her thighs, she stopped. Shivering, she observed Sylvie swimming circles around her. Sylvie's muscular body brushed against her leg. She resurfaced, playfully splashing Hélène's face with seawater.

Hélène could feel her soaked T-shirt plastered to her chest. She looked down. Horrified, she realized her erect nipples were pointing directly at Sylvie, with drops of seawater streaming off their tips.

When she stumbled against a wave, Sylvie gently lifted her

up, holding on to her tightly. Just then, the descending sun's rays lit up Hélène's face. She shivered as Sylvie cupped her cheeks in her hands, peered into her eyes, and kissed her tenderly on the lips.

Mon Dieu. Is this really happening?

Hélène took a deep breath and kissed her back. Their tongues mingled; awkwardness turned to tenderness, which turned to passion. Hélène couldn't get enough of her. Like an animal's acute awareness, her senses perked as their bodies rubbed against each other in the ocean. Her mind went blank as Sylvie attacked her throat with her tongue while they grabbed at each other with their hungry hands...

Hélène woke with a start. Something was tickling her neck. *Mmm, that's nice.* She lifted the straw hat from her eyes and yelped, "*Mon Dieu!* You naughty thing..." Chaussette was licking her throat. "What do you think I am? Friskies?" Hélène's face was warm. "Stop it!" She set her cat on the wet grass. While she was dozing, the sprinkling system had sprayed the entire garden—including her. Peering at her soggy white T-shirt, she noticed her nipples standing as erect as obedient soldiers. Then she remembered her daydream, and the fragrance of Sylvie's wet skin mingled with the salty ocean air. Not only did it create longing, which she felt deep inside, but she started to worry about tonight's tête-à-tête dinner. She turned off the sprinkler and sloshed her way into the house.

"*Mince*, it's already after eleven!" She looked at the clock. "I hope it's not too late, *bébé*," she told the fuzzy ball at her feet. "Maman has to go shopping before the market closes!"

Hélène pedaled to the market as fast as she could. Once there, she rushed to her favorite stands before the merchants packed up their goods. Squeezing past the crowds, she emerged with two straw baskets overflowing with farm-fresh groceries.

Too bad she wasn't there. She glanced at the fresh flowers tucked under her arm. *But I'll be seeing her tonight anyway.* The thought made Hélène's skin tingle. Then someone called her name. Her heart beat faster. She swung around to see Paul and Ramon, the hairstylists from her friend Jimmy's salon. The couple was wearing matching outfits: tight white shorts, leather sandals, and "JIMMY'S CUTS" tank tops.

Hélène tried not to look disappointed.

"Nice to see you too," Paul said with a smirk.

"I didn't mean..." Hélène stammered, trying to force a smile.

Ramon glanced around. "Maybe you were expecting someone else?"

"*Non.* It's just that I've never seen you guys here before." Hélène returned their kisses.

"That's for sure," said Paul.

Ramon added with his strong Spanish accent, "I'd love to come here on Saturdays, but it's impossible with customers lining up to—"

"Make them sexy for their Saturday night *rendez-vous!*" added Paul, running his fingers through Ramon's wavy hair.

"I see Jimmy's got you out here advertising." Hélène pointed at their lime-green tank tops. The muscle-hugging shirts sported a colorful image of their boss waving scissors over his head.

"*Ouais*, but I'd rather chill the advertising. Maybe we'd get more Saturdays off. *N'est-ce pas,* Paul?"

"Great idea. *You* tell Jimmy then." Paul tapped his boyfriend playfully on the chest.

Hélène's groceries were growing heavier by the minute. She peered over their shoulders. *Maybe she's still around. Somewhere...*

Ramon followed Hélène's eyes until they landed on a man staring directly at them. "Could this be..." Ramon began, flashing the man a sweet smile until a blond woman with a baby carriage grabbed the man's hand. "I guess not," he muttered, turning toward Hélène. "Anyway, where's your hubby? I'd *love* to finally meet him!"

"Yeah, me too," added Paul.

"Sorry, you're out of luck. He's on a business trip."

"*Ah bon.*" Paul's smile faded. "So, you're all by your lonesome?"

Hélène nodded. "But actually, I'm enjoying my freedom. I never really get any."

"You never get any *what?*" Paul winked.

Hélène flushed as her thoughts dashed back to Sylvie. She mentally pushed her emotions aside and sneaked a last, desperate look around the marketplace.

"Stop embarrassing us!" Ramon punched his boyfriend playfully in the arm.

"*Aiie*, that hurt!"

"Good, you deserve it." Ramon rolled his eyes at Hélène. "Sorry about that. He can get so obnoxious sometimes. Sex is all he thinks about on weekends."

"What? Sex on weekends? Only weekends?" Paul spread his arms wide. "How dare you insinuate—"

"Shh, *mon chéri*, or you're spending the rest of your weekend alone." Ramon blew him an exaggerated air kiss. Then he looked at Hélène and hooked his muscular arm around her shoulder. "Wait a minute. Now that you're free, why don't you join us? We're headed to our favorite café."

Paul's eyes lit up. "*Ah oui*, what a fabulous idea! You *must* come with us, Hélène. You'll absolutely *adore* the place." He winked at Ramon.

Hélène scanned the marketplace. Hardly any shoppers were left. She checked her watch. "*D'accord*, but I can't stay long. I'll get my bike."

Ramon's dark eyes hardened. "He left you without a car?" He eyed Hélène's overflowing baskets. "That's unforgivable. You'd think he'd have the decency to take a taxi."

"Before you get all worked up, it's not what you think. My car's at home, but I never use it anymore. I'd rather use these." Hélène pointed to her thigh muscles. "I want to keep them strong and healthy and…" Then she glanced at Paul, sitting in his wheelchair, listening to her ramble about developing her strong, healthy legs.

I'm such an idiot! She stammered, "I'd rather…*Eh bien*."

"Hey, it's okay," Paul smiled warmly at Hélène, whose face burned with embarrassment.

Ramon slapped her on the back. "Seems as if you've radically changed your lifestyle. Not like you were a lump of lard or anything, but...Anyway, you'll tell us all about it at the café. *Vámonos*," he added, grabbing her baskets.

"And don't worry about your bike. We'll bring you back here later." Paul smiled warmly.

I can be such an idiot sometimes. Hélène watched his biceps bulge as he wheeled over the cobblestones. But then she chuckled when she saw the image on the back of Ramon's tank top: the three hairstylists at Jimmy's Cuts were all wearing the same tight tank tops, mini shorts, and straw hats, and Ramon was suspended in the air, clicking his heels together.

The three gay Musketeers. Good thing Marc isn't here with me today. He has so little tolerance for anyone who's not like himself. Then she bit her lower lip. *I've been thinking that more and more lately.*

Ramon pulled his van into the café parking lot. "*Super*, it's all ours." He entered the blue disabled parking space. A buzzing sound erupted as the van's metallic ramp lowered to the ground. Ramon untied the straps fastening Paul's wheelchair to the floor of the van and rolled his boyfriend down the ramp.

Hélène had never thought about how people in wheelchairs got in and out of cars. Her eyes fell on Paul's broad shoulders. *He sure is strong. I wonder if there are cars that can be driven with hands only, like an oversized, motorized wheelchair?* She made a mental note to search for it on the internet as the three headed up the ramp to a peach-colored café with huge windows.

"Nice name." She pointed to a flashing neon sign, CAFE HOM@LONE, above a dangling rainbow flag.

"Just wait till you get inside. You're in for a real treat!" Paul winked.

"*Incroyable*," murmured Hélène when they entered the café. *How unique. So, this is what gay bars are like?* Through the dimness, she squinted at the rainbow-colored walls, gigantic potted plants, and sculptures of nude men in compromising poses. Disco music blared from a jukebox.

Hélène's smile collapsed as soon as she bumped into something. "*Pardon*," she whispered, stepping back. "What the?" she exclaimed to the coat rack. Her hand smothered her giggles. *Now, that's original.* Like smooth branches on a tree, a dozen wooden phalluses stuck out from the rack at all angles—in all colors and sizes. She noticed a pink umbrella dangling from one of the sturdier, mushroom-nosed branches.

"Such nice…decorations!" Hélène's fingers swiftly brushed off all imaginary impregnating substances she might have rubbed against.

Ramon grinned. "Cool, *non?*" He led her to a booth beside the window. "Sit here. You don't want to miss the scenery. You won't believe what kinds of exotic specimens—"

"Stroll by," interceded Paul, wheeling his chair to the booth.

"I can only imagine." But when Hélène looked out the window, she gasped. There was Frank, the homeless man she and Sylvie had come across a while ago in the street. She had been shocked at how Sylvie had treated him, with such respect and genuine concern. She had even held his hand and asked him how he was. How could she have guessed that these two people from radically different walks of life—at least from all outward appearances—were friendly acquaintances? She cringed inside. *How could I have been so ignorant about homeless people?* Thanks to Sylvie, she realized they deserved respect just like anyone else—they all had their own unique situations.

She held her breath. *That's him all right.* He was wearing the same tattered clothes as the other day and clutching a wine bottle. To her surprise, just as he passed the café, he stopped, squinted at Hélène, then winked.

Hélène felt a trickle of sweat run down her neck. She glanced at her companions, but they were too busy checking out sexier, cleaner folk. *C'est bizarre. Everywhere I go, I see signs of Sylvie.* To emulate

Sylvie's kindness, she quickly winked back at him. He nodded his scruffy chin at her and shuffled down the sidewalk.

Just then, a young guy with razor-short hair and tight jeans strolled past the window.

"Get a look at this fine piece of—" whispered Paul.

"Decoration!" added Ramon, straining to see properly.

When the young man sauntered into the café, both Paul and Ramon stared at the white jeans passing their booth.

Paul licked his lips. "Baseball butt."

"*Non*. Hockey. Ice hockey. Definitely," insisted Ramon.

With a deep sigh, Hélène directed her gaze toward the street. She despised sweaty male sports, mainly because Marc was so obsessed by them. Through her glasses, she noticed the blackness of Frank's soiled, bare feet as they inched across the street. Every few steps, he paused to take a swig of wine. At last, he leaned against the wall, sinking like a waterlogged ship as his weary body descended to the sidewalk.

Hélène followed his outstretched toes with her eyes. Then she gasped as she looked at the blue and white building behind him. "*Mon Dieu!*" *It's the Greek restaurant where we had lunch. Sylvie and I sat at that small table in back of the garden. We were all alone and...* She covered her gaping mouth with her fingers.

"I knew you'd love it here. View's amazing, *non*?" Paul cracked a smile. "Hunks like these are to whimper and die for!"

Then he seemed to notice an element of sadness in Hélène's expression. "*Ma puce?* You all right?" He placed his fingers over hers. When she didn't answer, he turned to Ramon.

"Maybe this wasn't such a good idea. It might be too much for her. Look at her face, it's as red as a hot poker in a—"

"Shh, Paul. That's not it." Hélène fanned the air. "It's just that…See that restaurant across the street?"

Ramon's long lashes fluttered with recognition. "Where are our manners, Paul? Here we are babbling about hunky this and hunky that, and it's already well after noon." He turned toward her. "You must be starving, *ma chérie!*"

"*Garçon!*" he shouted, flicking his wrist at the waiter.

Hélène shook her head. "*Non, non.* It's not that. It's just…" She lowered her voice. "You see, I came here the other day, and—"

Paul frowned. "You've been to this café before?"

"Are you kidding?" Hélène snickered. "Let me finish, *d'accord*? Actually, I ate at that restaurant over there." She pointed out the window. "It's Greek and—"

"I know, it's delicious, isn't it, Ramon?" Paul interrupted.

"Let Hélène finish her—"

"Wait! I get it!" said Paul. "The waiter *hit* on you! Don't worry, that's a Greek thing. They do that to all their customers. It's good for business." He tapped Hélène's wrist. "Don't you worry. We won't tell your hubby, will we, Ramon? We *adore* going there. Those two waiters are absolutely gorgeous, *n'est-ce pas*? Especially the hairy—"

Ramon tweaked Paul's chin. "Let her tell her story. Something's bothering you, *ma chérie*. Don't worry, we won't tell a soul. You'll feel much better once it's out."

Hélène raised her eyebrows at the word choice. "Out?"

Ramon smiled. "It's written right here." He pointed to a small crease in the center of her forehead. "Nothing that some detoxifying, anti-stress herbs can't fix." His arm went around her shoulders. "Once they seep into your system, we'll discuss things calmly and—"

"*Salut les filles!*" A waiter with a ponytail and closely trimmed, peppery beard sauntered over to their booth. He air-kissed Paul and Ramon with an obnoxious smacking sound.

"*Salut*, I'm Georges," he purred, extending a highly manicured hand to Hélène. "Welcome to Café Hom@lone."

Hélène glanced at his low-cut red sneakers. *He smells like oil paint and cinnamon rolls. A true a-r-t-i-s-t-e.*

"*Alors*, what'll it be this time, girls? Coffee…tea…or *moi*?" The waiter twirled his ponytail at the trio.

Ramon cleared his throat. "We'll have one of those calming detox teas for our lady friend, and the usual for us, Georges."

"A Dainty Bather for *Mademoiselle*, and two Erect Cliffs for my favorite stylists," recited Georges, batting his curly lashes. His eyes settled on Ramon's chest. "*J'adore* those shirts! Can I get one?"

"Only if you behave yourself." Paul whacked him playfully on the elbow.

"*Moi?* I'm a perfect angel." The waiter winked at the threesome and sashayed off. "Back in a jiffy!"

"You'd never guess he owned the place," snorted Paul. "With those silly sneakers. And who says 'jiffy' anymore?"

"His charm must work on the customers, though." Hélène eyeballed the packed café.

"Sure does." Ramon nodded. "Now, back to you. What's going on?"

"*Eh bien...*" Hélène glanced around nervously. "Where's Jimmy today?" She averted Ramon's eyes.

"Sneaky, Hélène. Don't change the subject."

"*Non*, really. Where is he?"

"At an international hairstyling contest, so we get the weekend off." Ramon grinned. "It's the first time we've closed on a Satur—"

Paul perked up. "And get this, he brought his new—"

"Pair of scissors with him!" interrupted Ramon.

Paul made a face. "Of course he did, but he also brought—"

"*Mon lapin*, let's not bore Hélène with trite chatter."

"What's the problem?" asked Paul, pouting. "Jimmy and Hélène are old buddies! You don't know anyone in the gay scene anyway, *n'est-ce pas*, Hélène? Besides, you're going to tell us all about your—"

"Actually..." Hélène lowered her eyes. "I—"

Just then, Ramon's cell phone rang. His eyes lit up when he gushed, "Speak of the devil! How's it going over there? We were just talking about you."

"*Alors*, he's having a good time?" asked Paul.

"Sounds like it." Ramon nodded. "He was out of breath anyway."

Paul snorted. "That's probably a good sign."

Hélène gave the couple a quizzical look.

"And he got the bronze medal with his new scissors!" Ramon beamed.

"*C'est super*," added Paul.

"So, he's at an international hairstyling contest?" asked Hélène, relieved the conversation had switched to Jimmy. "That's so exciting. Where is it?"

"In Lo—"

"Miss me?" Georges, approaching with three steaming mugs of tea, winked at Ramon. "*Voici.*" He set a mug in front of each customer.

Hélène's eyes widened. Each ceramic mug was shaped like a muscular, naked man. *How am I supposed to pick this thing up?* She tried not to appear squeamish at the challenge of handling the mug without poking certain male body parts with her fingers.

"*Aiie*, it's hot!" she yelped, withdrawing her hand.

"You bet it's hot, *bébé.*" Georges flashed her a cunning grin.

"Don't worry, *ma puce*, it can't hurt you. It's just tea: a natural remedy for stress," reassured the waiter, licking his lips. Then he laughed. "*Mais évidemment!* This isn't your specialty, is it, *Mademoiselle?*" He grinned. "Of course, other lesbians come in here too. Couples mostly. Funny, I don't remember seeing you—"

Ramon cleared his throat. "Georges, Hélène is a former classmate of Jimmy's."

Georges squinted at her. "Really? Maybe you can do something about this. I can't stand it any longer!" He flicked his peppery ponytail at her like a horse flicking flies.

"I'd love to, but that's not really my specialty."

"It isn't?" Georges scratched his head.

Hélène laughed. "*Non.* But I *could* translate your menus. Jimmy and I went to translation school together, way back when."

The waiter's eyes lit up. "No kidding! That must be why he speaks such good French. Hey, this reminds me…" His nostrils flared with excitement. "I know a gal who translates so much, her fingers cramp up. So, get this." He whispered, "She translates with her tits. And those things really stick out. She does it like this, by hitting the keyboard with her knobs. Like this…Control, Alt, Delete. You know—"

"Thrilling," interrupted Hélène, forcing herself to remain calm. *This guy is really getting on my nerves. Why can't we just sip our tea?* "Most of us still do it the old-fashioned way, with these." She wiggled her fingers in the air.

Paul stifled a giggle. Ramon looked away nervously.

Georges wiggled his thick fingers back at her. "I bet you *do!* You naughty little lass!"

Ramon broke in. "Back off, Georges! Hélène's not only a translator, but she's a very loyal customer of ours and quite married."

"To her *husband.*" Paul pointed to Hélène's wedding ring.

"*Ah bon?* How silly of me!" The waiter crossed his arms over his chest. "I just assume everyone is…Forgive me, *Mademoiselle.* I mean, *Madame. Oh là là,* now I've put my foot in it." He sashayed away from their booth.

Hélène spoke in a hushed tone. "That's the first time anybody thought I was a…You know, a…" She coughed, realizing she was unable to say the L-word. Not even here, in a gay café with her two companions who happened to be gay. Very gay.

Why can't I say it? wondered Hélène, wiping a trickle of sweat off her forehead. *Sylvie and I kissed the other day. She's all I can think about. I'm completely obsessed with her. And I can't even say the L-word. What's wrong with me?* Feeling her cheeks flush, she turned her gaze to the wall.

"Hey, come back to Earth. Our tea's getting cold," said Paul.

Ramon nodded. "*Alors,* time to tell Uncle Paul and Uncle Ramon what's on your mind."

"Just pour out your problems, honey." Paul smiled genuinely.

Hélène sighed. "I don't know where to start."

"How about from the beginning?"

"Lots of things have changed for me recently." Hélène took a deep breath. "I've been exercising. First, I started biking, you see, then I started swimming lessons." She wasn't even going to bring up Hilde, the psychic, and the possibility of having a brother. It was often on her mind, but she wasn't ready to do anything about it yet. Besides, if she told these two, they'd be on some kind of crazy genealogy hunt within seconds.

"Swimming lessons!" Paul burst out. "*D'accord!* Gorgeous, athletic bodies in tight little bathing suits. Excellent!"

Hélène flinched.

"It's exciting, right, Hélène?" Paul leaned closer. "That's it, isn't it?" He smiled as he studied her. "*Oui, c'est ça.*" He nodded emphatically. "Ramon, Hélène's infatuated with someone in her swimming class."

Hélène could feel the blood rising in her cheeks. "Anyway, so I'm taking these swimming lessons…" Her voice trailed off.

"Go on," prodded Ramon.

"*Private* ones."

Paul stopped swirling his tea. "*Ah oui!*" he blurted, fanning his face. "It's like a sauna in here, *non?*"

"Cut the antics, Paul," said Ramon curtly.

"Yeah, you're getting all worked up for nothing. It's not at all what you're thinking."

"And why not?" asked Paul, dabbing his forehead with his napkin.

"Because my swimming teacher's a woman," Hélène whispered, shutting her eyes. *She's a woman all right.* She imagined Sylvie glistening wet in her bathing suit, standing so close; she smelled the chlorine on her smooth, olive skin. Hélène suppressed a sigh as her hand fluttered to her chest.

Paul leaned forward. "What did you just say?"

Hélène cleared her throat and repeated slowly, "My teacher's a…woman."

Paul batted his long, dark eyelashes at Ramon as if to send him a secret message.

"Young, pretty…A *woman!*" repeated Hélène, twitching as the word reverberated down her spine. *She certainly is a woman. Actually, she's a Greek goddess, in the flesh...* Hélène felt another jolt of electricity.

Paul shook his head. "*Ah non*, that's too bad."

Ramon brushed a strand of hair from her eyes. He leaned in, whispering tenderly, "I'm not so sure about that."

Hélène held her breath when she realized her fingers were trembling. She looked into the mirror above their heads. Her eyes were like the sea: moist and clear, with a deep shade of blue. They always got like that whenever she felt strong emotions. Ever since she was a toddler, people commented on how stunning her blue eyes were—after she spent a few minutes in the bright sun, or had a migraine, or cried—even behind her thick glasses. As an introvert, she hated being so transparent; her eyes unlocked the doorway to her soul. She knit her eyebrows. *I feel so vulnerable right now. And so stupid.*

"You okay, *ma chérie?*" Ramon put his hand gently over hers. She exhaled at the comfort of his touch. Instantly, her fingers relaxed.

"Welcome to the club." Smiling tenderly, Ramon gave her a warm hug.

Paul's eyebrow shot up. "What club?"

Ramon winked at his boyfriend but didn't go into detail.

"*Non, non.* You've got it all wrong!" stammered Hélène. "She's just a friend, really..."

"*Ah, that* club!" Paul chuckled. "Now I get it."

Hélène's fist pounded the table, rattling the spoons and mugs. "Well, I don't! Where in the heck did you get this idea that—"

Paul smiled. "Just look at her, Ramon. She's getting all nervous and—"

"No, I'm not!" Hélène raised her mug. Her fervor sent her Dainty Bather tea slicking over its edges.

"You dig her, it's obvious." Paul leaned across the table. "Let me give you some advice, *ma puce.* Just take the plunge!"

Ramon held up his hand. "*Attends.* I think she needs some—"

Hélène's nerves were fraying. "You're terrible. I don't even know if..." She clenched her teeth. Did she really want to say the words out loud? If she couldn't talk to her friends, who would she talk to?

"Take a sip, *ma chérie.* It'll calm you down."

Hélène obeyed. After a gulp of tepid tea, she whispered, "*Enfin...*We had lunch at that restaurant over there." Her eyes widened. "Oh my God!" A mouthful of Dainty Bather tea spewed through her teeth. "Her car." She pointed her spoon at the VW Bug parked across the street. "It's the yellow one."

Ramon whistled. "Cool car. A bit ancient, but it's—"

"Shh! It's her. My swimming teacher!" Hélène gasped as Sylvie emerged from the Greek restaurant. Her heart was racing. *What does she do, live there?* Sylvie was standing in the doorway, laughing while flinging her hair. *She's flirting with someone.* Hélène tried to control her anger.

A young woman with a dark, blunt haircut strolled out. She was stylishly dressed in high heels. Hélène held her breath. The woman grabbed Sylvie's arm, then whispered into her ear. They burst into laughter.

Hélène studied the young woman's shapely legs. *They sure seem intimate. Who in the heck is she?* Sylvie had said she wasn't with anyone, but that didn't mean she wasn't dating. Hélène hadn't even thought to ask. *And it's none of my business, really.*

"Which one is she?" asked Ramon and Paul at the same time.

"That one." Hélène pointed to Sylvie. "The beautiful one."

"But they're both superb!" said Paul.

Hélène's stomach lurched. "The taller one."

Paul squinted. "You mean the older one?"

"*Ah non!* You guys, I think they're together!" The words resonated in her mind, like an echo. *How could they be together? And how come I didn't know about this? I bet there's a lot of things she doesn't tell me. How many girlfriends does she have?* Hélène shook her head to try to reason with herself. *Why should I care, anyway? All we did was kiss. And I fully regret it...Don't I?*

"Don't say that," said Ramon. "They're probably just—"

Hélène grabbed her hair in frustration.

"And don't do *that!*" added Paul. "If Jimmy saw you ruining your new hairdo, he'd—"

Hélène flashed him a dirty look.

"Like I said, they're probably just close friends, right, Paul?" Ramon winked at his boyfriend.

Paul shook his head. "No way, Ramon. She's right. Look at how the taller one's…Ouch!" He leaned down to rub his shin under the table. "You nuts or what? That *hurt!*" But then he glanced at Hélène.

"*Ah oui. Bien sûr*, Ramon, you're right. They're just buddies. How silly of me to jump to conclusions."

"I hope she can't see us in here!" Hélène ducked down to retrieve a huge pair of plastic sunglasses from her bag. She promptly placed them over her glasses. *The last thing I need is for her to think I'm spying on her. Our relationship is already troubled as it is. I can't let her see me in here, in a gay bar!*

"Let's not get paranoid, *chérie*." Paul pursed his lips to sip his tea.

"But I've got to hide!" gasped Hélène, huddling over Ramon's lap. "Do something, Ramon. Camouflage me!"

Ramon put a thick, leafy plant on the windowsill to block the view. "*Voilà.* You're all set."

Hélène sat up and peeked through the leaves.

"*Mince!* She's getting into Sylvie's car." She watched as they moved around each other. Then the woman bent over and was clearly trying to get something from the floorboard as Sylvie hovered behind her, laughing and pointing.

"I'm going to be sick." Hélène covered her mouth while diving under the table. Crawling on all fours, she emerged on the other side and sprinted toward the ladies' room.

A few moments later, Ramon scooted out to let her back into the booth. "Feeling better, *ma chérie?*"

Hélène peered through the leafy plant and sighed with relief. "*Oof*, looks like they're gone." Her hand gravitated to her lips to muffle an abrupt Dainty Bather burp. "*Pardon!*" she whispered, wiping her lips with her napkin. "*Désolée, les mecs.* I hardly expected that."

"No problem." Paul chuckled. "Everyone gets indigestion."

Ramon smiled tenderly. "Life can be so unpredictable. Anyway, I'm sure there's nothing between them. Probably just sisters…"

"*Eeew.*" Paul screwed up his face in disgust. "I think they were too friendly for *that.*"

Hélène tried to ignore that last comment by contemplating the leaves on the window plant. "I don't remember her mentioning any sisters," she murmured, poking her nose at a leaf.

"I've got an idea." Paul winked at Ramon. "Just ask her, '*Eh bien*…Who are you sleeping with lately?' "

"Brilliant idea. You're so subtle, Paul." Hélène plucked the leaf and flung it at him.

"Why not? That would clear up any doubts, wouldn't it?"

"Actually, I'm going over to her place for dinner tonight and—"

"*Ça alors!* This is getting better by the minute." Paul rubbed his hands together. "What fun, inviting you for a drink. This is so—"

"Paul! Let's get back to helping Hélène." Ramon lowered his voice, ignoring his boyfriend's scowl. "Though, for once, he's right, Hélène. You could just ask her if she's seeing someone. In a tactful manner, *bien sûr.* Like after a glass of wine…"

Paul shook his head. "*Non.* Drain the bottle. Then attack her. Besides, who cares who she's sleeping with? If you're lucky, you're next in line. She's superb!"

Hélène tossed another leaf at him. "This is serious, Paul." She lowered her eyes. "I'll just cancel dinner and—"

"Let's not get drastic, *ma chérie.*" Ramon lifted Hélène's face. "So, you really like this woman?"

Hélène thought about it. *Do I like this woman?* Before she could answer, she felt nauseous again. Her stomach twisted into a knot. She rested her face on her crossed forearms. "Guess I do."

"Louder. We can't hear you," Ramon whispered into Hélène's ear. "*Encore.*" But she just lay on the table, silent. "You asked for it." He wrapped her hair around his fingers and pulled her to an erect position. "*Alors?*"

Hélène gave him a stern look. "I like her." *It's true. I really like her.* Hélène felt it in her gut. She felt it in her soul. *So, what's she doing with that other woman?*

"Much better." Ramon held up his mug. "Here's a toast. To Hélène and her *private* swimming teacher."

"Who's really hot." Paul rubbed his hands together.

Ramon narrowed his eyes. "To a long—"

Paul giggled. "Orgasmic…"

"Cut it out, Paul. I'm trying to be serious." Ramon continued, "Here's a toast to a long—"

"Friendship!" Hélène lowered her voice. "I don't know that I want anything more than that. Not yet."

"That's hardly romantic." Ramon paused. "How about a long lifetime of—"

"Underwater vibes!" blurted Paul.

Ramon grinned. "*Oui*, I like that. 'Underwater vibes.'"

A shiver slid through Hélène's body as her thoughts went to Sylvie's muscular body, her warm touch in the water, the attraction she felt whenever she approached. *Such strong vibrations. Something about them makes me feel so alive, so awake.* She nodded with approval.

"Cool! To underwater vibes, then." Ramon lifted his mug again.

"Bottoms up!" Hélène tipped her mug, exposing a pair of bare ceramic buttocks. Even though her tea was cold, it did wonders for her morale. "Thanks, guys. I feel so much better."

"Told you so," said Ramon. "Each tea has its own special effects."

Paul smiled. "We're heading home now. You've got to relax before your hot date and…*eh bien*, Ramon and I just downed two potent Erect Cliff teas, if you get my drift."

"That's enough!" interrupted Ramon. Before Hélène had time to blush, he was waving his white napkin, summoning the bill.

CHAPTER SEVEN

As soon as Hélène set her grocery baskets on the kitchen table, Chaussette was licking her ankles.

"*Désolée, bébé!* I was heading home, but guess what? Paul and Ramon invited me out for tea. What a unique café. You would've adored it!" She poured cat food into Chaussette's bowl. Scratching her cat's ears, she glanced at the clock.

"*Ah non,* it's already four thirty!" Hélène raced up the stairs. "What am I going to wear?"

Chaussette jumped on her mistress's bed, licking her lips in anticipation of an intriguing fashion show. The music was already on. Hélène emerged from the bathroom, prancing around in a new outfit before the full-length mirror. She wore a slinky, low-cut black dress with a red-feathered boa around her neck. *Makes me look cheap.* Chaussette shook her head in disapproval.

Then she appeared in an oversized Mickey Mouse T-shirt with flared, red and green checkered polyester pants, embellished by a light pink backpack with a miniature Barbie doll hanging by a noose. Chaussette gagged.

"Right. Not sophisticated enough." Next, she tried a shapeless, pale green velvet dress with puffy shoulders and a thick green ribbon in her ponytail. As a final touch, she wore a massive pair of red plastic glasses. Chaussette yawned.

"Too intellectual, *non?* I look like a German teacher." She whipped off the glasses and flashed a naughty grin. "Maybe something sexier?"

This time, Hélène reappeared in a tight, deep-cut, transparent blouse over a lacy thong and black fishnet stockings. While she danced provocatively alongside the mirror, Chaussette gagged until a fur-ball laced with saliva popped out of her mouth.

Hélène winced at the new decoration on her bedspread. *"D'accord.* Looks like I'm in drag." She reemerged in charcoal slacks and a tailored blue blouse. The neckline opened in a tasteful manner, revealing a slender pearl necklace between Hélène's breasts. "Guess the classic, natural look will have to do."

Chaussette licked Hélène's finger in agreement.

❖

Clad in her new outfit, Hélène pedaled up to a row of tall apartment buildings in Forest—a quiet area of Brussels renowned for its wide, tree-lined streets. Like the others in the neighborhood, Rue des Pépins was graced with dozens of plush pine trees. She had been riding for at least a half hour; as soon as she stopped, she noticed how hard her heart was pounding. *Is this from exertion or nerves? It's time to stop...or drop.* She searched for Sylvie's building.

"Numéro douze. Voilà," she muttered, folding her map into her coat. She was about to ring the buzzer when a young man emerged from the building. He gallantly held the door open so she could amble in with her overflowing baskets of food. Once he left, she paused in the hallway to collect her thoughts. She hesitated for so long the sensor lights went out. Shuddering, she held her breath. *Restons calme,* she told herself, with a pounding heart.

Okay, let's get this over with. She shuffled her feet over the pavement until she felt the smooth doors of an elevator. To her relief, the lights went on as she entered. She pushed the button next to *S. Routard.* On the third floor, she gazed at the bronze doorbell. *I'm really here.* She dropped her baskets and raised a finger. Then she froze. *Think it through. How bad can it be?*

Inhaling deeply, she pretended to ring the doorbell. Then she smiled, kissing an invisible Sylvie on both cheeks. *Bisou, bisou...*

She pretended to hand her the yellow roses and book of poems she had carefully selected for her.

"Just a little something to thank you." Her heart was beating faster now. She ran her fingers through her hair. *Mince! That was awful. Let's try it again.*

"*Bisou, bisou...Salut!* I know you like yellow so..." Just then, the hall lights went out with a click. *Not again! Stupid automatic timers. Oh well, better get it over with.* She blindly extended her finger, trying to ignore the pounding in her ears. *Riiiiing.*

At least the doorbell works.

Riiiiing, riiiiing.

Hélène waited a bit longer. She squinted at her watch in the darkness. The fluorescent hands read 8:06. She hesitated, then pressed the bell one last time. Finally, the door cracked open. Hélène peeked in but couldn't see Sylvie. It sounded like someone was screaming—in Greek. *Maybe I made a mistake. What if it wasn't tonight?* Hélène started to panic. She was just about to leave when the door swung open. There stood Sylvie, clad in a low-cut white cashmere sweater and black jeans. Hélène's heart jumped. Her hostess was holding a cell phone to her ear and yelling in Greek. At first, she ignored her guest in the doorway. Finally, after a long tirade, she flashed a quick smile at her and pointed to the interior of the apartment.

Hélène entered cautiously. *Not exactly the welcome I expected.* After Sylvie slammed the door, she continued gesticulating and yelling into the phone. *Wish I spoke Greek. She seems really upset. These should comfort her.* She placed her Greek poetry book on a nearby coffee table and handed her the exquisite bouquet. Without even a glance, Sylvie snatched the yellow roses and waved Hélène toward a bright red sofa in the living room. Hélène's shoes sank into the plush, yellow carpet, which matched the room's yellow and orange walls. Flowers were everywhere, in all shapes and colors—especially orange and yellow.

Sylvie was still holding the bouquet. *She hasn't even looked at it yet.* Hélène tried hard to suppress a frown. *Maybe I should've gone with chocolates after all.* To add to Hélène's dismay, her hostess began shouting even louder in Greek, gesticulating with the roses in her hand. The more violently she spoke, the more violently they shook.

Hélène gasped as yellow petals began soaring around the room. She stood in shock as she scrutinized this new, chilling version of Sylvie. Then, ever so tenderly, Hélène began collecting the flower petals strewn around the room. She tried to push away the heaviness in her heart, which felt as if it had just been shoveled into a freezer.

At last, Sylvie put down her cell phone. "Welcome to my pad." She bent down to kiss her kneeling guest. But Hélène turned her cheek away.

"Sorry about that." Sylvie dropped to her knees. "My mother's always so inquisitive. It's impossible to get her to hang up, especially on Saturday nights."

"Don't worry about it," muttered Hélène, forcing a smile. "I had no idea Greek was such a *lively...*" She stopped mid-sentence when her eyes fell on Sylvie's perfectly round, brown breasts trapped in her low-cut, white sweater. She couldn't help staring, which not only troubled her thoughts, it distorted her speech. "Such a...*lovely...lively...uplifting* language!" She thrust a handful of yellow petals into Sylvie's hand.

"What's this?" asked Sylvie as she stood up.

"Your bouquet of flowers."

"*C'est pas vrai!*" Sylvie stared at the petals in her hand. Then she looked down at her other hand, which was choking the bare flower stems. "*Ah*, this is awful. I don't know what got into me."

"That was some fight you were having."

"Fight? We weren't fighting." Sylvie laughed. "That's just our language."

"Sure that was your mother? Sounded more like a lovers' quarrel to me," said Hélène, rising to her feet.

Sylvie's eyes grew wide. "I can assure you, it was Mama all right." She frowned. "And I'm so sorry about your flowers. I go overboard sometimes. I just lose my head." She swept a wild strand of hair behind her ear. "No wonder you were so upset. I was noticing how your eyes changed color like that, and I realized—"

"What do you mean?" Hélène flinched. *She noticed my eyes?*
"*Ouais*, they're normally sea-blue. But right now, they're more like steel gray bullets."

Hélène snickered, recalling her destroyed bouquet. *Bullets... If she wants bullets, I'll gladly give her some. I can't believe she destroyed my lovely flowers like that.*

"Don't believe me? Just take a look." Sylvie led Hélène to a gold-leafed mirror.

"You're right, they do seem gray. Maybe it's because of your bright yellow walls?" Hélène took a deep breath as she tried to ignore Sylvie's warm hand, which was still grasping hers. "Anyway, where did that come from, 'steel gray bullets'?"

Sylvie looked deeply into her eyes. "*Je ne sais pas.* It just popped out."

"Amazing what just pops out sometimes." Hélène tried to keep her eyes off Sylvie's nipples. *Speaking of steel bullets.* "You're rather poetic," she added, trying not to blush. *I hope she can't read minds because mine is on her cashmere sweater.* As a reflex, she started speaking quickly to lessen the tension in the air. "Marc says he can read me like a book when I'm mad. I hate being so transparent."

Sylvie leaned in. Hélène could feel her warm breath on her cheeks. *She even smells like flowers.* She stiffened.

Sylvie was still staring at her. "He's right; you're not very talented at concealing things. I think it's cute," she whispered into her ear.

Hélène felt her cheeks sizzle.

"*Vraiment*, I'm so sorry about these." Sylvie shook the bare flower stems. "Guess I let my emotions get the best of me." She squeezed Hélène's hand. "Hey, you're burning up. Don't tell me you biked all the way here?"

Hélène nodded. "It would help if I could take off my coat."

"I'm such the perfect hostess." Sylvie smiled, revealing her dimples. "No wonder my mother gets angry at me. Where are my manners?" She helped Hélène remove her coat.

"*Ah*, much better," said Hélène, wiggling her shoulders. "It's not too far, really. A half hour or so."

"If I'd known, I'd have picked you up."

I think you already did, thought Hélène, staring at her gorgeous dimples. She thought it more prudent to respond with, "That's nice of you, but I've got a car. I just felt like getting some exercise."

Sylvie lifted one of Hélène's baskets. "You certainly did. This is *heavy*! Are you planning to make me dinner for three weeks?" She winked, then hauled both baskets into the kitchen.

Hélène's face flushed. *Three weeks, in this apartment? With her?* "I wasn't sure what you liked," she stammered, "so I got a bit of everything. Guess I overdid it."

"How Greek of you. We're excessive—and expressive—in all that we do."

"*Ah bon?*" Hélène responded sarcastically. "I hadn't noticed."

"Look at all this. You're amazing!" Sylvie sniffed at the piles of vegetarian dishes. While her hostess inspected each savory serving, Hélène checked out the bright yellow kitchen walls, rows of colorful flower pots, and Sylvie's mini-balcony loaded with plants. Hélène admired her refrigerator door, plastered with photos of a fat orange cat and a few pictures of Sylvie with friends.

"Mmm. These herbs are superb!" Sylvie dangled a few green strands in the air.

Hélène kept her attention glued to the refrigerator. She spotted a few shots of Sylvie and the waiter at the Greek restaurant. As she looked the photos over, she felt her heart thumping. Most of them were taken at the restaurant; others were presumably in Greece, with rows of white houses overlooking the sea. They reminded her of her Santorini picture.

Everyone looks Greek. Am I her only non-Greek friend? Am I even her friend? Or am I just one of her throngs of students? Hélène glanced over her shoulder. Sylvie was swirling her finger in one of Hélène's sauces. It came up white. *Yogurt dill.* As she tenderly licked it off, Hélène's neck began to tingle. With a guilty gulp, she turned back to the photos, though her mind was freshly imprinted with images of Sylvie's tongue.

Suddenly, she felt a lump in her stomach. *I wonder if she invites all her students here?*

Hélène waited until the licking noises subsided. When she finally turned around, her hostess had vanished. She first checked the balcony. *Empty.* Then the living room. *Empty too.* Shrugging, she gravitated back to the refrigerator where another photo caught her eye. Sylvie's arm was around a woman's waist; judging from the huge smile on her face, Sylvie was in bliss.

I knew it. She felt a pang in her heart when she recognized the young, sexy woman who had been laughing with Sylvie outside the Greek restaurant. Only a few hours ago, the pair had seemed just as glossy—and stuck together—as the paper they were printed on.

Hélène's pang grew sharper. Posing together on a secluded Greek beach, the Kodak couple appeared young, dark, and perfect. Hélène's breathing quickened as her eyes scrutinized the photo, tracing the women's unruly tresses down to their youthful bodies, adorned with scant bathing suits.

Hélène shut her eyes to block out the scene she had just witnessed—the two sexy women leaving the Greek restaurant, arm in arm. *Flirting. Giggling. Glued together.* She shook her head in disgust. Despite her efforts, no matter how hard she shook, she couldn't empty those distressing images from her mind. *Mince. I think I loosened a filling,* she realized, feeling the metallic taste in her mouth.

"Everything okay?"

Hélène jumped at the throaty voice over her shoulder.

"*Eh bien...*I'm just getting started. Besides, there's no rush. You're probably not hungry yet anyway." Hélène grabbed a pastel apron.

Sylvie chuckled. "You're wrong there. As usual, I'm starving. I could eat a hippo right now." She grabbed a large basket of organic mushrooms.

"You probably had a late lunch or something, *non?*" Hélène's curt voice sliced through the air. Her fingers trembled as she tied her apron around her waist.

Smiling, Sylvie leaned on the counter. "*Non.*"

Really? Hélène exhaled loudly, went straight to the sink, and started furiously scrubbing a cucumber with a brush. After a moment of silence, she pointed it at Sylvie accusingly. "Are you *sure* about that?"

Sylvie frowned. "Sure, I'm sure. What's going on?"

"Nothing," Hélène said coolly.

"*Quoi?* You don't believe me?" asked Sylvie, approaching her.

"Never mind. Drop it." Hélène went back to washing the cucumber. When she heard a thud, she whirled around to see dozens of tiny white mushrooms littering the red tile floor. Sylvie stood next to her, hands open and mouth gaping.

"I didn't mean literally!" Hélène snickered as the two women kneeled to the floor. Side by side, they began picking up the mushrooms.

"I warned you, I'm terrible in the kitchen. Poor little guys," said Sylvie. "*Regarde*, no bruises!"

She held a mushroom in front of Hélène's face; the smell of fresh dirt and musty fungus made Hélène's nose twitch. She sneezed loudly, and they both burst into a fit of giggles.

"Whew! For a moment there, I thought you were mad at me." Sylvie reached for another mushroom just as Hélène did. When Sylvie's hand landed on Hélène's, they gazed into each other's eyes.

Oh my! As soon as Hélène got a whiff of Sylvie's spicy, sexy perfume, she snatched the mushroom and abruptly stood up.

"*Aïe aïe aïe.*" She grasped her forehead as the kitchen started spinning. She leaned on the counter to balance herself.

Sylvie jumped up. "*Ca va?*"

Her blurry face was swaying before Hélène's eyes. When Hélène tried to step forward, she fell back just as Sylvie's strong, confident hands wrapped around her waist. *She feels just like she looks. Rock hard*, thought Hélène, remembering their recent intimate afternoon at the beach. Powerful emotions flooded her senses—she felt even more queasy. And as soon as she inhaled Sylvie's spicy perfume again, she knew she had no choice. *Gravity's calling.* She smiled wearily as her body collapsed into Sylvie's muscular arms.

❖

When Hélène's eyes fluttered open, her arms were laced around Sylvie's neck. Abruptly, she attempted to pull herself away.

Sylvie released her gently.

"*Désolée.*" Hélène hid her trembling hands behind her apron. "I think I'd better eat something. I...I forgot to have lunch." *Unless you count a Dainty Bather tea in a gay bar.*

"Three square meals a day keeps the doctor away," said Sylvie, peering into her eyes with obvious concern. "I'll give you a hand." She reached for a yellow apron, but Hélène snatched it from her.

"*Pas question!* No way. A deal's a deal. I'm making dinner for *you* tonight!" Hélène shoved two casserole dishes into the oven.

"But—" Sylvie began to protest.

"While these are cooking, why not give me a tour?"

Sylvie opened her arms. "Of course. *Mi casa es tu casa.*"

"You know I can't speak Greek; it's such a complicated language—" Hélène averted her eyes from Sylvie's breasts. *Lively, lovely, uplift...*

"*M'enfin!* That's not Greek, it's Spanish."

"*Ah bon?*" Hélène licked her lower lip. "So, you speak Spanish too?" *How sexy.*

"Just a little." Sylvie hesitated, then began brushing imaginary crumbs off the kitchen counter. "I used to go out with someone from Spain."

"I see." *Someone,* thought Hélène, noticing Sylvie's flushed cheeks. While her hostess's fingertips were chasing illusory bits of French bread, Hélène stole a few precious moments to admire Sylvie's silky dark hair. Her eyes followed its tips, tracing the soft curves in her sweater. A chill ran through her body. *What would it be like to be that "someone"? Even for a just day—or a night?* Despite the warmth in the kitchen, she shivered again.

Sylvie's fingertips came to a halt. Her husky voice broke the silence. "So...shall we?"

"Shall we what?" Another chill swept through Hélène's body—a notch lower.

"Take the tour."

Hélène gulped. "Sure, but first you have to explain what '*Mi casa* blah, blah, blah' means."

Sylvie gazed into Hélène's eyes. "*My* house is *your* house." She grabbed her hand. "Let's start with the living room."

CHAPTER EIGHT

G reat colors." Hélène pointed at the yellow walls. "Look at all these flowers…and books!"

She's like a kid, thought Sylvie, amused at how Hélène commented on nearly everything in her cozy apartment. That's what she was like, though; deeply visual, and she always seemed in touch with the natural world around her. The few times they'd spent time together outside the pool, she'd noticed the way Hélène's fingertips would trail along flowers on their path or the way she'd turn her face to the sun to catch an errant sunbeam. Even now, Sylvie watched her zoom in on her bookcase the way she seemed to zoom in on anything she was curious about. Hélène's fingers danced over their titles, stacked by subject. Many were in Greek; the French ones were dedicated to poetry and exotic plants. *Those date back to the late 1800s.* Sylvie watched Hélène caress their faded cloth jackets. *And they smell their age.* Someone had once said you could tell a lot about a person by simply looking at their bookshelf. Sylvie wondered what Hélène thought about her collection. It was a strangely vulnerable feeling.

Hélène spun around. "These are all yours? I never would've guessed you read so much."

"Is that supposed to be a compliment?" asked Sylvie, feigning offense.

"It sure is! Just look at all these on poetry and flowers."

Sylvie broke into a smile as she put on one of her favorite CDs with soft, modern Greek music. This always put her in a good mood. She approached Hélène, who was on her knees inspecting the French poetry section. Leaning forward, Sylvie whispered into her neck, "What did you think? All I do is swim laps and chow down gyros?"

Hélène stood up abruptly. "Don't be silly. We just haven't had a chance to talk about these things." She flashed a bashful grin. "Yet."

"What kinds of things?" asked Sylvie. *Let's see what she has in mind. I wonder what would happen if I got closer.*

Hélène took a step back, banging her derrière into the bookcase. "*Eh bien*…Things like…*Enfin*, books, poetry, music, art—"

"The most important things in life." Sylvie stared straight into Hélène's glistening eyes. "*N'est-ce pas?*" *It's funny how we like the same things. Yet we're exact opposites in many ways. Her eyes are so very blue. So clear and inviting. I've never seen eyes like these.*

Hélène side-stepped her gaze. "I'm impressed."

"If that's all it takes to impress you…" Sylvie moved closer. Having Hélène in her personal space was so intimate, so intense. For all her quirkiness, Hélène had a refreshingly open soul, and Sylvie couldn't stop herself from being drawn to her. *She's so fun to tease. I can't help myself. I wish we could get to know each other better without all this tension. If we could just have normal conversations, despite our obvious differences, we could get along fine. Even more than fine…*

Hélène looked at the wall of books. "Marc couldn't care less about those things. All he's interested in are car engines, muscles, stupid sports and—"

"I see." Sylvie sighed internally. Every time she thought they might be getting closer, Hélène brought up Marc, creating a barrier between them. *Who's interested in Marc, anyway? Why do I always care about women who care about men? Who are married to men? Who cares a flying fig about men anyway? I much prefer cats. They're more fun.* As soon as she thought of cats, she remembered her own. "*Attends*, you haven't met Marigold yet! Let's go track her down. Bet she's hiding under the bed. Next stop: the sleeping quarters." Before she realized what she was doing, she grabbed Hélène's hand and hauled her toward her bedroom.

❖

Hélène attempted to breathe naturally, nearly stumbling on the hardwood floor as they traversed the hall.

"*Voilà, ze* bedroom." Sylvie flung open the door to a spacious, dimly lit room.

Hélène entered cautiously, registering pleasure as her feet sank into the plush carpet. *I love what this place does to my feet.* Despite her initial nervousness at being in such intimate quarters with Sylvie, she felt her stress melt in the cozy, bohemian atmosphere. Rainbow-colored candles and sticks of incense dotted the sparse wooden furniture; a tiny window with linen curtains overlooked the park across the street; the orange glow from an overhead Moroccan lamp softened the setting. While she took all this in, she felt Sylvie's eyes on her. She felt her warmth. And even without looking, she could feel her smile.

Just as Hélène was realizing this, Sylvie squeezed her fingers. Hélène squeezed them back. And when her eyes adjusted to the dimness, she caught her breath. Above the huge bed in the center of the room, she noticed an impressive display of photos all glued together like an oversized collage made from fashion magazines. The collage covered the entire wall behind Sylvie's bed.

"Now you know my hobby: photography." Sylvie spread her arms and spun around the room like a butch ballerina. She flashed a coy grin.

Hélène stood transfixed. The collage was made entirely of black-and-white photos. But that wasn't what stunned her. She didn't mind black and whites, although she considered them a waste; only full color could bring out the beauty of flowers. What shocked her was the fact that all of the photos were of nude women in a variety of poses. She felt her ears grow hot. Some of the poses were benign; others, outright scandalous. All of the women—nearly life-sized—had something in common: they were uniquely and terribly attractive.

Hélène gulped. Instantly, she felt the women's stares on her own body. It was a strange sensation. *Shouldn't it be the other way around?* The room seemed crowded. Like self-adjusting camera lenses, her eyes went sharp, then blurry, as they reacted to the unanticipated stimuli. Sylvie's gaze was on her too.

"How creative," Hélène finally stammered, avoiding Sylvie's eyes as she pulled her hand away.

"Thanks." Sylvie clasped her hands behind her back. "I worked hard on these."

Hélène imagined the effort Sylvie must have made to render the pictures so perfect. Despite the awkward positions some of the women were in, they seemed at ease in front of the photographer. *You worked hard on what? The pictures or the models? They sure seem to be enjoying themselves.* Instead of being humiliated at baring their birthday suits to the world, they were beaming at the camera. In fact, some were winking, while others were tipping their hats and licking their lips. *They're flirting with her!* Hélène's fingers rolled into fists, ready for combat. *Some hobby this is...Where did she find these women?*

After a pensive pause, she rubbed her hands together and replied shrewdly, "I bet you did."

At last, Sylvie broke the prickly silence. "My grandmother made those," she said, pointing at the embroidered pillows piled on her bedspread.

But Hélène wasn't interested in the pillows; her mind was focused on what lay underneath: Sylvie's enormous bed. *This thing takes up two-thirds of the room. Voilà, another hobby.* Her gaze shifted to the Moroccan lamp suspended over their heads that cast a warm glow on Sylvie's face, highlighting her strong cheekbones. Hélène drew in her breath when she noticed how the glow traced the alluring contours of her body in the soft atmosphere. *So, that's how she gets this special effect.* She glanced again at the photo collage, then her eyes descended on the piles of embroidered pillows. *At least, to start with...*

"Where's that naughty girl of mine?" Sylvie's voice interrupted Hélène's thoughts. "Come on out, *ma chérie.* Maman has a friend she wants you to meet!"

Hélène snickered. "Maman?"

"I know. It's silly, but I can't help it. She's my—"

"I do exactly the same thing. Drives Marc up the wall," said Hélène, relieved at the diversion from ruminating over nude models and Sylvie's enormous bed.

Sylvie dropped under the mattress. "It's so dark in here; I can't see a thing. Can you flip that switch by the door?"

"*Bien sûr.*" Hélène flipped the switch. Swiftly, her eyes adjusted to the orange flicker of Moroccan lamps in each corner of the room. Sylvie was kneeling beside the bed, face down. Behind her was a pile of rumpled clothes in a corner. Hélène stifled a giggle. *So, she's not perfect after all.*

"Can't seem to find her. *C'est bizarre.*" Sylvie stood up and, following Hélène's gaze, strategically positioned herself in front of the rumpled clothes. Just then, a chubby orange cat crawled out from under the bedcovers. "*La voilà!* Here's Marigold." Sylvie pulled the cat onto her lap. "Isn't she a sweetie?" The furry pet rubbed her neck against her hand.

Hélène felt a warm tingle in her heart. "Absolutely adorable. I can hear her purring from here."

"Gets louder the nearer you get." Sylvie peered up at Hélène. "Come and hear for yourself." She tapped a spot next to her on the spacious bed.

Hélène froze. *Mince alors. Un, deux, trois...* Counting silently, she eased herself onto the edge of the bed.

"You're too far, silly." Sylvie giggled. "Come closer."

Hélène obeyed. When she was an inch away from Sylvie, her body stiffened.

"Pet her. She loves to be scratched behind the ears."

Reluctantly, Hélène leaned toward the cat on Sylvie's lap. When she touched the soft orange fur, the cat purred even louder.

"*Tu vois?* She eats it up," whispered Sylvie.

They stroked the feline ceremoniously, as if huddled together on a church pew instead of a king-sized bed. The silence was deafening. *This is so awkward.* Hélène tried to avoid Sylvie's eyes while trying to breathe. Her chest was thumping so loudly, it resonated in her ears. *My body's making noises louder than the stupid cat's.*

"Just listen to that," said Sylvie.

Hélène cringed. *I knew it. She's listening to my heartbeat. Why did I come here after all? Couldn't I have stayed home like a normal wife or gone out with Cecile? That would've been more relaxing. Even hunk hunting with Cecile would've been less stressful than this. Just the two of us, I mean, the three of us, here, sitting on her huge bed.* She stroked the cat, hoping the trembling in her hand didn't show. Deep down, she wanted to dash from the room, but somehow, she couldn't force herself to move.

"She's in ecstasy." Sylvie leaned closer. "Goldie's such an intuitive cat. You must give off really good vibes."

Her Greek accent slid into Hélène's ear like fragrant honey. When she said the word "vibes," Hélène nearly buckled under her tender, chocolate eyes. She could feel the warm air seep through her smooth lips, caressing the skin on her neck. As they gently stroked the cat together, Sylvie's spicy perfume entered her nostrils. Hélène froze. *She said ecstasy. Oh my gosh, I think I'm going to burst. Un, deux, trois…*

Just then, their fingers touched. Hélène felt Sylvie's body twitch; she kept her eyes glued on the cat. *I can feel her looking at me.* Her ears started pounding; she closed her eyes.

Their fingers touched again. This time, Hélène felt the hairs on her neck stiffen. The strong electrical current between their bodies intensified. Her nipples hardened. She started to sweat. *I can't take this anymore.* She jerked her hands away and leapt from the bed.

"Time to get cooking, *non?*" She wiped her clammy hands on her apron. Without waiting for an answer, she sprinted out of the bedroom.

❖

Hélène was slicing carrots when Sylvie tiptoed into the kitchen. *Time to liven up the party.* She wanted to break the tension so they could have an enjoyable evening. "Thirsty?" Sylvie blurted, sneaking up behind Hélène.

"*Ah!*" shrieked Hélène, raising her chopping knife, nearly grazing Sylvie's nose. "What the heck do you think you're doing?" Sylvie laughed nervously. "*Désolée.* But you really seem to have the jumps tonight. Am I that terrifying?" *Most women don't seem to think so. But Hélène's not like most women. She's more of a strange bird.* She could tell Hélène felt the friction between them, and she knew it must scare her. And truth be told, it scared Sylvie too. She knew better than to get involved with a straight woman. She knew the cost to her heart. But standing there in her kitchen, she simply couldn't help breathing in Hélène's lovely scent and moving closer to her.

Hélène bit her lip. A flash of worry seemed to cross her brow. Abruptly, she held up a bottle of white wine. "Here. This is from the market. But it's probably warm by now."

"I'll just stick it in the fridge for a minute," said Sylvie, trying not to wonder why Hélène quickly changed the subject. *Guess that's my answer: she thinks I'm dangerous. Or maybe I'm reading into things. Maybe she just wants a friend, and I'm really making her ill at ease.*

"I looked for that Greek stuff at the market but—"

"It's impossible to find retsina there. But this looks great." Sylvie admired the bottle's fancy label. "Let's save it for dinner." She placed it in the refrigerator. "How about a traditional Greek cocktail?" *This should make her relax. Me too.*

"A homemade Greek cocktail?" Hélène wiped her hands on her apron. "Sounds intriguing. Is it strong?"

"Usually. But I can make yours less potent. You'll like it—I promise." Sylvie chuckled under her breath. *I bet she never drinks hard alcohol. But it's Saturday night, and her husband's out of town. Who cares about that jerk anyway?* Tonight, Hélène was with her. And that's all she needed to think about.

Hélène looked at her contemplatively for a moment, and Sylvie wondered what was going through her head. Then her eyes began to glisten in that unique way Sylvie knew meant a mood change. Like an Olympic medal winner with her country's flag, Hélène waved a carrot in the air triumphantly.

"Sounds *fabuleux*." Hélène took a huge bite out of her carrot. "Let's live it up tonight!"

In the living room, Sylvie held the ouzo bottle up to the light, then she unscrewed the top and sniffed. One whiff brought her straight to Santorini. Grinning with fond memories of teenage adventures on the sun-scorched sand, she poured the Greek liquor into two tall glasses filled with ice. After adding pineapple juice and grenadine syrup, she mixed the cocktails with a long, silver spoon.

"What's taking so long? This is thirsty work, you know!" called Hélène from the kitchen.

Sylvie, who was standing at the living room buffet, glanced at the kitchen door. *I couldn't.* She shook her head. *I really shouldn't.* After a pause, she opened the ouzo bottle again. Another whiff made her dark eyes twinkle. *She did say she wanted to live it up.* Chuckling, she emptied the bottle into one of the glasses. After giving the cocktail a few twirls, she inserted a tiny yellow umbrella to cover up her dirty deed.

"*Désolée, les apéritifs fait maison* require precise measurements," Sylvie replied, slipping into the kitchen. She added a fresh pineapple slice to each glass. "*Voilà.* Fresh from the islands," she offered with a mischievous flash of dimples.

❖

"Mmm, how lovely. You're spoiling me!" Hélène accepted her fruity cocktail with the paper umbrella.

"Hope you like it," said Sylvie, clinking her glass against Hélène's. "*Santé!*"

Their eyes met as they took their first sip. When the liquid hit her lips, Hélène stifled a gasp. *This tastes like acid.* Burning her taste buds, the alcohol rushed to the back of her throat. She tried to block it with her tongue, to protect her insides. Then she forced a smile. "Amazing."

"Tasty! Isn't it, though?" Sylvie took another sip. She approached the kitchen counter, covered with food, bowls, pots, and utensils. "Now, what can I do to help?"

"Just keep me company while I chop." Hélène pinched her throat discreetly. She glanced at her drink. "On second thought, maybe you could set the table?"

As soon as Sylvie left, Hélène raced to the sink and dumped out her cocktail. Holding her nose, she squirted liquid soap into the drain and turned on the faucet full blast. She chucked the umbrella and ice cubes into the trash and filled her glass with tap water. *Ah, much better,* she decided, relaxing against the counter. *Tap water never tasted so good.*

Sylvie waltzed in. "Table's ready." Then her eyebrows shot up. "*Ca alors*, you really *were* thirsty!" She peered at Hélène's empty cocktail glass. "I'm impressed. Don't worry, there's plenty more. I'll go make you another one." She grabbed Hélène's glass.

"*Non, non!* It was really *incroyable*, but..." Hélène protested. "That was more than enough. I wouldn't want to get drunk and silly." She could tell by the look on Sylvie's face that she wasn't fooled, but she still stumbled on. "Dinner will be a few more minutes. Why don't we relax in the living room?" Getting out of the close confines of the kitchen seemed like a good idea. She followed Sylvie to the living room, and while Sylvie went to put on music, Hélène looked over the bookshelves once again.

She's definitely got taste, decided Hélène. *Except for that horrendous cocktail she makes.*

Sylvie had dimmed the lights, put on some soft tunes, and transformed the room in a handful of minutes. Hélène smiled approvingly at the décor: an orange linen tablecloth, gold napkins, eggplant-colored twisted candles, and a magnificent spray of wildflowers.

"You've got an eye for decoration."

"I make do with what I've got. It's not much, but it's cozy."

"You're like me. You like to surround yourself with beautiful things," said Hélène, caressing a yellow daisy.

Sylvie peered over her shoulder. "Hear that, Goldie? You just got a compliment."

Hélène glanced at the kitty, curled up in a tight ball on the sofa. "She's so lovely." Then she noticed a picture on the wall—a sensuous, nude woman posing under a palm tree. Hélène gulped. "As are other things."

"Guess you could say I appreciate anything that's..." Sylvie looked straight into Hélène's eyes. "Beautiful, original, and full of life."

Just like you, thought Hélène, feeling her cheeks grow hot.

"Speaking of beautiful, check this out." Sylvie handed her a black-and-white photo.

"*Regarde*. That's us, at the Greek restaurant." Hélène inspected the photo of the two of them. Sylvie's arm was around Hélène. They were both grinning.

"Developed it myself. Just for you."

"For me? *Merci!*" Hélène smiled quickly, then her lips froze as a streak of jealousy entered her mind. Something about the photo was bothering her, but she couldn't put her finger on it. She brushed it aside and concentrated on the moment. *What about the photos in the bedroom with all those beautiful nude women?* A chill swept over her body as dozens of images of attractive women filled her mind. She imagined Sylvie standing with her camera so close to their bare skin. She shivered at how she might be tempted to touch their soft, slender bodies. Maybe Sylvie even stripped down herself to get to know her models in the most intimate way possible, like some famous artists did with their muses. She imagined Sylvie naked in all her splendor and gulped. "Do you develop, um, *all* your photos?"

"*Ouais*. I use my bathroom as a darkroom; it's just the right size. And I rinse the pictures in the bidet."

"In the bidet?" Hélène's features screwed up; she glanced at the picture between her fingers. "Gross!" she exclaimed, flinging it in the air. The picture landed under a small table with a fishbowl on it. Hélène wiped her fingers on her apron.

Sylvie chuckled. "Don't worry, that's the *only* thing I use the bidet for," she added, handing back the picture.

Hélène set the photo down, unable to deal with the emotions it raised, and went to the fishbowl.

"How adorable!" Hélène admired a pair of goldfish.

"Boo!" Two immense brown eyes with fluttering lashes popped out at her from inside the fishbowl.

"Ah!" yelled Hélène, jumping back.

Sylvie, who had pressed her eyes to the glass, giggled. "Got ya!"

"Did anyone ever tell you," asked Hélène, trying to suppress her racing heart, "you can be a real pain sometimes?"

Sylvie crossed her muscular arms. "*Bien sûr.* Apparently, that's what gives me my charm."

"At least you're original…And full of life." *And beautiful,* thought Hélène, fingering an imaginary knot forming in her throat.

"*Merci.* So are you."

Hélène shook her head. "Come on. I'm the most boring—"

"*Non,* you aren't." Sylvie's expression turned serious.

"*Mais si.* Compared to you," Hélène countered. "You swim like an athlete. Or a mermaid. Or whatever. Faster than anyone I know. And you're such an artist. Just look at all your stunning pictures. You've got taste. And style. And originality. How many people do *you* know who start their car with a screwdriver? Only you. And you come from an exotic island where people like me can only dream of—"

"So what? That doesn't mean anything. I was born on Santorini. You were born in the capital of Europe and—"

"It was hardly the bustling, cosmopolitan capital that it is today."

"You know what I mean. You're an artist too. Just read some of your poems. And you swim like an athlete. Each day, you're faster than the day before."

Hélène felt the lump tightening in her throat. She hadn't been complimented so thoroughly in a very, very long time, and she had no idea how to respond. She peered at the pair of goldfish in the bowl. "They're sure going at it."

Sylvie knelt next to her. "They do that all day long. It's like they're dancing. Wish I could do that, just swim around and never grow tired. Looks like so much fun."

"But that *is* how you swim. You're like a big Greek fish." Hélène laughed. "What're their names?"

Sylvie pointed to the tiny black one. "That's Yin." Then she pointed to the big white one. "And that's Yang."

Hélène's eyelashes fluttered. "A boy and a girl. *C'est romantique!*"

Sylvie giggled. "Sorry to disappoint you. They're both females!"

Why doesn't that surprise me? "Now *that's* original." Hélène watched the two fish nibble on each other. *And intimate.* A shiver raced through her body. *This is déjà vu. You're like a big Greek fish...* She hastily stood up.

"Obviously, they know it's supper time." Hélène disappeared into the kitchen and promptly reappeared with steaming dishes in each hand. "Who's ready for my healthy, home-cooked, vegetarian meal, paired with some wild-caught fish? We're talking fiber here. Not fluff."

"You sound just like a commercial."

"*C'est bizarre.* I don't even watch TV."

"Neither do I," replied Sylvie, pointing to her stereo, then her immense bookcase. "That's my TV."

She's a lot like me. On a sudden high, Hélène waltzed back into the kitchen, leaving Sylvie to pour the wine.

As soon as Hélène had placed the last of the platters—fresh halibut laced with steamed organic broccoli—on the table, she felt two arms wrap themselves around her waist from behind.

"Just one more thing." Sylvie's words slipped into her ear. Delicious words with a slight—yet sexy—Greek accent. "To help set the mood."

Hélène caught her breath. She could feel Sylvie's muscular

arms tighten around her body, pulling her close. With Sylvie's firm breasts pressed against her back, Hélène imagined her lips on her neck. She shivered as her nimble fingers moved around her waist. She looked up at the ceiling as if sending off a prayer to the heavens while trying to keep her body from trembling. The heat between their bodies traveled up her spine. Sylvie's hands left her waist and moved to her back. Then they slid over her neck. She held her breath until her ears were about to pop to release the mounting tension.

"You won't be needing this anymore," whispered Sylvie gruffly in her ear.

Hélène heard rustling, then felt something light drop to the floor. She looked down. Her apron was draped over her feet like a limp rag. *That's it?*

"*Voilà*, that's better," said Sylvie, pulling away. "Here."

Hélène turned around, trying to not let her disappointment show at the cessation of contact. Her fingers trembled as she took her wineglass.

"Cheers," said Sylvie, flashing her dimples.

Hélène's cheeks flushed as she clinked her glass against Sylvie's. *So, all she was doing was untying my apron.* The wine's cool crispness soothed her nerves as it ran over her tongue. She swished it around in her mouth, hoping to numb the lingering excitement that their brief, awkward embrace had awakened in her. Sylvie's eyes lingered on hers.

"*Bon.* Let's get down to business," Sylvie said abruptly, plopping ample quantities of each dish onto their plates.

Hélène sat down. "I told you it would be vegetarian, but the fish seemed so fresh today." She averted her gaze. "I hope you don't mind."

"Not at all." Sylvie grinned. "I love everything that comes from the sea."

"Well then, *bon appétit.*"

Sylvie dug her fork into the halibut. "*Incroyable!* This is just as good as Yaya, my grandma's!" She waved her fork for emphasis. "*Vraiment.* You said you could cook, but I had no idea you were a *cordon bleu!*"

Hélène's eyebrows shot up. "Flattery will get you everywhere, *ma chérie*," she whispered, blushing.

"No, really, this is so *delicious*. And I've had fresh fish before, believe me. Yaya used to..." Sylvie paused until tiny teardrops slid onto her lower eyelashes. She reached for her glass.

"Go on. Please tell me," urged Hélène gently.

"My grandma," Sylvie croaked. This final word prompted a plump tear to run down her cheek. Sylvie's expression grew pensive. After an uncomfortable pause, she stuck her fork into a vegetable casserole.

"Mmm. This looks great." She seemed to force a grin. "Anyway, enough about me. Let's talk about you. That way, I can enjoy all of these magnificent dishes while you explain." Sylvie waved her fork in the air, carving figure eights with cheese-covered broccoli.

Hélène held her breath. *What does she mean?* "Explain what?"

Sylvie cocked her head. "About you. Let's start with your culinary talents, for example. Your husband is so lucky." She picked up a forkful of halibut. "Must be great to come home to such tasty dishes."

Hélène covered her mouth to suppress her giggles and wondered if she detected a hint of judgment in Sylvie's tone. "If you only knew! Every night, he drags himself home from the gym, reads the paper, wolfs down his food—"

Sylvie looked puzzled. "Wolfs down?"

Hélène laughed. "Sorry about that. Your French is great. But I guess you're not familiar with that expression?"

Sylvie shook her head.

"That's funny. For some reason, I was sure you would be." Hélène giggled bashfully as she took another sip of wine. "*Eh bien,* it means 'chows down,' 'tucks in,' 'inhales'..."

"Thanks. I get it." Sylvie made a face.

"You seem to enjoy your food, yourself." Hélène stifled a laugh and pointed her fork at Sylvie's half-empty plate.

"Athletes need to eat to stay in shape." Sylvie puffed up her chest. "It's a pain, really."

"*Ah non!* You sound just like Marc." Hélène took a robust sip of wine. "I make him all these healthy meals, like this one, and he either wolfs down his food without looking at it, or he rants about its lack of taste and takes off to watch TV with a couple of beers instead."

Sylvie frowned. "You've got to be kidding," she said between bites. "I'm not at all like that. Look how I'm enjoying this." She licked her lips. "I know guys can be brutes, but nobody's *that* bad. He sounds like a cliché. Maybe some character you concocted to spice up a new poem?"

Hélène contemplated the idea. "I wish. But it's true. That's exactly how he is. Anyway, I write about nature, not humans. Humans are too complicated. And even if I did, I certainly wouldn't write about Marc." *That's for sure.*

"That makes sense. Why write about your husband? You live with him every day. You see his underwear, his—"

Hélène waved her napkin. "*S'il te plaît!* You're making me lose my appetite!"

"*Mais non*, what I mean is…" Sylvie glanced at one of her nude pictures on the wall. "If I were a writer, I'd focus on what interests me." Her eyes began to sparkle. "That's why I don't write. For me, it's easier to just take pictures of—"

"I see." Hélène nodded, feeling the heat in her cheeks. *She spends her time taking pictures of nude women in her apartment. It's obvious that's what interests her the most. Wonder if she's planning to shoot me next?* Hélène felt a drop of sweat run down her back as she imagined herself posing naked before Sylvie's camera. She shivered as she focused on Sylvie's sparkling eyes, trying to avoid her adorable dimples, her full lips, her perfectly fitted cashmere sweater…

"Anyway, if you wrote about him, nobody would buy your poems." Sylvie took a gulp of wine. "Too darn depressing." Then she bit her lip. "*Ah*, I'm sorry, Hélène. I shouldn't have said that. But he does sound—"

"Different." Hélène made a face. "Is that what you were going to say?"

"*Non.* He sounds like a *monstre.*" Sylvie shrugged, her expression serious.

"*Un monstre?*" Hélène laughed self-consciously. *Is Marc a monster?* The thought made her heart race as adrenaline swept through her nervous system. Feeling her eyes moisten with emotion, she glanced at Sylvie's plate, which was nearly empty, and took another bite of cold halibut. *Do I say such terrible things about him? Are they true?*

"*Je suis désolée,*" stammered Sylvie. "I did it again. I had no right to—"

"*Non.* You're right." Hélène felt her throat tightening. "And sometimes it's really embarrassing. Especially when he overreacts in public." She gulped at the thought.

Sylvie reached across the table, but Hélène pulled her hand away from hers. "Let's leave Marc out of this, *d'accord*? I want to enjoy this evening." Hélène picked up her wineglass.

"*Our* evening." Sylvie smiled broadly.

She has the most charming dimples. The thought made Hélène's cheek twitch. It twitched even more when she noticed her glass was empty.

"But maybe you *should* talk about it." Sylvie refilled Hélène's glass and then her own. "Sometimes people need to talk when things aren't—"

Hélène raised an eyebrow. "Aren't what?"

"Aren't right."

Hélène glanced at her half-eaten halibut, her appetite gone. Did she want to have this conversation with Sylvie, of all people? It felt awkward, like talking to a crush about another crush. "I don't want to complain, it's just that…" Her eyes filled with tears, rendering her vegetables blurry.

Sylvie cleared her throat. "So, how long have you been married?"

Hélène sniffed discreetly. "Twenty years." Then she took a generous sip of wine. For some reason, it tasted sweeter now, and softer. *This stuff flows down my throat,* she realized, appreciating how soothing it was to her palate.

Sylvie nearly choked on her wine. "Two decades?" She used a napkin to wipe the wine from her mouth. "I mean, that's wonderful. But that could explain why—"

Now that Hélène had started, it was like a tap she couldn't turn off. "And since he basically ignores me, I usually just talk to Chaussette. At least *she* listens to me. That makes him furious!" The wine's effects were working wonders on her ability to communicate. She took another deep sip and, giggling, squeezed her legs together to remain vertical in her chair.

"So, he hates cats?" Sylvie glanced at Goldie nestled on the top of the sofa.

"*Ah oui.* He can't stand animals." Hélène tried to focus on the goldfish, but the glass bowl appeared to be swimming. Her voice grew weary. "He doesn't even like kids."

Sylvie swept a strand of hair over her ear. "So, that's why you don't have children?"

Hélène sighed. "I wanted them, but Marc always said..." Like a distracted preschooler, she began rearranging the last of her vegetables with her fork.

Sylvie paused, then spoke ever so gently. "I'm sorry, that was rude of me. I can be so tactless sometimes."

Hélène shook her head. "Don't worry about it. He always said..." She tried to keep her lips from trembling as she lined up her peas like soldiers in formation at boot camp. "He'd leave me if I got pregnant."

Sylvie's eyes grew darker; she clenched her fork until her knuckles were pale.

"You see, his mother is extremely controlling." Hélène gestured with her knife. "Abusive, even. Marc never wanted to be like her. He suffered so much growing up. So ever since he was old enough, when he was just a kid really, he promised himself he'd never become a..." Her voice faltered as she struggled to get the word out: "Father."

"That must be hard for you," Sylvie replied softly, reaching across the table.

This time, instead of pulling her hand away, Hélène let herself be comforted. But the gesture backfired. Just feeling Sylvie's warm fingers over hers sent urgent messages to her brain, stirring up areas in her body that normally remained unsolicited at dinner time. Hélène squirmed as sparks of electricity shot down her spine. Inhaling deeply, she tried to remain still by concentrating on the twisted candles separating her from Sylvie. Their yellow flames danced before her eyes, just like the sparks inching down her vertebrae, yearning to ignite something deep inside her. The sensation, like a tenacious tickle, was unbearable.

Hélène sighed heavily as Sylvie's fingers gripped hers. Drops of sweat trickled down Hélène's back, merging to the spot where the heat ignited her thighs, its flame licking at an illusory, veiled wick trapped between tender folds of skin. Her head began to spin.

Just then, Sylvie gave Hélène's fingers a strong squeeze, thrusting the imaginary flame to its target. Hélène's hidden wick ignited at last, giving her body a jolt; she jerked her hand away from Sylvie's and grasped her water glass—to put out the fire as elegantly and discreetly as possible.

After quenching her thirst, Hélène twirled a strand of hair and ever so slowly, continued her story. "*Alors*, after a while, I got used to the idea of never becoming a mother." She leaned forward. "You can't really change people. Especially Marc, he's so stubborn. At least I have Chaussette to keep me company."

Sylvie glanced at Goldie, who was licking her paws. "But it's not the same, is it?"

"Of course not. But what about you?" asked Hélène, trying to sound cheerful. "Planning to have kids?"

"Not yet. I've still got some time to—"

"That's right; you're still young." Hélène peered at Sylvie's low-cut neckline where her smooth, dark skin contrasted perfectly with her white cashmere sweater. Hélène's mouth began to water as a flood of warm feelings washed over her. In an unconscious attempt to either drench the flame or feed the fire—she wasn't sure which, in her dizzy state—she grabbed her empty wineglass and slurred, "And when you find the right—"

"Person to settle down with," said Sylvie, "then I'll think about it more seriously. But for now, I just want to enjoy life." With a swift flick of the wrist, she refilled Hélène's wineglass.

When the last drop in the bottle fell into Sylvie's glass, Hélène giggled loudly. "*Oh là là!* You know what we say in Belgium. Whoever gets the last drop of wine in their glass will have a baby within the year." She lifted her glass. "*Félicitations*, Sylvie! Congratulations!"

"I completely forgot about that old wives' tale. Otherwise *you* would've gotten the drop," said Sylvie, raising her glass.

"Too late!" Hélène licked her lips. "No offense, but this wine goes down lots faster than that *redbeaner* stuff of yours."

"*Redbeaner*?" Sylvie furrowed her brow. "You mean retsina!"

"That's what I said, *redbeaner.*"

"You need Greek lessons, *ma chérie.* Anyway, here's to our gorgeous cats."

"And to us," slurred Hélène.

"You bet," added Sylvie. "*Efthymíes!*"

"*Efthymíes!*" They clinked their glasses together. Giggling, Hélène guzzled down the chilly liquid, feeling free and relaxed in a way she hadn't in ages. "Now it's your turn. Bottoms up!"

Sylvie complied. But before she could set her glass down, Hélène snatched it from her.

"*Attends*, what are you—"

"There's one drop left." Hélène peered inside. "You've got to get that last one."

Sylvie grinned. "What for?"

"Just do it."

"But I—"

"For me," said Hélène with a slow wink. As alcohol mixed with desire flooded her system, her marriage woes faded conveniently into the background. She held her breath as she focused on Sylvie's perfect lips poised over the rim of the glass.

"*D'accord*, you're the guest. Whatever makes you happy," Sylvie replied, sucking the last drop from her glass. "Not bad," she remarked, licking her lips. "But I still prefer *redbeaner.*"

CHAPTER NINE

When the meal was over and the silence reigned with things unspoken, Hélène gathered their plates and went to the kitchen. "Might as well do some of these dishes while we digest our dinner."

Sylvie moved up behind her. "You sure?" she whispered in her ear. "I thought we'd relax on the sofa and—"

"I'd feel better if we got some of these out of the way." Hélène leaned against the sink to steady herself.

"If you insist." Sylvie grabbed a dish towel.

"This way, we'll have room for dessert."

Sylvie gave a hearty laugh. "Dessert? Are you trying to kill me?"

Hélène swiveled around. Her eyes glimpsed Sylvie's lean figure while her mind tried to block images of what lurked under her sweater. "Don't be silly. Fruit salad can't kill you." She glanced down. "Besides, there's ample room in your jeans." She remembered when she had first seen Sylvie's slim waist. Sylvie was pulling on her jeans in the locker room, and Hélène had thought: *she could fit a fist or two in there*. Then Sylvie had tightened her belt, squeezing the denim gap.

Sylvie crossed her arms. "Since when have you been looking at the way my jeans fit?"

"We share a locker room. I know your secrets," murmured Hélène, smiling as she coyly twisted a strand of hair around her ear.

Sylvie's eyes sparkled. *"Ah bon?* Which ones, smarty-pants?"

"Hmm." Hélène concentrated on her gorgeous dimples. "All of them." She giggled.

"*Oh là là!* You're swimming in dangerous waters now. You're still my student." She leaned toward Hélène, narrowing her eyes like a predatory shark.

"And *you're* my teacher," retorted Hélène, giggling even harder. "And my lifeguard." She flung a handful of sudsy water at Sylvie. "See! You never know when that skill might come in handy."

"*Je vois.*" Sylvie rubbed the suds off her face. "At last, I've found a way to cool off and sober up. I'll invite you over to do the dishes!" She snapped the tip of her dish towel at Hélène's leg.

"*Aiie!*" Hélène shrieked, rubbing her thigh. "You brute!"

"*Désolée*, but you bring out the brute in me."

When Sylvie leaned forward, Hélène jerked back, ramming her butt into the hard sink counter. Drops of sweat slid down her back. *What's she going to do to me now?* Guardedly, she lifted her eyes to meet Sylvie's shimmering eyes. Their noses were an inch apart. Hélène held her breath, waiting for something she knew she couldn't have…hoping for something she knew she shouldn't have.

Just then, Sylvie pulled away. "That was the best meal I've ever had. And even though your husband complains about your food, I bet he has a hard time staying thin."

Hélène stood blinking at Sylvie. *What the…Now she sounds like she's trying to sell something on TV. What happened to the "you bring out the brute in me"?* But she went along with the change in subject. Thinking about the kiss that could have happened wouldn't do any good. "Are you kidding? He's a stick. All he does is work out at the gym. Plus, he's such a picky eater—he couldn't get fat if he *tried!*"

Once the dishes were done, Hélène and Sylvie sat together on the sofa with Goldie, the fluffy orange cat, sandwiched between them, purring heavily. On the coffee table was a large bowl of freshly cut fruit salad, two yellow mugs, and a yellow teapot.

"*C'est intéressant.* You say you're not athletic. Could've fooled me," said Sylvie, stirring honey into their tea. "Swimming every day, biking to work. You're as athletic as one can get."

Hélène shrugged. "But it's all new. I mean, just look at this body. Not very convincing, *eh?*" Hélène poked her finger at her belly. It bounced back, like rubber. "But you...You've got such a nice body, if you don't mind me saying so."

"I just swim. And jog a bit." Sylvie grinned.

"It's obvious you've always been a swimmer. I'd *die* for a body like yours!"

As Sylvie handed Hélène her mug, her arm touched Goldie's head, whose ears shot up. "Watch out, it's hot."

"*Aiie!* You're right." Hélène quickly set her mug on the table.

"And all the guys must think so too."

Sylvie stared at Hélène. "What are you talking about?"

What does she think I'm talking about? It's obvious. "Your body."

"What about my body?" Sylvie's eyes widened.

Hélène blushed. "Like you said, 'it's hot.'" *Hotter than ever. Where am I headed with this conversation? I'm treading toward dangerous waters.*

Sylvie chuckled. "Thanks for the compliment, *ma chérie*, but I meant the tea."

Hélène put her hand over her mouth. Sylvie's dimples surfaced as she stifled a giggle, then her expression grew serious. "You don't realize how much your body has changed in the past few weeks. Swimming's made a real difference, Hélène."

"I don't know. Look at this." Hélène pinched her stomach. "After a meal like that, it's all—"

"Maybe you don't see a difference, but I do. And everyone else does too."

"*Je ne sais pas.*" Hélène shrugged and blew into her steaming tea.

"I'll show you then. Move over, Goldie." Sylvie nudged her cat until Goldie meowed and jumped off the sofa. Then Sylvie slid next to Hélène and took the mug out of her hands. Like an expert, she grasped Hélène's forearm, unbuttoned the cuff of her blouse, and rolled up her sleeve. *"Tu vois?"* She held up Hélène's arm. "Just look at this bicep! With all those workouts in the pool, plus biking—"

What does she think she's doing? Hélène's cheeks grew crimson. She jerked her arm away. "Stop teasing me!"

Sylvie furrowed her brow. "What do you mean? I'm just trying to show you—"

"Listen." Hélène rolled down her sleeve. "First of all, I'm not used to people looking at me. And I'm certainly not used to people touching my body like—" She wanted Sylvie to keep touching her. Everywhere. But she couldn't just let that happen, could she? The alcohol was confusing her, making her want things...her emotions were mixed up like weeds in a flower bed.

"Attends. I'm not just anybody; I'm your swimming coach, remember?" Sylvie spoke calmly and smoothly. "It's my job. I *have* to touch you, to make sure you do the moves correctly. *D'accord?"*

"But tonight, we're nowhere near the pool."

"True." Sylvie nodded. "We're not. That was just an example."

Hélène felt the wine racing through her veins, intensifying her temper. It had been a long time since someone got to her like this. *Even with Marc, I never lose control. He does.*

She snapped, "I don't need any more examples from you."

"But what about your husband?" Sylvie's voice quickened. "So, maybe he ignores you at dinner, but don't tell me he doesn't touch you in—"

"This isn't the time or place to talk about this," Hélène hissed, feeling her expression harden. *Mon Dieu, I'm turning into him. How did this happen? Everything is fine. Then she says something that makes me snap. Like him.* She looked at Sylvie coolly. *What's wrong with me? Why does she get under my skin like this?*

Sylvie leaned back. "Okay," she replied softly. "It was wrong of me. Sorry I brought it up."

Hélène could barely stand the next few seconds of prickly silence.

Suddenly, Sylvie perked up. "Anyway, you should be proud of your progress. You're definitely heading in the right direction."

Hélène glanced at her sensuous lips. She could hardly control her trembling hands. *And just which direction might that be?*

❖

Sylvie coughed, breaking the unbearable silence. She gazed into Hélène's eyes. "I think you just need more confidence, so—"

Before she could finish her sentence, Hélène was in her arms, burying her face between her breasts and making sniffing noises into her sweater. She hesitated, her hands in the air, before finally holding Hélène to her. If ever there was a moment full of mixed signals, this was one. She'd thought Hélène kept bringing up Marc to put a barrier between them, but she realized it was the exact same thing she was doing whenever she started to feel desire overwhelming her. It wasn't fair to either of them, and now she'd made Hélène cry. *Smooth. Very smooth.*

"*Ma pauvre chérie*," she said, pushing a few strands of blond hair behind her delicate ear.

"It's just so hard…" began Hélène with a snort.

"*Je sais.* Your husband seems—"

"He's an insensitive brute," murmured Hélène between sniffles. "I can't remember the last time he touched me, except for a kiss on the forehead when he returns from work. I mean, the gym. And that's only 'cause he wants his beer."

Sylvie stiffened. "You mean, you two never even have sex?"

"You kidding? The last time he…" Hélène stopped abruptly. "Never mind. That doesn't count. He changed his mind all of a sudden and, which…" She shook her head from boob to boob. "*Enfin*, let's just say it didn't work out." Tears dripped from her cheeks onto Sylvie's porous sweater.

"You're trembling…I know what you need." Sylvie tightened her arms around Hélène. "Just relax," she whispered, tenderly kissing the soft flesh on her neck. Sylvie closed her eyes to taste the sweetness of Hélène's skin. *I know I shouldn't be doing this, but I can't help it. She needs comfort right now, and…Mon Dieu, I need more of her.* As Sylvie pressed her lips to Hélène's neck and inhaled her sweet scent, she felt her thigh muscles tighten. With each passing second the tension rose in her chest. Her heart felt as if it was splitting open; to resolve this conflict, a swift decision needed to be made between her rational mind and her physical body. Sylvie's soul knew she desperately needed Hélène, despite the deep, dark souvenirs of past hurts from married lovers lurking in her memory. Even though everything in her conscience told her how wrong it would be to be intimate with Hélène right now, her body's increasing tension made her push forward with desire.

When Hélène started to move away, Sylvie pressed her head down again. *"Ca va,* just relax," she insisted, squishing her face against her chest. *I'll let my fingers do the talking.*

Sylvie let her instincts take over, sliding her hand inside her blouse. Hélène's body was shivering, but her head stayed down. Sylvie put her ear to Hélène's back. *At least she's still breathing.* Caressing her shoulder, she gradually worked her fingers toward her breast. Finally, she reached her target. Her nipple was hard. She flashed a naughty grin, rolling the nipple lightly between her fingers as she pressed her head against Hélène's back. "I *told* you I'd teach you the breast stroke," she whispered gruffly.

This made Hélène giggle, prompting Sylvie to reinforce her tactile explorations. *I have no idea if she's aroused, but at least she's awake...A broad awakening. Let's take a peek.* She lifted Hélène's face, removed her glasses, and studied her deep blue eyes—which were distant and dreamy, as if she were half asleep. Ever so slowly, Sylvie approached Hélène's lips with her own, parting them for a tender kiss. But before they could touch, a song began to play. Sylvie pulled back abruptly. *Who turned on the stereo?*

Hélène flinched. *"Mince."* Her eyes popped open like a porcelain doll's. She sat up.

"Attends." Sylvie looked around the room. Then she chuckled. "Relax. It's just a cell phone." She parted her lips again. But when she leaned in, Hélène turned away.

"I have to pick it up," Hélène said, patting around the sofa with her fingers. "Help me!" she ordered, flipping over on the sofa.

Buttocks up and nose down, she grazed the carpet aimlessly with her fingers, searching for something.

After a moment, Sylvie cleared her throat. "*Eh bien,* is there something wrong?"

"Funny. Really funny." Hélène waved her hands in the air. "Where in the heck did you put my glasses?"

Sylvie plucked the glasses from the coffee table and plopped them on her nose. "*Voilà.*" The moment was a cold shower. Sylvie sighed with frustration. *Why in the heck does she need to answer her phone at this very minute? We were just getting warmed up.*

Hélène adjusted her lenses as she rose to her knees. "That's got to be Marc," she said, looking frantically around the room as the song continued to play. "*Mince,* where's my phone?"

"Got to hand it to him." Sylvie rolled her eyes. "Dude's got perfect timing."

Hélène flashed her an annoyed look. "Aren't you going to help me?"

"Don't answer it, *ma chérie.* He'll leave you a message," whispered Sylvie, caressing Hélène's cheek, trying to retrieve the mood they'd begun crafting between them. *She's hot.* She smiled inwardly. *That was quick. Is she hot because of me or because of that idiot husband of hers? Let's hope it's me.*

Hélène jerked her head back. "But what if it's an emergency?"

"Isn't he on a business trip? He's a grown man. What kind of emergency can he get into?"

Hélène put her hands on her hips. "You never know. It's Saturday night. Maybe—"

"Maybe he's having a good time." Sylvie extended her open arms. "Like us." Instead of dropping into them, however, Hélène began racing around the room like a madwoman. *Red flag alert. Just when we're about to make out, he calls. Then she acts like a lunatic. Why am I always attracted to women with intimacy issues? What the hell is wrong with me that I keep making this mistake?*

"Maybe he forgot something at home!" Hélène exclaimed, running into the hall. She thrust her ear against the closet door. "It's in here!" she shouted, opening the door and grabbing her phone from her coat pocket.

Technology sucks. Sylvie had never liked cell phones. She only agreed to get one because her mother insisted on it. "But it's way after midnight. What could he possibly need at this hour? Don't answer it." To persuade Hélène, she placed her lips at the back of her neck and blew her hot breath onto her tender skin.

But Hélène was already talking. "*Bonsoir, mon chéri.* What's up?"

Sylvie crossed her arms and exhaled in frustration. *Mon chéri? Really? If they're not having sex and he's such a jerk to her, why is she calling him that? Especially in front of me.* The lack of awareness and respect made Sylvie's head ache. "I know it's late. Sorry you were worried. Actually, I'm at a girlfriend's…I was just about to leave. But why are you calling? Anything wrong?" Hélène turned to face the wall.

Trying to ignore the red flags in her conversation, Sylvie began plucking tiny tufts of white cashmere from Hélène's blue blouse. *I'm not listening. Just preening a bit. Like right here.* Her fingers reached an intimate spot under Hélène's arm. She leaned closer, frowning as Hélène stood as stiff as a plank.

Hélène spoke curtly. "*Non*, I didn't call you. How could I? You didn't even tell me where you're staying."

That's it, get mad at him. Sylvie nodded.

But then, Hélène softened her voice. "Just to wish me 'good night'? That's so *sweet* of you!"

How pathetic. If that's not a wet blanket… Sylvie withdrew her hands and stalked into the kitchen.

"Why does Maman always get into these kinds of situations?" Sylvie mumbled to the cat in her arms. Adjusting her buttocks on the kitchen counter, she crossed her legs. "What's wrong with me?"

Meanwhile, Hélène finished up her phone conversation in the other room. "You too, get a good night's sleep…*Quoi?* I miss you too. See you on Monday. *Bonne nuit, mon chéri.*"

Sylvie closed her eyes to block out the kissing noises. *Control yourself.* She felt her veins pulsating on her temples with rage as she heard Hélène tiptoe into the kitchen. To Sylvie's surprise, Hélène began petting Goldie, who was nestled in her arms. *She comes in as if nothing had happened.* The steady caresses in her lap made the tiny hairs on Sylvie's neck bristle. Gradually, she let herself relax. She closed her eyes as Hélène's fingers ran through Goldie's soft fur. As usual in conflicting situations, she was at a loss for words. In her frustration, her heart and mind stood at opposite ends of the playing field. *I'll just be like Goldie right now. Let it go and deal with it later.*

All was peaceful until Hélène announced abruptly, "Never mind," and withdrew her hand.

Sylvie's eyes popped open. "*Quoi?* What did you say?"

"I said 'never mind,'" Hélène repeated, louder this time. She began piling her dirty Tupperware and utensils into her grocery baskets.

Sylvie opened her mouth to say something. But nothing came out. *Never mind what?*

"It's late. I should go."

Sylvie pushed Goldie off her lap. "But we haven't even had dessert, and—"

"*Je suis désolée.* I'm not hungry anymore," stated Hélène curtly, staring at the refrigerator. "Know what?" she blurted. "Just invite someone *else* over. To eat it with you."

Sylvie's face reddened. "Don't be ridiculous! I want to eat it with you." *What's wrong with this woman? She's acting like she's mad at me. But what have I done? She's the one with a husband she was making kissing noises at.* She placed her hand on Hélène's shoulder. "Forget about the phone call. Let's go back to the sofa and—"

Hélène shook her hand off her shoulder. "You'll have no problem finding someone else to..." Her head was bent over her baskets as she filled them, with her hair falling into her eyes. "To share your sofa with. *En fait*, you've probably already had lots of—"

"What are you talking about?" asked Sylvie, reaching toward Hélène. *Don't tell me she's jealous. How can she be jealous when she's the married one? The one who answers phone calls from her husband at midnight while we're practically making out on my sofa? Besides, who could she be jealous of?* She caught Hélène's arm as their hands locked in midair, suspending a Tupperware container full of carrots.

"You should be with someone young. And cute. *Pas avec moi.* I'm as old and worn out as…" Hélène let go of the carrots and picked up a gray, natty dish towel. "This." When she twisted the towel, a few drops of sudsy liquid trickled to the floor. Throwing down the towel, she turned her back on Sylvie. "And just as useless."

Sylvie whispered in her ear. "Don't be ridiculous." She whisked Hélène around and wiped a tear from her flushed cheek. *Why is it that I'm supposed to comfort her right now when I haven't done anything wrong? Why is she being so irrational?* She pushed her own irritation away in an effort to make things right between them. Maybe once Hélène had calmed down she could figure out why she'd acted so bizarre.

"But it's true," replied Hélène, grabbing her baskets. "Thanks for having me over," she mumbled, hurrying from the kitchen. She grabbed her coat and reached for the doorknob, but before she could turn it, Sylvie's hand was on hers.

"*Attends,*" said Sylvie, gently pushing Hélène against the door. "I think we should talk—"

Hélène placed her finger over Sylvie's soft lips. "Some other time. When we've had less to drink."

"But I just want to tell you that—"

"It's not a good time, Sylvie. We hardly know each other."

"*Je sais.* That's why—"

A phone rang. Sylvie's eyebrows shot up. Startled, Hélène looked around the room. Pulling her cell phone from her coat, she announced curtly, "It's yours."

Sylvie couldn't imagine who it would be. *I sure as hell don't have a husband checking up on me.* "Wonder who it could be? It's so late."

"*Ouais*, I wonder," hissed Hélène, grabbing the doorknob. Before Sylvie had time to react, Hélène was running down the dark hallway. *Why is she trying to get away from me? What have I done to her?* Sylvie groped the wall. With a click, the hall light came on. Before Hélène could reach the elevator, Sylvie was grasping her shoulder, pulling her back. "Wait! I'll come down and open the—"

Hélène spun around. "I can find my way out. Go answer your stupid phone!"

Sylvie stood motionless, as if Hélène had just slapped her. Numbly, she watched her run for the stairs, descending them two by two. There was nothing else she could do—until she noticed an orange ball escape through the doorway. She hollered, "Goldie! Get back in here!" then slammed the door with frustration.

❖

Sylvie was lying on her side on the sofa. Wrapped in her arms, Goldie was licking the tears dribbling over her paws. Sylvie's mind lingered on the day she had realized, as a teenager, that a heterosexual lifestyle was like deep-sea fishing—she disliked both. After that day, unlike the other girls in her class, she avoided all hairy-chested men—the only option in Greece. They left her indifferent. She vowed to never dangle her legs in front of men's eyes, nor their fishhooks, which they seemed to cast everywhere she went, even leagues away from the sea.

Her dream was to remain as free as a dolphin. *I'll never get attached*, she had promised herself. And now, she realized, even without the dreaded instrument of torture—a deep-sea hook—dangling before her eyes, her dream had become a self-fulfilling prophecy. This thought made her cry even harder, until—through blurry eyes—she glanced over and spotted a lone cherry in her bowl of fruit. She picked it up by its stem and twirled it, observing its plump perfection. Goldie followed the shiny red ball as it moved through the air. The fruit's sweet yet tangy taste on Sylvie's tongue whet her desire for more. She flashed a naughty smile as her teeth entered the pulpy flesh of the forbidden fruit. *Maybe I should just give up on love altogether. Is it a self-fulfilling prophecy that I'll be alone forever? If I keep falling for straight, married women, I'll always end up single. Just like this lone cherry in my fruit bowl.*

The cherry's tart juice perked Sylvie's taste buds. She licked her lips and tried not to think of the way Hélène's had felt against them. *So, what am I going to do about it? Be bold and go find a real lesbian?* But was that what she really wanted? Or was she addicted to the chase, which was why she only went after women who were unattainable? This thought saddened her even more. Would she ever find someone who loved her? Only her? She held her kitty to her chest. "Why is love so difficult, Goldie?"

A church bell rang three times, indicating the early morning hour. The only other activity in the peaceful, sleepy neighborhood was in Dionysos Taverna, where Sylvie—wide awake and perched on her barstool—was gesticulating wildly. Vassilios, the waiter, was sitting next to her, simply nodding as he poured her endless shots of ouzo. The liquor swam through her system, transforming her into a babble machine. Her words spewed forth like an uncontrollable stream, only pausing when she took a swig in a vain effort to numb her hyperactive tongue. She was trying to soothe her nerves after the disastrous dinner with Hélène. Despite her naturally calm demeanor, she poured out all her frustrations to Vassilios about how the evening had ended and how she couldn't stay in her apartment thinking about Hélène anymore. At last, the potent liquid took effect. Her tongue seemed to numb, and at last, Dionysos Taverna grew silent. A lone tear dribbled down her cheek.

"Shh," whispered Vassilios, holding her tightly in his arms. He smoothed the hair behind her ear and gently kissed her forehead.

Sylvie's dizzy head tipped sideways, landing on his broad shoulders. The last thing she remembered, besides a musky masculine odor mixed with Greek spices and ouzo, was squeezing her eyes to shut out the vertigo and everything that reminded her of Hélène.

Chapter Ten

Kneeling in a pile of dirt, Hélène wiped her sweaty hands on her jeans as she scanned her garden for weeds. Finding a hidden tuft, she reached down and yanked on a new handful.

She frowned at the fresh scratch in her dirt-encrusted fingertips as she jerked her hand back. Then she remembered the saying *no pain, no gain.* Feeling better with each handful, she crawled over to an enormous weed and pulled. It wouldn't budge. Standing up, she struggled with all her might.

"*Voilà!*" She uprooted the intruder as clods of soil rained around her. "*Enfin!*" She shook her lifeless victim by the neck. As she sat in the garden, Hélène eyed the unfortunate weed, strangled by her dirt-covered hands. Then she remembered the voice. *Déjà vu.* Like a powerful wave, her thoughts swept backward. When she shut her eyes, she could see the elderly woman leaning on a wooden cane, two paces behind her. Memories of that bizarre, rainy day returned to Hélène so clearly. She remembered how the muddy blooms she had thrown in the air in fury had torpedoed the elderly stranger's oversized, floppy pink hat. *Hilde.* She had often wondered about their chance meeting that day and their strange conversation in Hilde's cozy home over steaming cups of tea. The elderly woman had revealed so many obscure details about Hélène's life, it was scary. But was it real? Was Hilde real? Did she even believe in psychics? She decided to do some digging of her own.

Hélène shook the dirt off her jeans and entered the house. *It's got to be here somewhere.* Like a sleuth, she headed up the stairs to her bedroom, Chaussette in tow. Perched on a stool, she shuffled boxes on the upper shelf of her closet. At last, she found what she was searching for.

She carried the tattered, dusty white box to the bed. Thoughtfully, she lifted the lid. Inside the box, buried beneath a layer of faded newspapers, were a half dozen cassette tapes. She sighed with relief. *Why didn't I think of this before?*

She hadn't wanted to touch the box since Maman died. Those were Maman's personal items. If she had wanted Hélène to listen to the cassette tapes, she would have said so. But then again, Maman had passed away so suddenly, she hardly had time to leave instructions. And Hélène had been her only surviving family member. Or so Hélène had thought, until she met Hilde, who revealed an entirely different story.

It had been ten years since Hélène had last touched that box, the day after the funeral. She had used that same stool to stuff it safely in the back of her closet. Hélène shuddered at the memory. It had been a damp, dark day. A day of mourning. A day she could never forget. She inspected the dust on her fingertips. Gray. Just like Maman's ashes. She shuddered again, painfully aware of the loneliness gnawing at her soul. *I miss her so much.*

She took one of the cassette tapes from the box. Then she frowned. *None of these are labeled. Maybe they're blank.* As if called by a mysterious, exterior voice, she squeezed her eyes shut. *Why didn't I do this before? Somehow, deep down, I must've known Maman was hiding things from me.* Now, after yanking weeds, digging her fingers in the soil, and her bizarre conversation with Hilde the psychic, she was having this strange déjà vu experience. She felt a profound hole growing inside her heart, filling her with deep sadness. Her intuition was kicking in—she desperately needed to know what was on these tapes after all these years. As if in a trance, her eyes popped open, and she raced down the stairs, two by two, to the kitchen. *Only one way to find out...*

She inserted the tape into the radio-cassette player. *Glad we didn't toss this prehistoric contraption.* Chaussette, who had beaten her to the kitchen, stared intently at the tape's initial crackling noises while Hélène held her chest to steady her pounding heart. At last, Hélène heard a voice. *Maman?* Her heart beat faster.

Non. It wasn't her. But it *was* a familiar voice, an elderly woman's voice. Hélène crinkled her eyes as she listened, trying to decipher the sounds on the old recording. The woman spoke in a soft tone with a slight Flemish accent. She was explaining about her garden. A beautiful garden, full of exotic plants and flowers. *It's not Maman, but I know her.* The motherly warmth radiating through the woman's voice had a soothing effect on Hélène. She felt her body begin to relax. Then, abruptly, the voice stopped.

Hélène stood for a long time in the kitchen, staring at the radio-cassette player. She listened to the woman's deep breathing, which sounded more like a throaty rattle than a series of breaths. Then she glanced at her forearm. The tiny blond hairs stood upright. Whenever something rang true, whenever she knew her intuition was right, she got goose bumps. This was one of those moments. *Mon Dieu.* Gulping, she realized who this woman was. But how could it be possible? *C'est Hilde! How could Maman have known the psychic?*

Just then, Chaussette, who was curled on a chair, cocked her ears. Her tiny body twitched at a sudden slam; then she froze.

"Hélène, I'm home!"

Before he could find her, Hélène shut off the cassette player and raced out the kitchen door. She rushed into the garden and knelt in front of the plants. She didn't know why, exactly, she felt the need to hide the cassette from him. Or why this feeling of frustration was stronger than being glad he was home. She'd deal with that later.

"You're back early. It's only Sunday," she said when Marc sauntered into the garden. He was wearing freshly ironed jeans and a black turtleneck sweater. Like a robot, he flashed her a curt smile and pecked her on the forehead. *"Bonjour, chérie.* Tomorrow's meeting was canceled. Good news, *non?"*

Hélène raised her hand to block the sun. *"Oui, je suppose.* But what does—"

"I'm so glad to be home. I missed you," said Marc, not seeming to notice that his wife was sitting in the dirt.

"*Ouais.* Me too, but—"

"I got this for you." Marc handed her a brown paper bag.

"How sweet," said Hélène, holding up an extra-large *I love London* T-shirt adorned with a red heart. "*Merci.* It's adorable."

"Glad you like it." Marc glanced toward the kitchen. "Anyway, I'm headin' back in. Game's about to start."

Hélène waited for him to leave before trying on the T-shirt. It drooped over her shoulders. *I'm swimming all right.* She wiggled out of it, leaving dirty-finger smudges on the white cotton circling the heart. Had he really not noticed how much weight she'd lost? Or how hard she'd been working to follow Dr. Duprès's orders to change her habits and get healthy?

A football announcer's voice blared through the open door. Then Marc hollered, "Hope it's the right size. Not too small, is it?"

Hélène exhaled through her teeth. "*Non!* It's perfect!"

"I thought you'd like it. Check out the back. It's cute."

Hélène scrunched her nose when she saw the photo. *Cute, eh?* An obese blond woman sat on a bar stool, licking her lips. She held a pint of beer in one hand and a huge piece of fried fish in the other. In front of her were five plates piled with fish and chips and five empty beer mugs. Under the photo it said: "But does London love me?"

"Very cute," muttered Hélène sarcastically. *At least it's reassuring. He won't hit on any English women if they're all like that.* She sighed and attacked another weed, which brought her thoughts back to the cassette tape tucked in her pocket. *What on earth was Hilde's voice doing on Maman's tape? Why was she talking about her garden? What other deep secrets will the tapes reveal?*

As she cleared the garden of all unwanted shrubs, she tried to stay focused on the glorious sensation of being outside, among her flowers, instead of the overwhelming feeling that her life was spinning out of control. To her frustration, she realized she had more questions than answers about what she wanted in her future.

❖

That evening, after doing the dishes, Hélène wandered upstairs to work on her latest poem. Humming at her desk, she rubbed the tips of her slippers together, ignoring Chaussette's furry body bobbing on her thighs.

She flipped the pages of her botanical dictionary to find just the right word. *M...Magnolia...Ma...Marigold...*

"*Merde!* That's the last thing I was looking for." She slammed the dictionary shut, which startled Chaussette, who dove under the bed. Images of Goldie, Sylvie's chubby orange cat, filled Hélène's mind. Then her thoughts went to Sylvie and that soft cashmere sweater she was wearing at her place. *Why is she always invading my mind?* She tried to stop the intense feelings these images brought her. Once again, her efforts backfired. She clenched her pencil in frustration. *I wonder what she's doing right now?* Their evening had ended so terribly, and Hélène wondered just what Sylvie thought of her. The alcohol had taken over, and she'd let irrational jealousy ruin what was promising to be a most interesting evening. *But what was I thinking? Maybe Marc's call came just in time to keep me from doing something I would regret later.*

Just then, the phone rang.

After three rings, Mark yelled over the TV, "I'm not here. Unless it's Maman."

"As usual," groaned Hélène, reaching for the phone. But when she saw the number, she gasped. "*Non, non.* Not her!" A knot formed in her throat. The phone rang again.

"Would you *please* pick the darn thing up?" hollered Marc.

But Hélène couldn't do it. *Strange that I was just thinking about her. I really want to know how she is, especially after our disastrous dinner last night. It's just that...* She could almost smell Sylvie's soft scent on her skin. Despite her efforts, she couldn't get her deep, chocolate eyes out of her mind. Then she saw herself running through the dark hallway and down the stairs, trying to get away from her. Her heart was beating wildly. *Non! Not now. I can't talk to her!*

Finally, after the eighth ring, the phone stopped. She sighed with relief—until the answering machine kicked in. With her hands on her hips, she braced herself, ready to fight her rival like a rebellious cowboy.

"Hélène, it's Sylvie. I didn't get a chance to thank you for last night. Dinner was delicious. Also, I'd like to talk to you. So, when you hear this, please call me. *Merci.*"

Hélène stared at the answering machine, pressing her lips together. *What can I say to her?* Her heart was still thumping. She shook her head. *I've nothing to say to her.* Before she could stop herself, she pushed the erase button on the machine.

Afterward, no matter how hard she tried, the words in Hélène's poem no longer made sense. Finally, she threw down her pencil. "*Zut!* I can't concentrate, and it's all *her* fault!"

Just then, the noise from the TV downstairs went silent.

"*Whose* fault is it?" Marc called out.

Hélène cleared her throat. "Ah…Just some stupid salesperson. You know how they are. Everyone's home on Sunday nights, and they figure—"

Hélène never thought she would welcome the sounds of a beer can opening and the volume rising on the TV, but she did. She exhaled mindfully, trying to get her creative juices flowing again. But after another few painful minutes, she gave up. *I need some fresh air.* Peeking under the bed, she whispered, "Maman is going out for a little while. Be a good darling, *d'accord*?" She blew her kitty a kiss, shut off the computer, and tiptoed down the stairs.

Marc was so absorbed in his football game, he didn't notice when Hélène said good-bye. Instead of answering, he jumped up with a "Go for it!" Popcorn flew around the room as he flung his arms in the air.

"Never mind," said Hélène, extracting buttery kernels from her hair while she crunched her way out of the room.

❖

As Hélène pedaled furiously through the dark streets, the cool night air soothed her hot cheeks but not her temper. She sped past the Atomium with its shiny metallic balls in the form of a gigantic atom, lit by spotlights and reflections from the full moon. Ignoring the silhouette of shabby wooden boats lining the canal, she headed toward the Grand Place at the city center. Instead of slowing down, she zigzagged between throngs of tourists, nearly crashing into an Asian tour guide holding up a tiny flag. An entire busload of tourists squealed in Japanese, flashing pictures of Hélène as she rode off.

After a frenzied half hour, Hélène reached a secluded street and slowed down. Her heart was racing. Breathing heavily, she straddled her bike and gazed up at the full moon.

"Stunning," she whispered. Then she began to shiver despite the sweat running down her back. She hugged her shoulders. *Better get a move on before I catch a…Attends, this street looks familiar.* She rode over to a street sign. Rue des Pépins. Then she gasped. She checked the numbers on the buildings. *Six…eight. Oh my gosh, I'm only a block away.* Before she could stop herself, her legs were pedaling furiously down the street. As soon as she reached Sylvie's apartment building—number twelve—her cell phone rang.

Hélène grimaced. *The game must be over.* She pulled out her phone. But when she saw the unfamiliar number, she scratched her chin. When the ringing stopped, she put her ear to the receiver. There was a beep, and then a message:

"Hélène, it's Sylvie. I left a message at your place earlier, and since you didn't call me back, I thought I'd try your cell. Thanks again for last night. And, like I said…*Eh bien,* I'd really like to talk to you. It's kind of urgent, actually. Sorry it's late, but call me back, *s'il te plaît.*"

"She's too much!" Hélène slammed her phone shut. When she spun around, she hit her ankle on her bike stand. "*Aiie!* Stupid bike." She shoved the offensive object behind a tree. It landed with a thud, ringing its bell. She gave the bike a sharp kick; the bell rang again. "That's what you deserve, bringing me *here,* of all places."

It was an unusual occurrence for Hélène to lose her temper. She hardly ever did it with Marc, and she certainly had ample reason to blow her stack with him on a daily basis. With her shoulders locked as tight as a solid iron gate, she stuck her fists in her pockets and paced in front of Sylvie's building. *I've nothing to say to her. Why does she keep calling me?* Hélène knew deep down that she was being unfair to Sylvie. She was angry at her, but she was even more angry with herself—for letting herself fall for Sylvie. It had all started out innocently enough. She had admired Sylvie for her courage, her physical strength, and her genuine kindness toward others. She was the exact opposite of Marc. But then, at some point during their daily swimming lessons, she had realized that this admiration she felt for Sylvie was stronger than ever. It had transformed itself into attraction: physical, emotional, and even spiritual. Her whole being cared for Sylvie in ways that she had never cared for anyone before. She was mad at herself for letting this happen. Her life had been so much easier when it didn't get tangled up in emotions. Caring for Chaussette, writing her secret poems, even dealing with Marc's terrible moods was easier than facing the truth. She didn't want to admit that she loved Sylvie with all her heart. She just couldn't do that. And it was all Sylvie's fault.

Feeling her gut churn with angst, she cocked her head and spat her anger at the moon. "What nerve!" *And I can't believe I pedaled here, of all places. What a messed-up night.*

With a huff, she whipped out her phone to listen to the message again.

"Hélène, it's Sylvie. I left a message at your place earlier, and since you didn't call me back, I thought I'd try—" *Shut up!* Hélène shoved the phone back into her pocket, muffling Sylvie's voice. The message stopped as Hélène approached a brick wall under a massive pine tree across the street. Impulsively, she jumped up and straddled the wall as if it were a horse. Its hard bricks felt cold and rough under her thighs. She hugged her tense shoulders for warmth as her eyes penetrated the tree branches. A woman was pulling the curtains shut in a fourth-floor apartment. Hélène squinted. *It's her!*

Hélène's heart flipped. Then she gasped. "What the?" A young woman approached Sylvie from behind. Sylvie stopped tugging on the curtains and slowly turned around.

At that precise moment, Hélène's stomach lurched.

I can't watch this. Hélène tried her best, but she couldn't stop staring at the window. She cringed when the young woman started dangling a cherry in front of Sylvie's mouth. Sylvie was shaking her head, but the woman kept insisting.

How disgusting. Hélène scowled as she watched Sylvie give in, taking the fruit between her teeth. *That's it, gag her with your cherry.* Then Hélène realized, *Wait, that's my cherry! That chick's stuffing Sylvie's face with my fruit salad!*

As if she had read Hélène's thoughts, Sylvie glanced outside and shut the curtains.

Hélène glared up at the moon. *Why did you bring me here to see this? I've had enough suffering for one day, merci.* She was about to slide off the wall when she heard a noise. She stopped just in time to see Sylvie and the woman leaving the building. Sylvie was pulling a yellow suitcase on wheels.

Hélène remained crouched on the wall, mesmerized.

The younger woman was carrying a small plastic cage. A cat meowed loudly from within. "Shh, Goldie," whispered the woman.

Hélène felt dizzy all of a sudden. She lost her balance and fell behind the wall with a thud. *Ouch! That landing's gonna give me a magnificent bruise.*

The two women stopped walking and briefly glanced in Hélène's direction, but she was conveniently hidden behind the wall. She peeked over it, in the shadows, to observe them.

Sylvie shrugged. The pair continued until they reached a black car parked nearby. Hélène—crouching in the grass—held her breath. Her heart was pounding. *Please, don't let her see my bike.* She peeked over the wall again. To her relief, Sylvie was busy stuffing her suitcase into the trunk. Then she took the small cage and entered the car on the passenger's side.

This is ridiculous. Hélène's anger mounted; never before had she succumbed to such lowly tactics: crouching behind a wall and spying on someone, and in the middle of the night, no less. Shivering from the damp night chill, all she wanted to do was run away, but she didn't dare move. There she stood, forced to observe Sylvie and the other woman—*probably her lover*—practically under her nose. Sylvie was gesticulating and speaking loudly, as usual, in Greek.

The woman replied just as loudly. To Hélène's dismay, she began caressing Sylvie's arm. *Non...non! Stop touching her!*

Growing increasingly frustrated, Hélène attempted to decipher their words. But it all sounded like gibberish. *I'm a professional translator. Why can't I get any of this?* She bit her lip in desperation. *Why in the heck didn't I study Greek in school? Of course, I opted for Latin—a dead language. Smart move.* Despite her lack of understanding Greek, however, she could tell Sylvie's voice sounded tired. Then the woman kissed Sylvie tenderly on the cheek.

I can't believe this. Hélène felt nauseous. Even without a translation, their body language told her more than she needed to know. She clutched her stomach. *No wonder she sounds exhausted. They've probably been at it since last night.* She tried to look away, but something kept drawing her gaze back to them. *Linguistic curiosity? Not exactly. I must be masochistic.* The knot in her gut tightened.

As the two women talked, Hélène noticed Goldie sitting in her plastic cage on Sylvie's lap. With horror, she saw that the cat's emerald eyes were staring out the window. They seemed to be aimed right at her head, which was just above the wall. *Please don't make a fuss, Goldie.* As if it had heard her silent wish, the orange kitty began to meow.

Alarmed, Hélène hissed. This only made the cat meow even louder. Hélène quickly ducked. To make things worse, the sudden movement pinched her intestines. The pressure shifted its contents, filled with a healthy, copious dinner. Hélène coughed once and then vomited violently behind the wall. She heard Sylvie's voice in Greek over the sound of her own retching. Her ears were straining to hear Sylvie's words, even though she couldn't understand them. She could feel the pressure mounting inside her body and her mind. *This is unbearable.* She was disgusted at how strongly her emotions were taking over, as if she had lost control of her life.

With tears in her eyes, Hélène lifted her weary head. When she peeked over the wall, she saw the younger woman pinching her nose. Then she whistled. Both of them were speaking rapidly in Greek and looking in her direction. Luckily, it was nighttime. Tree shadows camouflaged her presence until the woman drove away with Sylvie and Goldie. As soon as the car disappeared, Hélène's heart felt like lead.

Dragging herself over the wall, she wobbled to her bike. Glowering, she cast a final look at Sylvie's apartment. The moon's whiteness created an eerie reflection off the window where the two women had been standing so close together. *No wonder I got sick. Bien sûr, she had something urgent to tell me! She's going to sleep... no...live with that young Greek woman. I knew she would share my fruit salad with her.* Hélène felt even more nauseous. *Why doesn't she want to take care of me instead of her? It's my fruit salad, after all! Why are my feelings so messed up right now?* Deep down, she knew she was being irrational. She kept pushing Sylvie away; what right did she have to be angry that Sylvie was with someone else, someone who wanted her? Her heart wouldn't listen to reason.

Clutching her woozy stomach, Hélène began pedaling. When she reached the first red light, she gazed once more at the moon. Its pureness and splendor only made her feel worse. She clenched her jaw as fresh anger raced through her veins. Why couldn't she keep her mind off Sylvie and that woman? Even when she squeezed her eyes shut, she saw them laughing, holding each other, making a life together...

That's when it hit her. Standing in the middle of an empty street, lit by the moon, swallowed by the viscous darkness around her—a wave of sadness swept over Hélène. These profound feelings, initially camouflaged by anger, informed Hélène of the extreme darkness and loneliness in her life. *What makes my life so dark and empty? How did I even get here?* She pointed her face at the moon. "Give me some sort of sign," she demanded. *Is it her? Is it Marc? Or is it me?* The response came swiftly. It began with an ache in her bosom. Then Hélène felt a sharp pinch when a dam of tears broke loose, flooding her face. By the time the light turned green, her chest was drenched. *Génial*, she thought, scowling at the moonlight glimmering off its shiny pool. *It's me. I'm the one who's messed up. But it's her fault too. If we hadn't met, I wouldn't be feeling this way. I'd be just who I was a few months ago.* She squeezed her eyes shut before they generated a new surge of tears. Who was she a few months ago? The woman she had been before she'd met Sylvie was an entirely different person. Had she been so lonely and sad that she spent all her free time writing poetry about flowers to lift her spirits? Was that why she devoted her life to Chaussette, the only member of her family that actually cared for her after she lost Maman? Had her head been stuck so deep in the sand that she didn't realize how unhappy and lonely she was? She shook her head to chase these negative thoughts away. Who did she want to be now?

❖

When Hélène finally made it home, she slammed the front door. Even though it was after midnight, Marc still lay on the sofa, watching TV. It was on so loud, he didn't even budge. Neither did he notice when she appeared in the living room; he was too busy sketching two boxers fighting on TV.

Idiot. Hélène glared at the row of empty beer cans. *You didn't even notice I was gone.* She kicked off her shoes and trudged up the stairs. Ignoring her sticky clothes—imbibed with sweat and tears—she dove under the bedcovers. Chaussette crawled out from under the bed and promptly hopped on her mistress. Once she realized Hélène's distress, she nuzzled her face and tried to lick away her sadness—starting with her salty neck.

After a moment, the volume on the TV dropped. Then came a holler: "*Chérie*, did you go somewhere? That stupid phone hasn't stopped ringing!"

Hélène sighed. *I could curl up and die, and he wouldn't even know it.*

"I'm tired, Marc. *Bonne nuit*," she replied, realizing how exhausted she was. *I don't even have the energy to tell him what a jerk he is.*

"What'd you say?"

Hélène rolled her eyes.

Marc cleared his throat. "How obnoxious can salesmen get, anyway? It's Sunday night!"

You idiot. Hélène thrust her head under the pillow. Then she heard a muffled, "*Chérie,* could you check the messages? Just in case it was Maman? Could be important."

Stumbling out of bed, Hélène crawled over to the answering machine where a red light was blinking. "So important," she muttered. "Who gives a poop?" She lifted her leg in the air. Wiggling her big toe, she whispered, "Chaussette, *bébé,* look what Maman is going to do with all these important messages." Chaussette's eyes dilated, mesmerized by Hélène's toe as it hovered over the "Play" button. When she pressed it, a computerized voice announced, "You have three new—"

"Shut up," grumbled Hélène, hitting the "Erase" button. The voice then announced: "Erasing messages...Erasing messages... Messages erased."

"Good riddance!" Hélène fell back on the soft carpet. Exhaling deeply, she closed her eyes. *Thought you could play around with me, eh? We got cozy at dinner, but that was a huge mistake. Too much alcohol or something. It's all your fault.* She clenched her fists just as Chaussette came over to rub against her ear. She gently pushed her cat away. *Okay, maybe I'm being irrational. You've got the right to date whomever you please. It's true, I'm married. Perhaps I'm not being fair. But sometimes, life just isn't fair.* She scrunched up her nose in disgust. *Hah! Your little adventure with me didn't work, did it?* She smiled smugly. *You lose. I've erased you from my life. Forever. And if you think I'm ever going near your stupid pool again...* But as soon as Hélène pictured the pool, she had an eerie feeling the crystal blue water was calling her name. Her eyes popped open.

Directly above her, propped against her computer, was the painting of Santorini that she had found one day while biking to work. When she reached for it, she accidentally knocked an envelope opener off her desk.

"*Zut!*" she exclaimed as its sharp point pierced the carpet.

This must be a sign, she thought, studying the glistening silver blade. Its coolness felt nice in her sweaty palm. She closed her eyes again. *Non, that's silly.* She shook her head emphatically. Something seemed to rattle inside her skull, which scared her even more. *This is crazy. I'm losing my marbles.*

Then she got another idea. "I really shouldn't...But what the heck."

She grabbed her painting of Santorini and took a deep breath. Then she stabbed at the painting with the blade, poking holes in the sea, the white houses, the blue sky—until the small canvas looked more like Swiss cheese than a painting.

Then she shook the ruined painting. "*Voilà!* That's what I think of you and your Santorini!" A greasy croak erupted from the back of her throat. Hélène knew deep down how terribly she was behaving. She destroyed her painting of Santorini to get back at Sylvie. She knew it was unfair, but what was she to do? Sylvie made it crystal clear she wanted to be with her. But now, Sylvie wanted someone else—a young, attractive Greek woman—instead of her. It was as if she hadn't taken her desire for Hélène seriously in the first place... and that thought hurt more than it should have.

She held up the painting and squinted through its shredded sea. "Life really is unfair, isn't it, *bébé*?" As a response, Chaussette promptly took refuge under the bed just as Hélène dove on top of it.

She's ruining my life! Hélène punched her pillow with her fists. She didn't care that sweat was dripping off her body, soaking the sheets. She just wanted...well, she didn't know what she wanted. And that was even more infuriating. She curled around a pillow. *What is wrong with me?*

CHAPTER ELEVEN

Whenever Sylvie traveled back to her island, the excitement was always overwhelming. Brussels airport had always fascinated her: engines revving, busy people hurrying to catch their flights, teary kisses to say *au revoir*, *bonjour*, or *yassas*. But tonight, her excitement was stifled by sadness. When they left the check-in counter, Sylvie could hardly look at Aphrodite. Her creative mind kicked in—a protective mechanism she had developed as a child to keep her sane in a world she didn't always like or understand.

Like swarms of busy little ants, dozens of shoes in all shapes and colors crossed Sylvie's line of vision. Judging from their polished sheen, most of the travelers were there for business. She had always wondered why Belgians put so much effort into polishing their shoes. It was like brushing teeth—an automatic reflex. Many of her Belgian friends couldn't leave home without swiping their loafers with a soft cloth.

Sylvie glanced at her own feet as she walked. Her dark toes stood out against her modest leather sandals. The beige trim was scuffed, but she didn't care. She had always liked the natural, well-worn look. No wonder she felt like everyone could tell she wasn't born in Belgium, even before she opened her mouth. Her eyes registered the cotton, rubber, and plastic shoes of the travelers hopping on planes for pleasure. Those were the best. A mauve pair with leather tassels strode by. Realizing how the white marble floors would make a perfect backdrop, she fingered her camera strap pulling on her shoulder, prompting her to capture these images.

Wish I had time to get a few shots of those, she mused, remembering she only had thirty minutes before her flight.

When they reached the passport control checkpoint, Sylvie glanced at her watch. Luckily, only a few passengers were waiting in line. Clutching her passport, she quickly kissed Aphrodite on the cheek.

"You can do better than that, can't you?" asked Aphrodite, pulling her into her arms. "It's a long flight."

Sylvie grinned, thankful for the extra hug. "You're amazing, know that?" She pulled away. "*Ah oui*, I almost forgot." She reached into her jacket pocket. "You don't mind, do you?" She handed her cousin a small yellow envelope.

"Don't be silly." Aphrodite took the envelope, kissed Sylvie softly on the cheek, then held up the small cage. "Aren't you going to say good-bye to little *Mademoiselle*—"

Sylvie plugged her nose and blew air kisses into the cage. "How could I forget my little stinker!" she said, recalling the embarrassing scene an hour before, when they were leaving for the airport.

They'd been just about to drive off in Aphrodite's car when a strange noise erupted in the dark.

"What was that?" she had asked in Greek.

"Sounds like a wild boar," Aphrodite had whispered. "Any pigs in your neck of the woods?"

Sylvie had stuck her finger in the cage and stroked her kitty. "*T'inquiète pas*, Goldie. She's just joking." She had looked out the window again. "The noise came from behind the wall."

Aphrodite had gasped. "*Mon Dieu*, what's that horrible smell?"

"Maybe it really was a wild pig."

"*Non*, it's not outside. It's in here." Aphrodite had pinched her nose.

When Sylvie peered into the cage, she had cringed. "*Merde*, it's Goldie! Poor thing's got the runs. She's so intuitive. Just like Yaya. Telepathic even. She feels it when someone's upset."

Then Aphrodite had whistled. *"Ca alors.* Impressive cat. All the way to Yaya in Santorini!"

"You're amazing, Goldie." Sylvie had grinned as she held her nose. "Don't worry, little one, Maman won't be gone long." She had stroked her kitty warily as Aphrodite drove them straight to the airport.

Sylvie's thoughts returned to the present. She peered into Goldie's cage. "Maman is going to miss you so much. But don't worry, Auntie Aphrodite will take good care of you. I promise. It's only for a few days, and Maman will be back as soon as…" Feeling her throat tighten, Sylvie blinked, trying to hold in her tears.

Her cousin's hand squeezed her shoulder. *"Ca va, ma chérie.* Don't worry."

Sylvie's eyes were brimming. "But she's so fragile—she's already eighty-three, you know."

"She'll be fine, Syl, don't worry."

Sylvie gave Aphrodite one last hug and winked at Goldie. "Be good, little stinker." She did an about-face and marched toward the passport control booth. *I hate leaving Goldie behind. Luckily, she's in good hands with Aphrodite. But I wish Hélène would call. What's wrong with her? I hope she's okay. I swore off straight women for a reason. Somehow, though, I thought she was different. But I guess they're all the same.* She knew full well she should simply cut ties and leave Hélène to her straight, confused life. But as usual, her heart was disagreeing with her head. Discreetly, she wiped her eyes with her sleeve and showed the officer her boarding pass to Athens.

Hélène shoved the destroyed painting under her bed and dove back under the bedcovers. *Go ahead and move in with her.* "I couldn't care less!" She blubbered into the sheets as her eyes filled with hot tears. She smacked her pillow again before shoving her face underneath; a few seconds later, she reemerged, gasping for oxygen. When she rested her head on the pillow at last, it sank deeply into the down feathers. Within seconds, her body and mind surrendered to fatigue, and Hélène dozed off.

❖

Hélène was standing stark naked in the women's locker room, showering. Streams of warm water poured into her eyes—as if she were crying backward. Ascertaining that she was no longer the source of these tears, she shut her lids with relief. As the silky water caressed her tense shoulder muscles, her body softened and her mind gradually wound down. She began to wash, glad to get rid of the feeling of grime sticking to her.

All was fine until she heard a door slam. Next, she heard water running in the shower next to hers. She cranked up the warm water and continued soaping—until she heard a moan. She stopped scrubbing. The moan stopped. But as soon as she began soaping again, she heard another moan. Louder this time. *And it's coming from the shower next to mine.* Hélène's scalp prickled. She squinted at the blurry body on the other side. All she could see was water pouring down on someone who was washing herself very slowly. Another moan erupted. *Here we go again.* Hélène turned off her shower, listening attentively.

It's starting to get cold in here, she decided after a few moments, raising a forearm laden with soapy goose bumps. She took a step toward the shower curtain when she heard another long moan. Ever so cautiously, she poked her head through the shower curtains, which were decorated with tiny blue fish that seemed to move across the curtain.

Ca alors! Sylvie's yellow bathing suit was hanging outside the shower next to hers. Another moan erupted. She crouched on the wet floor and peered under the opaque glass dividing their showers. She saw Sylvie's tan feet. Her left heel was an inch from the tiled floor, its toes curled under tightly.

Then came more moaning, with heavy, rapid breathing. The

noises intensified. Hélène pressed her face to the wall. But all she could make out was Sylvie's hand pushing on one wall while the other soaped her body.

As she watched, Hélène felt warmness climbing up her legs. Then wetness tickled her delicate thighs like a soft feather, teasing them... *Am I a voyeur?* The reality of her situation hit her in the pit of her stomach. Actually...a bit lower.

Hélène felt the warmth riding her inner thighs as she heard another groan. "*Mon Dieu!* What's happening to me?" she gasped as her mind unraveled. *This is insane...* Her back flattened against the wet glass, her teeth clamped together. The tension in her belly swept downward...

Instantly, Hélène realized how little she knew about her body. She had only been pretending to be alive—until now. At last, she heard Sylvie succumb to an incredibly long, conclusive moan. To her surprise, the excitement building inside her reached a tipping point. At the same time as Sylvie, she struggled to keep herself silent as a deep wave of ecstasy flowed through her body, releasing her pent-up sexual feelings. When it was over, she felt physically drained but emotionally recharged. *Amazing. I never knew I had that in me.*

❖

Hélène's ears felt hot as she strained to suppress the memory of Sylvie's moans and groans in the shower. That dream was so realistic and so incredibly powerful. She wanted to forget about how it affected her body in so many unexpected ways. Delicious ways. Sinful ways. But it was just a dream, so she shouldn't feel guilty. Should she? Without wanting to explore these thoughts further, she glanced at Marc sleeping soundly next to her; his mouth emitted scratchy snores, like a cheap radio. With each exhalation, Chaussette's small body, bundled next to his head, rocked like a dinghy on the fluffy pillow.

Hélène brought her hand to her forehead. It was throbbing. Hugging her kitty to her chest, she slid from the sheets and snuck downstairs. In the kitchen, she fixed herself a stiff espresso with five spoonfuls of sugar. Leaning against the counter, she knocked back her head and guzzled the thick black liquid.

Chaussette, perched on a chair, watched her with a puzzled look.

"*Bébé*, what are you looking at?" Hélène gave her kitty a friendly tap on the nose. "Don't knock it if you haven't tried it." *So what if it tastes like melted tar. It does the trick.*

As Hélène felt the jolt of her espresso fix, she shut her eyes and pressed her fingers to her temples. *Ahh...It's been so long*, she thought, savoring the rush to her system. Ever since Dr. Duprès had asked her to give up her sugary coffee habit for medical reasons, she had been ingesting herbal tea instead, to her great regret. *This is incredible! I've cut out so many wonderful things in my life.* Her eyelids sprang open. "*Eh, bébé*. What else hasn't Maman done in a long time?"

Chaussette meowed.

"*Exactement*," replied Hélène, exiting the kitchen. "We haven't read the paper in weeks. Brussels could burn down and I wouldn't even know it. Let's see what's been happening in the real world."

When she opened the front door, however, she was startled to find—instead of *Le Soir* newspaper—a small yellow envelope. *What's this?* She bent down. In large, black letters she saw *To Hélène*.

With caffeine racing through her system, she ripped open the envelope. A picture fell out, landing on her toes. Ignoring it, she extracted a yellow card. It was handwritten with a black felt pen, with small, delicate strokes:

Dear Hélène,
You forgot this at my place.
I'm at a loss for words. Please forgive me for anything I might have done to hurt you. I'm not quite sure what I did wrong the other night, but whatever it was, it certainly wasn't intentional. I hope we can still be friends.

I hope I'll see you Saturday morning.
Take care, Sylvie

Hélène read the note carefully. Then she read it again. Her eyes lingered on Sylvie's name. "Sylvie..." she said out loud. Her jaw tightened as pangs of anger welled in her chest. She stuffed the note in her back pocket and picked up the photo—of Sylvie and her at the Greek restaurant. *Why is she punishing me like this?*

She shifted her weight from one leg to the other. Her sore muscles made her grimace. Through her caffeine-induced state, she was hit with an onslaught of vivid mental images—sour memories of last night's biking escapade to Sylvie's apartment. As if it were happening to her again, her muscles tensed in agony as her body remembered falling off the wall, hiding behind it, then throwing up with anger under the full moon. *And then she went off with that woman.*

Thoughts of Sylvie driving off with Goldie's cage in her arms made her nauseous again. To chase the all-too-vivid images from her mind, she knew she needed to do something drastic.

Friends? Because you've already got someone else. Before she could get a closer look at the photo, her trembling fingers—operating on their own—ripped the glossy paper in half. She caught a glimpse of Sylvie just as her fingers jammed her into her back pocket. *You're only fit to be sat on.*

With all thoughts of reading *Le Soir* forgotten, she slammed the door and returned to the kitchen to fix herself another stiff espresso and—in an effort to relieve her rage—sit on her swimming coach's smiling face.

Hélène knew deep down that her rage was illogical and unwarranted. Yet her feelings for Sylvie were more than complex; they were off the charts. She'd never, ever thought she would be attracted to another woman. The idea had simply never crossed her mind. She knew she was straight. Besides, she was married to Marc. This lesbian thing wasn't supposed to happen to her. It was fine for others; she had never criticized anyone for loving someone of the same sex. After all, she had several gay friends like Jimmy, Paul, and Ramon. She admired certain women, especially Sylvie—a strong, talented, and gorgeous woman. Who wouldn't admire her? But this admiration had taken an unexpected turn, transforming itself into something much more powerful. She had to admit, she was terribly attracted to Sylvie. And she deeply cared for her. Just the thought gave her goose bumps. *So, why am I so afraid to do something about it?*

Hélène knew her reasoning was irrational. *Because she makes me furious.* Unable to manage her erratic thoughts, she watched them jump around like a child skipping rope, which was incredibly annoying. *But what has she done to hurt me?* She considered the question, then frowned. *It's not all her fault. It's mine too.* Hélène realized again how much her life was out of control. She studied her nails and noticed her fingers were shaking. *Is this rage or anxiety?*

It had all started with feelings for Sylvie, Sylvie's situation with that beautiful Greek woman, and Marc. *What a complete jerk he is. Why has my head been buried in the sand for all these years?* Then her life got even more complicated when she met Hilde, the psychic, and listened to Maman's secret tape. *Why didn't Maman tell me I had a father and a brother?* The loneliness Hélène had been suppressing until now engulfed her. She needed to find the time to return to Maman's tapes and maybe even go back to the psychic. Maybe in Hilde's cozy home she could find at least some of the answers to the questions plaguing her.

She cradled her coffee mug between her hands. The warmth of its sweet, milky liquid, infused with its dark, earthy aroma, brought her back to reality—her terribly inconvenient reality. Hélène felt a deep longing for intimacy—true intimacy—for the first time in her life. *So, why do I feel as if I've just been kicked in the gut?*

CHAPTER TWELVE

Twilight descended gently on the Greek island of Santorini. Yet instead of taking in the familiar sea breeze, usually so refreshing, Sylvie's lungs recycled the damp, sticky air in Yaya's tiny bedroom. She was sitting on Yaya's ancient iron bed, which was abnormally high, pressing her knees together to keep her calves from dangling over its edge. The dimly lit space was sparse, except for a few religious objects and an oil painting of Santorini adorning its walls. A thin curtain hung from an iron bar over the room's only window, begging the full moon to grace its dusty lace with light.

Whenever a cloud passed, the light shifted, casting intricate designs around the room. When Sylvie was a child, she used to poke her fingers in the designs. But tonight, she ignored them. Her thoughts were focused on Yaya, whose fragile body lay under the hand-stitched, patchwork spread. Sylvie still couldn't believe her grandma had fallen ill. "Gravely ill," as her mother had explained over the phone on Sunday evening, confident that her daughter, who adored Yaya, would hop on the next plane to be at her bedside.

Sylvie clasped her fingers around Yaya's bony hand while she slept, trying not to notice how cold her skin felt. Through the dim light, she could just make out the thin white hair grazing Yaya's tender scalp, which rested like a soft egg on its embroidered pillow. Somehow, the elderly woman's wrinkles had softened, especially around her mouth. Their dark lines used to remind Sylvie of craggy mountain crevasses, but now, on Yaya's pasty skin, they looked more like light pencil sketches on a blank canvas.

Sylvie tried to block out the faint bursts of air seeping through Yaya's teeth, refusing to accept how vulnerable her grandma had become. *I've been away too long.* She tried to keep her lower lip from trembling. Yaya had always been so robust, but now, in the moon's soft light, her bent body resembled a helpless, wounded animal. Painfully, Sylvie likened it to the day she found the little bird outside the pool's locker room during a rainstorm, when its tiny body had grown cold in her hand.

Noticing the coolness of Yaya's fingers, she shut her eyes to push back the tears. *I hope she's not in too much pain.* Just then, as if she had heard her granddaughter's silent prayer, Yaya's fingers clasped Sylvie's hand gently. Then the old woman's eyelids fluttered.

Sylvie softly squeezed her fingers back and, trying to contain her excitement, whispered in Greek, "Yaya! It's me, Sylvie. I've returned to be with you."

The elderly woman shook her head as if she were sifting for a nugget of truth in the fog. Then her eyelids fluttered again. In a weak voice, she whispered, "My little darling." Her eyes slowly opened. "Let Yaya see you." But when her grandma tried to lift her head, Sylvie gently pushed her back to her pillow.

"Yaya. I'm right here." Sylvie lowered herself until they were lying side by side on the bed, which resembled a cot, it was so tiny. She wrapped her arm around Yaya and kissed her frail, moist cheek.

"There. Now you can see me better, can't you?"

"Sure. But you're sideways, honey. This is a first for us, isn't it? Sharing the same bed." Yaya's voice was hoarse.

"You've still got your sense of humor, Yaya. That's a good sign," whispered Sylvie.

Yaya cleared her throat. "I'm so glad you're back, my dear. Are you here to stay?" Despite the room's darkness, Sylvie knew her grandma's meaning. She hugged Yaya. "I wish I could, Yaya, but I've got a new job. I can only stay for a few days."

There was a long pause, then Yaya licked her feeble lips and shut her eyes. "You're just like me. Out of all your cousins, you've always been the one who resembled me the most. So hardheaded and determined. You'll live even longer than I have. I can see it in your eyes."

"Shh, Yaya, try to get some rest," said Sylvie, skirting the subject of death. *Yaya's going to live forever, if I can help it.*

"Let me finish, child. I can rest whenever I want. That's all I ever seem to be doing lately anyway. It's not every day that I get a chance to share my bed with you." She coughed dryly.

Sylvie chuckled.

"Talking about sharing beds..." Yaya squinted through the darkness. "Your eyes tell me you're suffering. You've lost something very dear to you recently. Something...or rather, someone. Am I right?"

Sylvie felt a knot form in her throat. "But, Yaya, it's dark in here. You can't—"

"Yes, I can and you have. Am I right, child?"

Sylvie nodded. "As usual."

Yaya tittered triumphantly. "I knew it."

Yaya had always been proud of her talents. Ever since she was a teenager, she had been referred to as a highly intuitive individual—a local psychic. The whole neighborhood relied on her predictions, from weather forecasts to suitable marriage partners, business ventures, school exams, health problems—anything they needed advice on.

Sylvie was used to Yaya reading into her future and giving her unsolicited predictions. She knew only too well she could never hide anything from her, even if she wanted to.

"So, let me give you a bit of grandmotherly advice," Yaya began, as she always did.

Usually, Sylvie accepted Yaya's suggestions gratefully; they almost always helped her. But tonight, she didn't want to hear the precious nuggets her grandma had to offer. She didn't want to talk about Brussels and certainly not her love life—especially her lack of one.

"We don't need to discuss this right now, Yaya. I think you'd better—"

"Hush, Sylvie. I might not get another chance to tell you this. So, listen carefully."

The knot in Sylvie's throat swelled. She held her breath and nodded.

Yaya's voice grew stronger. "If you want something bad enough, child, don't let anything stop you. Just go for it. I promise, in the end, you'll get it…some way or another." Drawing her thin lips into a weak smile, she gazed into Sylvie's eyes.

Instantly, the message hit its target, piercing the sweetest, most tender spot in Sylvie's heart. As she struggled to hold back her tears, Yaya continued.

"Remember all those trophies you won? That's exactly what you did. You went straight for what you wanted, despite the odds." Her eyes were sparkling now.

Seeing the moonlight glistening off their blackness, Sylvie shuddered. *I can't take much more of this.*

Yaya cleared her throat once more. "So, now, listen to Yaya. When you go home, do what I say. Don't give up. Go after your dreams, even if they seem impossible. Because…" The sparkle in her eyes clouded over. "When you reach my age, your dreams start to fade…"

Yaya shut her eyes. Within seconds, her facial muscles relaxed, and the faint sounds of air sucking through teeth returned. Relieved that Yaya had at last decided to rest, Sylvie held her grandma's bony hands and wept.

The next day, Sylvie spent most of the afternoon with her mother. Although Sylvie's mother had reached her late fifties, she possessed her daughter's dark, striking features and had aged gracefully. They sat tightly together on the sofa, poring over timeworn pictures in a family photo album.

Sylvie's mother's living room was modest, yet tasteful—typically Greek—with white walls, crisp lace curtains, and an embroidered carpet on the stone floor. Traditional Greek music filled the room. Occasionally, sunlight darted into the room through an open window, prompting Sylvie to glance outside at the fishing boats lining the harbor. How she missed those old boats. As a child, she and her best friend used to swim up to them and inspect their wooden hulls when nobody was looking. Even then, her artistic eye had captured each mosaic design as the paint faded and flaked off like dried onion peels in the sweltering sun. The red and green boats were Sylvie's favorites, reminding her of the M&M's candies she was forbidden to consume while in training.

It was tough to be in training nine months of the year. During swim season, especially before national competitions, she had to sacrifice two of her favorite things: chocolate and extreme heat, for they "sapped an athlete's energy," according to her coach. There was a third thing her coach said they shouldn't do right before a swim meet, but "you girls are all too young to worry about that one," he would say. Which wasn't entirely true, for Sylvie saw some of her teammates experimenting with boys, though that kind of opposite-sex activity hadn't interested her.

Since her coach couldn't get rid of the Greek heat, he did his best to keep the girls away from chocolate. Sylvie sometimes wondered if that was the real reason she had relocated to Belgium—for its smooth, dark chocolate. Now, remembering Belgium, she gazed out at the Greek blue sky; it was so glossy it appeared laminated. Such a contrast to the usual Brussels gray. She was about to mention this when she heard a soft, breezy sound. She turned to notice her mother's leaning head; like a sluggish fish, her eyes were shut, and her mouth was wide open.

Poor Mama, she's been taking care of Yaya so much lately. But who's been taking care of her? Sylvie adjusted her shoulder to prop up her mother's head, then she turned her attention back to the album. *I remember this.* She smiled at an old photo of herself. *I was as skinny as a string bean.* Her eyes settled on her prepubescent body, standing on the beach with three other swimmers in yellow competition swimsuits. Small waves crashed at their ankles. Behind them was a transparent blue ocean. The girls were laughing with their arms around each other. Warm nostalgia hit Sylvie. In the picture, she stood in the middle, thinner than the others, holding up a huge gold trophy. *We were as dark as chocolate in those days.* She chuckled to herself.

"Remember how proud you were that day?" said Sylvie's mother in a hoarse voice as she lifted her head and pointed to the picture.

"Ah, you're awake. Hope I didn't—"

"Remember, honey? It was the first time you won the nationals. Wasn't it?"

Sylvie nodded. It was one of the best days of her swimming career. She also remembered how self-conscious she had felt about her body. "Just look at those legs! I was as skinny as—"

"You were so happy, dear. And you deserved it too. Your father and I were thrilled when you brought home that big trophy."

"Yeah, but look how flat my chest was. I was so—"

"I wish you could be like that again, sweetie." Sylvie's mother peered into her eyes. She gave her hand a squeeze. "I know you're worried about Yaya. We all are. But just look at you. You've got circles under your eyes. You've never had those before. You're not getting enough sleep, are you?" She lowered her voice and leaned closer. "You know I would never stop you from doing what you want to do in life. And if your father were still here, neither would he. We've always given you freedom to roam. But I'm not sure living in Brussels is right for you, honey. I don't know, you seem so—"

Sylvie wiped the back of her neck; it was burning hot. "Mama, don't worry about me, *daxi*?"

"It's just that…Honey, you've always been like a wild bird. Impossible to tame. Even though I still hope you will become softer, more docile…and more reasonable. More like a woman ready to settle down and have a family. I hate the idea of you living alone in a huge city, far from our island, and I just wish—"

"Mama. Please stop. Don't you think we have enough to deal with right now, with Yaya sick and all?" As soon as the words left Sylvie's mouth, feelings of guilt came over her. She tried to avoid thinking about how Mama was taking care of Yaya on her own while she was living in Brussels, far away from Santorini and her family.

But the last thing she wanted was to move back home. Yearly visits to the island were enough for her. Sure, she missed the warm Greek sunshine on her skin. Any weather was better than the constant gray skies of Belgium. And she missed the freshly caught fish, tender olives, homemade retsina, and Yaya's sumptuous dishes.

Sylvie's life in Brussels gave her the freedom she knew she could never have in Santorini. She loved biking through the bustling streets of Belgium on weekends—taking romantic shots of kissing couples in parks as she rode past—then developing the black-and-white photos in her apartment. She was hooked on her early-morning runs to the park and teaching swimming lessons to rambunctious Belgian kids. But the best part was living alone in a quiet, residential part of town. She loved her apartment, which overlooked the lush pine trees on Rue des Pépins. Far from the nosy neighbors on her native Greek island, she could decorate her home as she wished, even with nude photos of gorgeous women on its bright yellow walls. Whenever she desired, she could invite anyone over to her place, no questions asked. And she adored living with her precious Goldie, whom she loved to spoil each week with fresh fish from the market.

After long days of teaching, Sylvie couldn't wait to sip tasty ouzo cocktails on her terrace and send wishes to the moon with Goldie in her arms. She enjoyed speaking French all day—how she loved that romantic language, especially in the poetry books she found in her local bookshop. She was happy hanging out at Dionysos Taverna with Vassilios and the others. But most of all, she appreciated having a life of her own, where she didn't have to slave over dishes in the kitchen, answer to a husband's incessant needs, or respond to well-meaning relatives about why she wasn't married or didn't have children at her age. She missed her family, but she still had her cousins, Vassilios and Aphrodite, to keep her company in Belgium. She only wished that Brussels were closer to the seaside.

Memories of family picnics at the beach brought her thoughts back to Yaya, who was once so strong. Now she could hardly lift her frail head from her pillow. She turned away from her mother in shame. *How could I have become so thankless? All I've been thinking about is Goldie and Hélène for weeks. What's wrong with me? Maybe I should move back home for a while. But where would that leave Hélène and me?* With that last thought, Sylvie's cheeks turned hot. Her mind struggled with guilty feelings, which made her clench her fist. *Why should I even care? She's married, and it's not me she wants.* Sylvie looked back at her mother, whose face fell.

"You're right. I'm sorry, dear." Mama lowered her dark eyes. But they popped wide open when they landed on Sylvie's white Greek fisherman's sweater, which accentuated her chest. "Well, I'll be darned. At least you filled out, honey!" Giggling, she playfully tapped her daughter's boob.

"Hands off, Mama!" Relieved for her sudden distraction, Sylvie returned the gesture. As they teased each other playfully, Sylvie tried to ignore her confusion about her current situation. She felt raw—torn up inside. Yaya had just told her to go after her dreams, even if they seemed impossible. But previously, when she had done that—and dated straight women—she only got hurt. *What would Yaya say about Hélène? I wish she could meet her someday. But would she like her?*

Sylvie became pensive. *What's wrong with me? That doesn't matter right now. Yaya and Mama need me here with them. I need to get my priorities straight.* She gave her mother one last poke in the boob and frowned. *Straight. How I hate that word. So, why am I letting Hélène get under my skin?*

CHAPTER THIRTEEN

Hélène crossed and uncrossed her legs under her desk, wound and unwound her hair around her pencil, and hummed a trite melody. She did everything she normally did to force her mind to focus on her scientific translations, but today, none of these tactics worked. Just when she threw in the towel, chirping sounds brought her to the window.

Two jaybirds sat harping in unison on a branch. "Can't concentrate around here with all that jabbering going on." She slammed the window. For some reason, the jaybirds reminded her of her last conversation with Sylvie. She checked her cell phone. "Nothing." She stuffed it back in her bag with a scowl.

I don't have time for you anyway. She grabbed a pile of documents and marched out of her office. Attempting to read her translations as she cruised down the hall, she failed to notice the copy machine that was being repaired in the hallway until she walked straight into it. Her forceful impact sent the wrenches and screwdrivers on it flying.

She yelped as her papers scattered. Glaring at the stunned repairman kneeling beside the copy machine, she reached down to collect her documents. But she stopped midair once she saw the object sprawled across her translations. It was a yellow screwdriver, just like the one Sylvie had used to start her car.

Hélène's thoughts drifted back to the day Sylvie had taken her in her VW Bug to her favorite Greek restaurant for lunch. Her eyes moistened. Leaning against the copy machine, she squeezed her eyelids shut. As if by magic, the flashback hit her before she could stop it.

"Time to go fishing." Bending over, Sylvie's fingers searched under the driver's seat. At last, her head popped up. "*Voilà!*" She waved a yellow screwdriver before Hélène's eyes.

She's weirder than I am. The thought made Hélène grin. Sylvie inserted the tip of the screwdriver into the ignition and flicked her wrist.

"*Mon Dieu!*" Hélène whispered as the engine revved up.

Sylvie flashed her a coy smile. "I lost the key a couple of years ago."

"I see." Hélène bit her lip. She tried to look out the window as they drove away, but her eyes kept cruising back to the steering wheel. Some magnetic force kept them focused on Sylvie's forearms as she maneuvered her car through the streets. Her smooth skin, with its tiny hairs leaning in the same direction, looked so soft. *I wonder if she knows how sexy she is?*

Hélène felt blood rushing to her cheeks. Something was buzzing nearby. She opened her eyes. *Where am I?* She looked around and realized she wasn't in Sylvie's car but in the hallway, leaning against the copy machine.

"*Désolée*, I think this might be yours." She thrust the yellow screwdriver at the puzzled repairman and headed toward the bathroom. After locking herself inside a stall, she sat down and wiped the tears from her eyes before they could hit her blouse. Slowly, she removed the crumpled black-and-white photo from her wallet. Half of it was missing. Sniveling, she fingered its jagged edges. *I shouldn't have ripped me off.* Smoothing out the creases, she inspected Sylvie's gorgeous, olive-skinned face. *She looks happy. But I bet she's even happier now...* The thought made her cry again.

A few moments later, Hélène wiped her eyes on her sleeve, pulled out the crumpled yellow card, and reread Sylvie's note:

Dear Hélène,
    You forgot this at my place.
    I'm at a loss for words. Please forgive me for anything
I might have done to hurt you. I'm not quite sure what I
did wrong the other night, but whatever it was, it certainly
wasn't intentional. I hope we can still be friends.
    I hope I'll see you Saturday morning.
    Take care, Sylvie

Saturday...Saturday... Hélène remembered Sylvie's words at the Greek restaurant: "Anyway, have you decided about lessons on Saturdays? We won't have the pool to ourselves anymore, but..."

Hélène counted the days on her fingers. *Today's Wednesday.* She covered her face with her hands. *What do I do now? And is she going to be there?* With everything that had happened between them, would Sylvie show up for their lesson on Saturday? If Hélène went and Sylvie wasn't there, it would devastate her.

A few hours later, Hélène stood straddling her bike in Cinquantenaire Park, observing a group of younger women in rainbow T-shirts doing aerobics. Hélène frowned at their coordinated moves to a Spice Girls song. Her body hadn't been wired to do aerobics. She knew she'd trip over herself—or someone else—if she tried to jump and kick at the same time. Adding music would only make things worse. She cringed, imagining the disaster.

Just as she was about to ride off, she spotted a woman with a ponytail. The woman was kicking higher than all the others and laughing. *It's her!* Hélène's heart sped up. But then she noticed the woman's legs. *Those aren't half as muscular as Sylvie's.* She sped home, forcing her body to outride the intense feelings of sadness plaguing her system.

❖

The next afternoon, Hélène swept away a pile of translations and removed her painting of Santorini from her bag. The multiple slashes reminded her of knife wounds she had once seen on an emergency-room patient when she was a teenager. Even though it had only been a TV show, the camera had zoomed in so closely that Hélène's body had started shaking. Blood oozed out of the slits until a nurse slipped on gloves and jammed them with a wad of gauze. Hélène had turned away abruptly, unable to look at the TV. She shivered at the vivid memory.

Let's be brave about this. Cautiously, she inspected the gravity of the slashes, then pulled out some scotch tape and mended the rips on the back of the painting as best as she could. After fifteen minutes of tedious work, she inspected the canvas.

"Parfait. I'm an alchemist." Smiling, she kissed the painting, propped it in front of Marc's photo, and tried to translate again. But her mind, drifting back to Sylvie, kept mulling over every detail of their intimate evening together. Especially when they were on the sofa, after the cocktails and wine, when they were beginning to touch each other—right before the phone rang. That moment seemed so real in her mind, it scared her. *What would have happened if Marc hadn't called just when...*

But each time she imagined Sylvie holding her, kissing her passionately, a voice in her head screamed *"Non!"* and chased the kiss—and all the scrumptious sensations it aroused—from her mind. These conflicting thoughts produced a blend of pleasant and unpleasant aftertastes that she couldn't figure out. She clenched her teeth. Where was this voice in her head coming from? Who was telling her *"Non!"* to shut off all these delicious sensations— the heightened arousal she felt around Sylvie—and replace these memories with guilty emotions instead? Was it Maman's influence? Was it her early Catholic schooling, where the nuns educated her to be ethically correct? After all, she was married. Yet Sylvie was so caring and kind. So selfless—the opposite of Marc. And such a gorgeous woman, a true Greek goddess. She was so incredibly attracted to her. Just thinking about Sylvie made Hélène's heart beat faster. To clear her mind, she took a deep breath and gazed back at the painting of Santorini. *So peaceful, so colorful. It must have been a perfect place to grow up.* This tactic worked, until she noticed Marc's photo behind the painting.

"What do you think you're looking at?" She stuffed the photo into her drawer. Even though her workday wasn't over, she grabbed her things, hopped on her bike, and rode straight to the pool. After scrutinizing all the cars in the parking lot, she had to admit defeat. She shook her head. Sylvie's beat-up yellow VW Bug wasn't hard to find. But it was no longer there. She shoved her hands in her pockets just as she was hit with a vivid flashback of Sylvie getting into the young Greek woman's car with her suitcase. *They were eating my fruit salad, they drove off together with Goldie, and they were laughing. They're certainly in love.* Frustrated at her inability to control the jealous feelings sweeping over her, her fingernails dug into her palms as she headed toward her bike. *Where did she go with that woman? Why isn't she at work?*

Half an hour later, she stood in front of Sylvie's apartment building. Once she had caught her breath, she dared to look up at the fourth floor. Sylvie's curtains were still closed. Sighing with despair, she glanced at the sky. *Might as well catch the sunset.* With a broad sweep, she swept pine needles off the wall with her fingers. Sunsets and flowers were Hélène's *crème de la crème*—magical and romantic. Dangling her legs, she observed the last rays of sunlight cast their orange fingers through the pine branches. She felt a subtle tickle on her skin as she watched the intricate designs of shadows dancing on the wall. Then she hugged her knees to her chest in a vain attempt to squeeze all thoughts of Sylvie from her system.

By four o'clock the next afternoon, Hélène was desperate. She still had no news from Sylvie. *So, maybe it's unreasonable for me to expect her to contact me after the way I treated her. I didn't answer her calls. But it was a mistake. I know that now. Anyway, don't I have the right to be unreasonable sometimes, like everyone else? Aren't Greek islanders supposed to be more in touch with their feelings than Belgians? Shouldn't she have female telepathy or something? She should know by now I want her to call me.*

Hélène knew very well she could've called Sylvie rather than waiting for her to call her back. But something inside her made her hold out. Was it female intuition? Stubbornness? She had overheard foreigners say that Belgians were more stubborn than other Europeans. What about Greeks? Were they stubborn too? She hadn't known any Greek people until she met Sylvie. She shook her head. What had she been doing these past twenty years? Taking care of Marc? Chaussette? *I sure haven't been taking care of myself.* This realization hit her hard. Her life had been passing her by, and she hadn't even realized it until now. They were precious moments... precious years, when she could've been traveling to other countries or getting to know foreigners in her own country, like Sylvie. But nobody else was like Sylvie...

Hélène sighed. *I haven't been living until now. I've been living in a cocoon. But that doesn't mean I'm not stubborn. Too bad if she's stubborn too. I'm not calling her.*

With incessant thoughts spinning out of control, Hélène spent her time swiveling in her office chair, banging her knees together. Instead of herbal tea, she knocked back multiple espressos, hoping the caffeine would jolt her body into bliss. To her despair, her liquid shock treatment backfired. The nervous buzz sparked a tic in her left eye. And her fingers twitched—as if playing an airborne piano—while constantly checking her cell phone for messages.

I'm becoming a stalker. Her conscience filled with doubts bordering on self-loathing. The tic had now invaded her face, spreading to her left cheek. She brought her fingers to her lopsided lips. *Hmm. I know what to do.* She fished in her bag for a mini bottle of rum. *Glad I saved this for a rainy day.* She congratulated herself for stashing away her *pousse-café*—the little bottle of liquor—after her last flight. Never mind it had been decades; it was time to numb her nerves.

When did I last take an airplane anyway? She glanced at the bottle's expiration date. *Zut. But who cares?* She gave the black top a twist. The sound of ripping metal brought back memories of her honeymoon twenty years prior, when she and Marc had flown to Ibiza, a tiny Spanish island. When she closed her eyes, she pictured the two of them—newlyweds—lying together on a flimsy double bed with rusty iron posts and a faded, carroty-colored bedspread.

She remembered the pink kimono she had purchased especially for the trip. It had been so hot during those ten days; she had felt more raw than sexy as the stiff cotton kimono rubbed against her sunburned shoulders, chafing her sensitive skin—which soon became pinker than the kimono.

They'd loaded the fridge in their three-star hotel room with mini bottles of Spanish liquor. They had laughed so hard as they tried to pronounce the Spanish names written on those bottles — *melocotón, fresa, melón, plátano*—while emptying their syrupy contents into each other's mouths. She remembered how dizzy she had felt with her head in Marc's lap. And the banana liquor didn't help. He had lifted the tiny bottle, aimed for her lips, but spilled the sweet, sticky liquid on his upper thigh instead. Suddenly feeling nauseous, Hélène blocked that dreadful scene from her mind and dumped half the bottle of rum into her coffee. She downed the bitter brew, grabbed her cell phone, and—before she could stop herself—dialed the number that had been sizzling in her mind for days.

On the sixth ring, instead of hanging up, Hélène mumbled after the beep: *"Bonjour*...Sylvie. *Eh bien*...I hope you're doing okay. *Désolée*...I'm sorry I didn't call you back. But I guess it's better late than never. Can you please call me back when you get this? I really need to talk to you. It's Hélène. *Merci."*

After stuffing her phone in her bag, Hélène dumped the rest of the rum into her mug, counted to three, and sucked the liquid dry. Instantly, a wave of calmness swept over her. *At least that should kill the tic.*

❖

That evening, Hélène wrote in her diary for thirty minutes straight while Chaussette's tiny body formed a tight ball behind her on Marc's pillow. Hélène couldn't make the pen move fast enough. At last, once she had emptied her thoughts about Sylvie, Marc, and her muddled feelings, she shook the numbness from her fingers and shut her diary. Turning over, she stroked Chaussette, who returned the favor with an enormous yawn.

Then Hélène went over to the answering machine. *I'll show you a thing or two about blinking lights.* She was tempted to kick the contraption senseless, but she knew it wasn't the machine's fault. It was her own. *J'étais stupide. I should've at least listened to her messages, before I erased—*

The phone rang. She grabbed the receiver, her heart pounding. "Dupont residence, Hélène speaking." The thudding of her heart resonated up to her ears. Then came a familiar voice. Without uttering the slightest greeting, she flung the phone down and yelled, "Marc, pick it up! *C'est ta maman!*"

With a massive sigh, she collapsed. Digging her fingernails into the carpet, she strained to swallow her sobs until a loud "What's gotten into *her?*" reached her ears from downstairs, making her bawl even harder.

Later that evening, while Marc was absorbed in his wrestling match, Hélène snuck back into the kitchen to listen to Maman's tapes for the umpteenth time. In desperation, she'd turned to the tapes instead of pining over Sylvie's absence the last two nights, listening to them in the privacy of the bathroom. At least there, Marc was least likely to overhear them. She wasn't about to share something so intimate with him. And to her bewilderment, each time she heard something new.

At first, Hilde was simply describing her garden. Then she would share precious information about Maman and her relationship with Hélène's father. Those details had her riveted to the machine. As she listened to their recorded conversations, she kept wondering why Maman had never wanted to reveal that her father was still alive, nor his whereabouts. Kneeling on the bathroom tiles, she hovered over the tape recorder, her hair tumbling over her cheeks like a curtain camouflaging her growing curiosity. Each tape made her feel raw with frustration at so many unanswered questions. *Why doesn't Hilde ever mention my brother? Why did Maman keep the truth hidden from me?* Despite her frustration, she cherished these clandestine moments.

Hilde's voice had a magical, mystical tone to it. And Maman's voice was so soft, so beautiful. Hélène wished she could share the secret of Maman's tapes, Hilde the psychic, and her father's and brother's existence with someone. Of course, she could share it with

Cecile, but something told her to be patient. A little voice inside her head kept insisting that she should share it with *her.*

Finally, Hélène couldn't stand waiting anymore. She grabbed her biking gear and slipped out of the house. Riding through the empty streets, she felt a sense of exhilaration. *Why didn't I do this earlier?* Then it hit her. All those painstaking hours she spent each night composing poems nobody would ever read. *Who am I trying to kid? I'm no poet. Why am I wasting my life? To get away from him? All he ever does is watch that blasted TV and guzzle beers. My life's a joke! Something has got to change...now!*

She was out of breath from pedaling so furiously. Before she knew it, she was standing in front of Sylvie's apartment building. She checked her watch. *Not bad, only twenty-two minutes!* But her triumphant smile faded when she saw that Sylvie's curtains were still closed.

On the way home, the breeze felt cool on Hélène's face, but it did nothing to cool her temper. *Bet she's a student of hers, like me.* Her mind ticked off all the reasons she should hate Sylvie. Then it began to prioritize them. She winced when she realized what she was doing. *Why aren't I thinking of all the reasons Sylvie should hate me? I led her on, returned her affections even though I was married. Even when I'm furious, I'm anal. I prioritize my reasons for getting angry instead of venting my feelings like a normal person. Why do I always have to evaluate everything? Why do I take everything so seriously? Why can't I just live?*

These thoughts made her speed up. *Good thing no cops are about.* She soared through another red light. *Wait a minute.* She stopped in the middle of the empty street. Straddling her bike, she looked in the distance at the Atomium—the Eiffel Tower of Brussels. A rainbow of colors illuminated the solid structure, with light beams floating over the metal balls. Hélène pondered the huge atoms. *Attends. Why am I angry at myself? I'm supposed to be angry at her. She's the one being sneaky. Ouais. What kind of teacher is she, anyway? She pretends to be my friend, and then...* She took a deep breath to let her emotions sink in. With her sleeve, she brushed away droplets of sweat on her brow. *I know I'm being unreasonable.*

I'm not giving her a chance. But I can't help but think...Now I know why private lessons are her specialty.

As she began pedaling, Hélène made up her mind. *Things were just fine in my life until she came along. She's insane if she thinks I'm going to show up for that stupid lesson on Saturday!*

CHAPTER FOURTEEN

The next morning, just like every other morning for the past few weeks, Hélène kissed Chaussette on the forehead before riding to work. To her surprise, instead of feeling weary after so much nocturnal exercise, her legs felt lighter the more she pedaled. Her mind felt lighter too. Abruptly, however, an idea popped into her head. In an unexpected moment of insight, halfway down the street, she did a U-turn and headed in the opposite direction. *Maybe it's the light*, she reasoned, gazing up at the sky. Like all Belgians, she appreciated every bit of sunlight falling on her country, for everyone knew those succulent rays might disappear in a sneeze. *Or maybe it's just the right time. Finally.*

She pedaled down unfamiliar streets until she reached a tiny brick house with pale-pink awnings overlooking a small, lush garden teeming with plants. A wrought iron bench sat in the midst of the lawn, facing the flowerbed, filled with rows of pink and yellow roses.

Hélène steadied herself, then rang the bell.

The door opened slowly. The elderly woman poked her head outside, exposing a familiar mound of gray hair bunched atop her skull. As soon as she saw her visitor, her light blue eyes lit up. "I've been expecting you. Just in time for tea, *ma chérie. Entrez.*"

Hélène nodded while lifting her chin as a rush of warm tears flooded her eyes. She couldn't help smiling at the humble, grandmotherly woman adorned in a powdery pink cotton house dress.

"Follow me." Hilde extended a withered, bony hand and, to Hélène's bewilderment, swiftly pulled Hélène inside her tiny brick house.

Whatever it was Hilde had to say, Hélène was ready to listen.

❖

After her intimate conversation with Hilde over countless cups of tea, Hélène pedaled away as recklessly as a ten-year-old. As she zigzagged down the hill, weaving between cars, people began honking. One woman called her a lunatic. Instead of insulting her back, Hélène started singing. Not normal singing, but loud, off-key, horrendous singing. She made up the words as she went along, chortling to herself; singing deliriously in public was something she had never attempted—not even in her dreams.

A poodle barked at her as she whizzed by. Its owner covered his ears. Giggling, Hélène kept pedaling and singing at the top of her voice. "I don't feel like going to work today. I'd rather have fun! I'll just mess around and play hooky. *Pourquoi pas?* It's Friday, and you only live once, *n'est-ce pas?* Thank God it's Friday! Thank God it's Friday! I'll just mess around and play hooky. *Pourquoi pas?* I'd rather have fun!"

I may not have much talent, but at least I'm original! She belted out the words until her throat felt raw. It wasn't the only thing that felt raw. Her conversation with Hilde had left her zinging with pain. Why hadn't Maman told her she had an older brother and father? And that they were both alive?

When Hélène had followed the psychic into her homey kitchen, Hilde had hummed a pleasant tune, just like the last time. They'd stood side by side, observing the iron kettle until it boiled, as if they had known each other for decades. Once again, Hélène had soaked in the peace that reigned in her hostess' cozy home.

Still humming, Hilde had prepared a tray with a steaming pot of tea, two pink earthenware mugs, a pot of honey, and two silver spoons and motioned for her to follow her with the tray.

Once again, she had ordered, "Sit here," and perched her cane in a corner before plopping herself in a chair. As they sat in the cozy room, Hélène had learned that her mother had met Hilde at a local botanical society meeting well before Hélène was born. They shared a love of gardening and often sat together at the society's monthly meetings. Once Maman had given birth to Hélène, she stopped going to the meetings, and the two women lost touch. Her mother had only learned about Hilde's intuitive abilities by chance. She mentioned them to Maman when they bumped into each other at the neighborhood supermarket when Hélène was six months old. It was right after her father had taken her older brother with him, slamming the door on Maman and little Hélène, never to return. He and Maman had gotten into a fight, one of many, apparently. This had been the last one. It had been devastating for Maman, but Hélène had been too young to remember.

Tears filled her eyes when she learned that her father lived on a distant island in another European country. Hilde wasn't sure exactly where, but he was very much healthy and alive. She had never known why he'd left them. Hélène's mother had never spoken about him, except to say that he had passed away. Why hadn't Maman told her the truth? Why had she been so secretive about Hilde and the cassette tapes? Her hands were clammy as she sipped her tea in Hilde's presence, trying not to choke with angst as the elderly woman unraveled each hidden detail of her family's past—and present.

The worst news was when she learned that her brother lived in Brussels. When Hélène found that out, she had asked where he lived exactly. While waiting for Hilde's response, she hadn't been able to look at the psychic, whose eyes were closed anyway. Instead, Hélène focused on the dainty, metallic lamp separating her from Hilde. To her distress, the soothing light warmed the room, but it did nothing to soothe her soul. Hilde had informed her that her brother was two years older than her and that he lived on the streets. When Hélène pressed her for the exact location, Hilde told her that he was most often seen near a popular ethnic restaurant, across the street from a busy, trendy café. He was a homeless nomad, and his name was Frank.

Why didn't Maman tell me I had an older brother who was homeless? And that he lived in Brussels, our city? I could've helped him! She thought of the man she and her friends had watched walk past the café that day. The same one she had seen with Marc near the market and later, on her way to the Greek restaurant with Sylvie. He could be her brother, a stranger people passed in the street every day, rain or shine, without noticing. They most likely didn't care about him. Worse, they could consider him a nuisance, a social outcast, like Marc had—like she had, to a certain extent, until she met Sylvie.

Just thinking about the magnitude of these hidden secrets enraged Hélène. She pedaled hard, even though she had no idea where she was headed. *In this state, it would be too dangerous to show up to work. Scratch that—I'd be too dangerous.* She felt the venom racing through her veins. *But who am I mad at most? Maman? Papa? Hilde? Frank? Screw them all!*

Before she knew it, she stood in front of a movie theater. *Why the heck not?* She locked her bike, went inside and—without reading the description—bought a ticket for the next movie playing. Then she headed over to the refreshment counter. *I think I'll treat myself to a few snacks.* She bought herself a liter of Coke, a package of ice-cream truffles, two bags of potato chips, and popcorn. She peered into her tub of double-butter popcorn. *A baby could bathe in this.* With overflowing arms, she waddled into the theater and plopped into the first chair she stumbled upon. Once her eyes adjusted to the dark room, she realized it was empty except for a couple of teenagers right in front of her.

Looks like I'm not the only one playing hooky. She snickered while shoveling handfuls of greasy popcorn into her mouth. With each crunch, she felt a surge of excitement. *I always wondered what it would be like to do this. C'est génial. It's fun being irresponsible for once,* she told herself, ignoring the artificial butter sliding down her chin.

"*Délicieux!*" she exclaimed, licking the butter as it ran down her wrists, buttering the ends of her shirt sleeves. A spontaneous fit of giggles burst forth, until Hélène noticed the movie screen. A masked man was holding up a butcher knife.

"*Quelle horreur!*" she gasped as the knife slid into the chest of a woman taking a shower. Cringing, Hélène squeezed her eyes shut and covered her mouth with her buttery fist just when blood spurted onto the white shower curtain. The woman's screams mingled with Hélène's. *This is fake!* she tried to convince herself, slurping her Coke to drown out the dying woman's last moans. But instead of waning, the woman's moans were getting louder. When Hélène dared to peek at the screen, she noticed the teenage couple in front of her. *Yuck!* She frowned in disgust as they necked passionately. *What's this? Mating season?* She brought her buttery fists to her ears to block out their slimy smooches as the pubescent lovers attacked each other's lips, cheeks, chins, and throats. Their enthusiastic embraces triggered a sudden repulsive response within Hélène, reminding her of her own lack of romantic connection. First with Marc, which was doomed from the start, and now with Sylvie. As she tried to block the sounds of their smooching, she couldn't help imagining Sylvie kissing her gorgeous Greek lover right in front of her.

Finally, clutching her lurching stomach, Hélène rose and yelled at them, "Munch on this instead of your zitty, spit-licking faces!" Flinging a handful of popcorn at the stunned couple—who paused just in time for their kernel shower—Hélène stormed out of the theater. Cradling her snacks in her arms, she slipped into another room. On the screen, an elderly couple was kissing passionately in a car.

"Not again!" shouted Hélène over their smooching noises. This time, before her dramatic exit, in a surge of jealous frustration, Hélène chucked her popcorn bucket at the screen.

I'll give it one last try. Hélène snuck into a third movie. This time, it was an old-fashioned Western. Forcing herself to ignore the two couples necking up front, she sat in the back and stuffed herself silly with junk food. After a while, she slowed her crunching and slurping while she scanned the empty seats around her.

What's wrong with me? she wondered at last, noticing the knot tightening in her throat.

Why do I feel so lonely right now? Instead of pondering plausible answers, she took the easy route and wolfed down the rest of her food.

CHAPTER FIFTEEN

Sylvie's mind decelerated as she wandered through the hidden pathway. How refreshing it was to just follow her feet for once. This was the path she had taken each day as a child—the one hidden by pine trees, known by only a handful of neighborhood kids. She recalled the secret ceremony they had held one afternoon, swearing to keep their secret for life. Under her white cotton bathrobe, she felt shivers of anticipation. What would she find when she pushed back those branches?

As soon as she poked her head into the clearing and saw the water's edge, she smiled. *So, they kept their promises after all.* Exhaling with relief, she wiggled her brown toes in the virgin sand. Shielding her eyes from the sun's direct rays, she gazed out at the water. Other than a few fishing boats dotting the horizon, all was clear. It was already late afternoon, with no traces of clouds overhead.

So incredibly blue. Sylvie listened to the water's tiny licking sounds while its coolness penetrated her toes, then her ankles. As soon as it hit her calves, she sighed, feeling the stress leave her body; all lingering thoughts seeped from her mind like soft honey. Sylvie tore off her bathrobe and flung it, along with her towel, onto the nearest branch. Then she dove into the seamless sea.

After a long moment, she surfaced. Like a slick water spider, her body advanced graciously, barely skimming the water's surface. After twenty minutes of effortless swimming, she emerged from the ocean and grabbed her towel. Chest pounding, she shut her eyes and simply breathed. *Délicieux*. Then, starting with her toes, she dried all traces of the sea from her bikini-clad body. To complete the ritual, she raked her fingertips through her wet hair, donned her robe, and crossed the warm sand again.

After a brief pause to examine the sun's rays smothering the horizon, she retraced her steps on the windy path, careful not to catch her robe on the prickly pine branches. Her soul was glowing with the energy of her youth, reunited with nature's wonders. Soon, the familiar sound of Greek music reached her ears. *This is bliss.* She hastened her pace until she reached a familiar café built on a terraced incline with a stunning view of the ocean. Slightly out of breath but with a warm feeling in her heart, she sat down at the closest table just in time to watch the sun dip its round bottom, cautious as a novice bather, into the ocean.

This was Sylvie's favorite time of day, when the sun spilled its golden light like translucent lava over all the white houses perched on Santorini's steep hills. After her refreshing swim in the ocean and ensuing trek to a nearby café, she was happy to simply relax in her chair while watching the sunset's show. Suddenly, however, the wind picked up, and a chill ran through Sylvie's body. Despite the reassurance of her familiar childhood surroundings and despite her workout in the water, she felt vulnerable and drained.

Within minutes, a young waiter appeared, shaking a metallic container like the one she used to mix Greek cocktails at home in Brussels. As she watched him pour the potent liquid into her glass, she reflected on her evening with Hélène. Even though several days had passed, she winced at the freshness of the memory—fresh as the pineapple slice lining her cocktail.

Sylvie contemplated her drink until her eyes misted over. Using her sleeve, she sponged up the unsolicited tears. Taking a deep sip of her ouzo cocktail, she closed her eyes to savor the exotic drink just as she had always done. But this time, instead of instant sweetness, a sharp, bitter taste washed over her tongue. Her trusted remedy had lost its charm as feelings of nostalgia swept through her.

She sniffed her glass. *What's the problem?* As she chomped

on her tasteless pineapple slice, she grimaced. *That's it.* This cocktail—even though it was prepared on her gorgeous, native island—reflected exactly how she felt inside: bitter. *If things had only worked out as I planned with Hélène...Why is my life so complicated? What would've happened if I'd stayed here in Santorini instead of moving so far away from my family? Would Yaya be better right now? Would Mama be happier? Would I?* She looked again at the white houses perched on Santorini's steep hills, wondering what would've happened if her life had taken a different course. Would she be married to some Greek guy right now? Would she have had children? Her thoughts ruminated on these questions until abruptly, they returned to even more pressing issues. *Now what should I do? Should I stay here or go back to Brussels? Why is it so hard for me to figure out what to do with my life?*

Tired of reflecting on past possibilities but also unsure how to figure out what the future held, Sylvie pushed away her cocktail and reached for her backpack, from which she extracted an old, tin box. She contemplated the box for a moment, then untied its frayed red ribbon. Next, she extracted a black and white picture. Thoughts of Dionysos Taverna in Brussels made her eyes soften, but they blurred when they hit Hélène's smile. A tear fell from her eyelashes onto the photo. She frowned as she wiped it off Hélène's cheek. *I'm ruining everything.* She placed the photo back in the box and took out a colorful postcard of Santorini. Just then, the street lights snapped on as the ocean consumed the last bit of orange in the sky. Slowly, she removed a fountain pen from the tin box and began penning her thoughts on the postcard:

Dear Hélène,
        Here I am in Santorini. I hope you're doing okay. I'm sorry I had to leave so suddenly, but

Choking back tears, Sylvie took a deep breath and continued.

as you know, Yaya, my grandma, is dying. It's so incredibly sad, for we have always been so close. Even though I'm with my family, I feel so alone here. And what's worse, I can't stop thinking

Abruptly, she held the card up to the light. Her fingers trembled as she tried to decipher her handwriting, which was normally neat. But tonight, it was a disaster. A knot formed in her throat. She glared at the card before ripping it to bits. Then she opened her palm. The light sea breeze swept the bits from her fingers. She watched them drift away, over the whitewashed wall and into the bushes.

At least they're biodegradable. When she could no longer see the bits of postcard, the knot in her throat finally melted. *I'll give this one more shot.* She eyed her favorite cocktail. She lifted the glass to her lips. But instead of soothing her emotions, the potent, fruity liquid delivered a flood of mixed memories. Her mind swept back to when she was a young and carefree islander, joyfully anticipating the future. The contrast between the two imaginary images of herself—younger and now—made her react more strongly than anticipated. She gulped with anguish as a hot tear slipped into her cocktail.

Discreetly, she glanced around the outdoor café. To her relief, nobody was there. She didn't feel like company right now. As if trying to remove debris from a roadblock, she moved her tongue around in her mouth. *Missed it.* She gave her tongue another swipe, trying to dislodge the pineapple bits stuck between her teeth. The slivers of stringy pineapple remained.

Aha! To Sylvie's surprise, her inconspicuous efforts had dislodged something much more serious than tropical fruit. With a renewed sense of energy pulsing through her, she now had the insight she had been searching for. *It's time for action. I've got to dislodge everything stuck in my way, starting with my love life...*

It was already dark when Hélène finally left the movie theater. Burping uncontrollably, she held her stomach as she lurched down the sidewalk. *Some diet, eh?* She let out a vicious cackle. *Wait,*

what's this? She stopped to listen to rock music blaring out of an open window. *Hmm. Seedy-looking place. But why not? I'm on a roll here.*

Before she knew it, Hélène had wobbled into the dimly lit SCUM BAG S&M BAR and approached the counter. A skinny waitress with blond dreadlocks, lime-green glasses, and a sequined "Scum Bag" T-shirt strode up to her. A sturdy, silver nose ring, suspended between the waitress's nostrils, wiggled in greeting as she nodded to Hélène.

Hélène nodded back, trying to keep her eyes off the tattoos stamped on every visible part of the waitress's body. The waitress stared at Hélène, cracking her gum and flashing her fake eyelashes. Before Hélène could protest, she grabbed the inside of her visitor's right arm and stamped it with black India ink.

"On the house," she declared, flashing her crooked teeth.

Today sure is bizarre, thought Hélène, noticing the young woman's left ear sporting at least forty metallic studs. She hardly noticed the waitress's grip until the studded-tattooed woman gurgled, "Cute, *n'est-ce pas?*"

Hélène gulped. "Who…Me?" She took a step back.

"*Non, ma chérie.* This ain't that kind of bar. I meant our logo. Designed it myself."

Hélène glanced at the black stamp on her arm. It revealed a collar and whip with the words SCUM BAG stenciled underneath.

"*Oui.* It's…precious."

"*Merci.* Ain't see you here before, missy." The waitress spoke in a distinctive Southern drawl while cracking her gum.

Hélène blinked. "I was just—"

"Thirsty, *non?*"

"That's it. I was thirsty." Hélène glanced around the bar. Through the dimness, she spotted dozens of bottles suspended upside-down. "I'll have a beer—"

"Bottle or tap, *chérie?*"

Before she could answer, someone's arm slid around Hélène's waist.

"Tap. Make that two, Jessie. It's on me."

As Hélène felt the stranger's warm breath on her neck, a titillating shiver darted up her spine.

The hand on Hélène's side was pale and delicate, with tiny black hairs gracing its wrist. Hélène's eyes drifted up the sleeve of the bulky leather jacket until they reached its owner—a young man in a white T-shirt and blue jeans, gussied up like a 1950s comic strip character. Hélène tittered when she saw the slick tuft of black hair sliding off his forehead—until she noticed the steel arrow pierced through his eyebrow and a studded chain around his neck.

Groovy. She shifted uncomfortably under the weight of the man's leather-clad arm.

"*Bonjour,* I'm Jeremie." The young man flashed her a cool smile and held out his hand.

Hélène tried to focus on his movie-star teeth instead of the steel chain around his neck. She managed a shrug and a weak, "*Bonjour.* I'm Hélène."

His hand was firm and warm.

"Why don't we go over there, where it's more comfortable?" Jeremie indicated a corner table in a dark, smoky area of the bar.

Hélène glanced at the two frothy beers in his hands. She gazed into his dark eyes. They reminded her of someone's, but she couldn't remember whose. His irises were deep, inviting…almost pleading. Her hand still tingled from the warmth of his fingers. *Why not? I can't show up at work now anyway. It's too late.*

She felt a rush of adrenaline as she followed him through tufts of smoke toward the back of the murky, crowded bar. She knew deep down she didn't want to do this. Everything inside her told her it was wrong. At the same time, she was desperate for companionship and for something—anything, at this point—to distract her from the mess her life had become.

❖

Three hours and twenty-two minutes after she had entered the bar, exactly one dozen empty beer glasses sat before Hélène and her new friend, Jeremie. Side by side in a red vinyl booth, they hadn't budged since they sat down. Jeremie kept Hélène amused with insipid jokes as she imbibed the alcohol he ordered.

Increasingly tipsy, Hélène studied the dried foam inside her empty glass. Giggling, she licked the foam off her finger, conscious of Jeremie watching her tongue slide gingerly over her lips.

Hélène wasn't used to such attention. But instead of feeling self-conscious, the beer made her feel powerful and...seductive. She raked her fingers through her hair as a fresh poem emerged in her mind. *I'm like a piece of toast. About to pop from a toaster. Hot, crunchy, ready to be smothered with butter and gobbled down... By some handsome stranger with a healthy appetite! Oooh là là!* The thought made her tickle all over. She felt the heat of Jeremie's warm body next to her own—and his breath lingering on her neck. It reminded her of someone else, someone she was trying desperately to forget, and the way her breath had tickled Hélène's neck in just the right way.

As Jeremie spoke, he threw back his head and laughed. Hélène concentrated on his fine lips, relishing each titillating moment while his gaze ran up and down her shirt. Shifting tautly from one buttock to another, she lapped up his words. Playfully, she tapped him on the shoulder and giggled louder. She felt herself glowing, radiating energy that seemed to pop out of nowhere. *Ouais, I'm toast all right. And he's about to gobble me...*

Just as Jeremie leaned in for a wet kiss, Hélène decided it was her turn to start making jokes. Even though she was so drunk she could barely keep her eyes open, she knew full well it wasn't his lips she wanted. The lips she wanted were soft and pink and smiled in a way that created dimples that made her knees weak. He frowned but politely laughed at her sad attempts at humor. After three more brews, Hélène couldn't stop rambling until her thoughts were swimming so fast, she clamped her lips to catch her breath. When she gazed into Jeremie's dark eyes, his long lashes mesmerized her like fine butterfly wings caressing her soul.

But when her body began to tremble, reality hit. Hélène realized why those eyes seemed so familiar. She burst into tears.

"*Attends*, what's going on?" whispered Jeremie into Hélène's ear. Tenderly, he dabbed at the wetness under her eye with his napkin.

"Funny you should ask that. But that's my line," said an oversized woman storming up to the couple. She wore a leather miniskirt and a tight black top under a leather jacket. With one hand, she hooked Jeremie by his jacket collar. Then she hauled him effortlessly—like a piece of lettuce—from the booth.

"*Alors*, who's the broad?" She nodded her bloated chin at Hélène, who averted the woman's eyes. "Thirsty little sleazebag, ain't she?"

Hélène cringed at the rows of empty beer glasses lining their table.

Chunky Leatherwoman lost her patience. Shaking Jeremie with her fist, she chucked her cigarette to the ground and stabbed it with her spiky heels. That's when Hélène noticed the woman's legs. *No wonder she's raging mad; those fishnet stockings are incredibly tight. I bet they're cutting off the blood to her head.* Smiling wickedly, she concocted a fresh poem. *Transforming badly stuffed sausages into fleshy wonders of...* But before Hélène could finish, Chunky Leatherwoman drew out a long black whip from her bag.

"You're paying for this, *mon petit garçon*." She thrust Jeremie toward the restroom. He flashed Hélène an "I'm sorry" look and obeyed his mistress, who was now cracking her whip on the floor as the bizarre couple made their way to the men's room. Meanwhile, all the other patrons cheered, "*Vas-y!*" and "*C'est ça*, show him who's boss!"

When the whipping sounds intensified behind the closed door, Hélène sighed. *Time for me to head home.* Despite her intoxication, Hélène gingerly stumbled her way through the bar without crashing into anything. Until she smashed into the waitress.

"*Pardon*," Hélène stammered as a cool beer wet her shirt. The unruffled waitress fluttered her fake eyelashes and cracked her gum as if customers rammed into her every day.

"Nice show you put on there, *chérie*. Where you goin'? The fun's just begun." The waitress indicated the inside of Hélène's arm. "You've got a stamp. You're one of us now."

Hélène interrupted her with an unceremonious burp. The odor of warm beer festering in her intestines brought her hand to her mouth. Knocking over a bar stool, she rushed outside.

"Come back soon, *chérie*. We'll be waiting for you!"

After three flailing attempts, Hélène managed to mount her bike. Then she toppled over. Lying on the cool sidewalk, she heard the pitter-patter of footsteps behind her. Next, a pair of strong arms lifted her onto her bike. Overwhelmingly tired, Hélène kept her eyes closed. Yet she felt surprisingly safe for the first time in ages, like a newborn wrapped in layers of soft blankets. Until a nasty odor invaded Hélène's nostrils—right before she passed out.

Hélène eyes popped open. She was moving. Her whole body was bumping up and down with someone's strong arms still grasping her waist. To her regret, the nasty odor smelled as pungent as ever. She glanced up to see where it was coming from.

Frank, the homeless man, held her tight to his chest while pushing her bike down a dark street. She shivered. *So, he's the one who rescued me. Why?* As Frank pushed, Hélène pondered her curious situation. *Why don't I feel scared? Who is this guy? Could he be my long-lost brother that Hilde was talking about?* That would be a coincidence, yet the thought warmed her heart. She had always wanted a brother. And he just might be hers. She shivered again.

She remembered how Sylvie had shaken his hand tenderly and addressed him by name. What a shock it was to learn she did this every time she saw Frank. *But doesn't he have germs?* she had wondered. Now, she knew so much more, thanks to Sylvie. *What's wrong with me? I'm such a loser. My heart's made of cement, not love.* She shuddered. *And what if he is my brother?* A familiar feeling of loneliness ran through her body. *In my present state, I can't really ask him, can I? And once again, I'm thinking about Sylvie. It's all my fault. I refused to answer my phone. Then I erased her messages without even listening to them.* She felt like kicking herself. *Where in the heck is she?*

As Frank continued pushing, a novel idea entered Hélène's brain. *Maybe singing will help. It will at least reduce the tension in this ridiculous situation. Like in a musical. There's always a good ending in musicals. Right?* In a shrill, off-key voice, Hélène started imitating *Annie*—from the children's musical she loved as a kid—with her own, homespun version. Frank's sunbaked lips grimaced as soon as Hélène burst out singing.

"Tomorrow, tomorrow…It's Saturday, tomorrow! I'll see you, tomorrow, Sylvie! I'll drown in your pool, but you'll save me, tomorrow, oh Sylvie, save me, tomorrow…Tomorrow, tomorrow… It's Saturday, tomorrow! I'll drown in your pool, but you'll save me, tomorrow, oh Sylvie, save me, tomorrow, Sylvie!"

Hélène knew her slurring words were incoherent, but she didn't care. She continued singing off key for several blocks until the surroundings looked familiar. Then she belted out the words even louder. For the grand finale, she lowered her feet onto the bike pedals—despite Frank's efforts to hold her back—and rammed her bike headfirst into her house. Just as her helmet slammed into the front door with a "splat," she let out a last "Tomorrow!" before her beer-logged body rolled neatly onto her doorstep.

When she fell with a thud outside the front door, Marc yanked it open and looked down at her with an expression of disbelief and disgust.

"Show's over!" she slurred with a lopsided grin.

"What the?" His eyebrows shot up. "Do you have any idea what time it is? Where the heck have you been, Hélène?"

"Nice to see you too, Marcie. I mean, Markie." Hélène winked. Then she hiccupped.

"Just get inside." Marc glanced at the neighbors' open windows. "Have you lost your mind?" He sniffed and looked at the man lurking behind Hélène in the dark. "*M'enfin!* Who in the heck… What are you doing with my wife at this hour?"

Marc stepped forward, pinching his nose. "Don't tell me you're Hélène's swimming teacher."

With a snort, Hélène rubbed the dust off her buttocks. "Hardly, *chéri.* This is Frank." She pointed an unsteady finger at her husband.

"Frank, meet Marc…" she began before losing her balance and tumbling into the house.

"What do you mean, have I lost my mind?" she added, colliding into Marc. "I'm sinking ash crearly as evah." She leaned against the back of the sofa to keep the world from spinning.

Marc slammed the door in Frank's face, then clenched his fists. "I'm going to…"

Hélène did a quick side-step. "*Quoi?* What are you gonna do to me?" Standing unsteadily, she punched circles in the air like a pro boxer on a losing streak. "*Hein?* Knock me out? *Hein?*" She stopped giggling when her fist grazed his cheek.

Instead of hitting her, Marc opted for the wall. Upon impact, he yanked his hand back. "*Aiie*, that *hurt*!" he yelped.

"*Chéri*, it's not convenient to hit the wall. We just had it repainted. Why don't you try—" She stopped mid-sentence. Marc's nostrils were flaring, with his pinched lips tight as a clothespin.

Marc poked her in the chest. "Your coworker Cecile left a message on the voice mail. You didn't go to work today, did you?" His beady eyes were glistening.

Hélène shook her head. She hadn't considered that her coworkers would be worried and call the house. But she didn't care about that right now. "Nope."

"*M'enfin.* Why the heck not?"

Hélène paused to watch the sweat sliding from Marc's forehead to his shirt. Slowly, she replied, "Didn't feel like it."

"You didn't *feel* like it? What kind of an answer is that?"

Hélène smiled smugly. "I felt like playing hooky, like in the movies. *Tu sais…* I never did that as a kid. In fact, I was such a good kid, I would—"

"Where'd you go then?" Marc began circling Hélène like a shark.

Hélène tried to remain standing, but her head was spinning. "To the movies," she mumbled, grabbing the sofa. "And stop whirling around me; you're making me seasick."

"To the movies," replied Marc, still circling her. "All day long?"

Hélène nodded, clutching her stomach.

"*Alors*, who'd you go with? That stinking jerk who brought you home?"

Hélène flashed him a blank look. "Where?"

"To the movies! And who in the heck is he?"

"*Ah*...My brother?"

Marc rammed his fist into his hand. "Tell me the truth, Hélène. Get serious!"

Hélène shrugged. "I am."

"Okay, you went to the movies all day long," Marc's nostrils flared. "*D'accord*. So, then what did you do? It's way after midnight!"

"*Attends*...I saw a horror film. *Non*...A romantic comedy." Hélène hiccupped. "*Non, attends*...A Western."

Marc sniffed at her. "You reek like an ashtray. Who the hell was that guy?" He jerked open the front door. "*Merde!*" he exclaimed, tripping over her bike as he raced outside. "Where is he? I'm going to squeeze his nuts to smithereens!"

"*Chéri*, who are you talking about?" asked Hélène, swaying in the doorway.

Scrambling to his feet, Marc began searching through the bushes. Hélène glanced at the "SCUM BAG" stamp on her arm. She rolled down her sleeve to conceal it just as Marc whirled around. He pointed his finger at her. "Enough lies! I know exactly what's going on."

"I...I...don't know what you mean..."

"And for God's sake, take this darn thing off!" Marc rapped his knuckles on Hélène's helmet.

Hélène unfastened her helmet and leaned against the door frame. The world was wobbling; her head felt like a warped record spinning on a record player. "What are you talking about?" she slurred. "I have no idea—"

Marc's nostrils flared as he sniffed her breath again. "I bet you—"

"Shh...*attends*," said Hélène, placing her finger on his moustache. "Before I forget. *Eh bien*...I need to tell you that...I'm not going with you to the market tomorrow. I'm going—"

Marc thrust her into the house before she could finish her sentence. He slammed the door, prompting Chaussette to dive under the sofa.

"Where? Where do you think you're going?" The lines on Marc's forehead deepened.

"I've got a swimming lesson at eight tomorrow morning, and we're going to—"

"Enough!" Marc grabbed her by the shoulders. "Why are you lying to me? I just went to the pool. You stopped your lessons last week."

"*Oui, mais*—"

"Stop lying to me!" Marc shook her hard. "What were you really going to do tomorrow? Who are you spending time with, Hélène?" Her helmet fell to the floor. He gave her one last glare, then let her go.

Hélène couldn't hide the fear in her eyes. Breathing deeply, she stared at his trembling hands. Tears streamed from Hélène's cheeks as she bent down to ease the tension between them.

"Come to Maman, Chaussette! Did Papa feed you dinner?" Hélène scratched Chaussette's tiny head, which was poking out from the sofa.

Like a furious lion, Marc paced around Hélène and her cat. He swiped a beer bottle from the table and sucked up the last few drops.

"You're going to have sex with someone, *non*? And it's not the first time either." His eyes narrowed. "I read your diary. I know you're seeing someone else. That's why you came home at this hour, completely wasted. I can't believe this. My wife's nothing but a whore!"

Marc's eyes were blazing. He hurled his empty beer bottle at the wall. With a loud crash, it smashed into bits, flying all over the living room.

"*C'est ça.* Get out of here! You *reek*!" he yelled, throwing the bike helmet at Hélène as she fled upstairs with the cat in tow.

❖

Once Hélène had locked the bathroom door, she tried to stop shaking as she cast off her clothes. This wasn't the first time she'd been upset by Marc's outbursts, and it probably wouldn't be the last. But maybe at least part of it was warranted? She sniffed at the alcohol stench surrounding her. *I'm starting to smell like him.* She made a disgusting face in the mirror. *I should've gone to work today.* Everything in her head was foggy, especially the series of events that had happened since that morning. Why had she played hooky anyway? As usual, her thoughts went back to Sylvie. That's why. She clutched her stomach.

In an effort to wipe away her worries, Hélène clumsily entered the bathtub. With a deep sigh, she fiddled with the knobs until warm water streamed from the shower fixture. While reaching for the soap bar, it slipped from her shaking fingers and dropped onto her foot. *Ouch!*

C'est bizarre. I don't remember getting a tattoo, she thought, staring at her forearm. She squeezed the soap between her fingers. It dropped again. When she bent over to pick it up, she slipped. Yet she hardly noticed; her mind was running on overdrive. *I'd better scrub this off before I get in trouble.* But no matter how hard she scrubbed, the "SCUM BAG" stamp on her arm remained.

"*Tant pis.* It's kinda cute anyway."

As Hélène's intoxicated state lowered her inhibitions, sensual feelings took over her body. She wiggled her buttocks to the bottom of the tub and ran her fingers over her stamped forearm. Instantly, goose bumps erupted on her skin. She shivered as the tiny hairs rose in unison. It made her think about how excited she was when Sylvie drove her to the Greek restaurant in Sylvie's VW Bug. She settled back in the tub with the chilly air surrounding her and closed her eyes for an impromptu, alcohol-induced dream.

Hélène was preoccupied with Sylvie's forearms as she firmly gripped the steering wheel. She felt a burst of pleasure each time Sylvie's arm muscles popped out with each swift maneuver. Ever so discreetly, she let her eyes wander up Sylvie's arm.

Her biceps are so round and smooth, so well defined.

Hélène wrapped her fingers around her own bicep and gave it a squeeze; its insignificance made her cringe.

The best part was when Sylvie shifted gears. *This is intense.*

Hélène's eyes lingered over Sylvie's strong fingers, and their power, as they gripped the stick propped between their bodies; the smooth control they offered excited Hélène.

She drives just like she swims...Skillful and fast.

To conclude her bathing experience, Hélène—clad in comfy, white cotton underwear—flung herself onto the bed. After her hot bath and so much alcohol, her body remained oblivious to the bedroom's chilly air. Her mind, however, seemed to have realized something very important. Despite her inebriated state, it had told her something clearly that she hadn't wanted to admit before. She needed more out of life. And she wasn't going to make any more excuses for Marc because she didn't want him anymore. She wanted—desperately needed—someone else. Splayed over the covers like a lazy rag doll—her thighs open and arms outstretched—she fell fast asleep.

CHAPTER SIXTEEN

I missed you," whispered Sylvie, squeezing her cousin tightly and kissing her cheeks. "And you too, little bugger," she said, scratching Goldie's head through the cat box Aphrodite was holding.

"Hope you've been a good girl." She swapped her suitcase for Goldie. "*Ca alors!* You certainly didn't starve at Auntie Aphrodite's!" she said with a chuckle as the heavy cat box strained her arm.

They conversed rapidly in Greek as they left the airport. Sylvie had to admit it was nice to be back in Belgium, even if the sun was, as usual, absent.

Half an hour later, Aphrodite drove up to Sylvie's apartment. Outside the car, they kissed cheeks again and hugged each other tightly. When Aphrodite pulled back at last, she wiped a tear from Sylvie's eye. "It was hard, wasn't it?"

Sylvie nodded. "Wish you could've come with me...I can't believe she's gone."

"Me neither." Sylvie pictured herself at Yaya's bedside in Santorini. Since she had left right after her grandma's passing, she hadn't had time to face the sadness lingering around her death. Just then, she felt a soft gust of wind caress her cheeks. "Everyone's going to miss her...Such an amazing woman."

"Coolest Yaya ever." Aphrodite smiled forlornly.

Sylvie's eyes watered up again. *And what about Mama?* She looked away.

Aphrodite touched Sylvie's cheek. "You okay? Want me to come up for a while?"

Sylvie shook her head. "I'll be fine. Thanks for everything." She handed Aphrodite a small paper bag. "Here. It's nothing much…"

"You didn't have to do that. What are cousins for?" Aphrodite peeked inside the bag and took a whiff. "Ooh! Homemade, *n'est-ce pas?*" She kissed Sylvie on the cheek before popping a succulent piece of baklava into her mouth. As she chewed, she held the bag out toward Sylvie.

Suddenly, a loud meow erupted from the cat box. "*Oui, bébé.* I've got a treat for you too," said Sylvie, peering into the box. "*Ah, non!*" She pinched her nose. "Time to get her inside. She's about to lay a travel turd. See you later."

Goldie's meows grew insistent as Sylvie rushed toward her apartment building. As she fumbled with her key to open the apartment building door, reality hit. During the entire flight back to Belgium, she had been dreading this moment, when she would return to her normal life. Now that it was here, she wasn't sure if she was ready to come back and face reality. Of course, she was thrilled to be reunited with Goldie. But what was she going to do about Hélène? She hadn't returned her calls. Was she going to show up for their first Saturday morning lesson tomorrow? Did she even want her to?

❖

Hélène slammed her hand down on her alarm clock. Glancing at her near-naked body, she moaned. "No wonder I'm shivering. Wish I had as much fur as you to keep me warm, *bébé.*" She kissed Chaussette, who was cuddled on her pillow, and crawled off the bed.

She winced as her hand went to her throbbing forehead. In a vain attempt to deter the pain, she pulled on her jeans and T-shirt and crammed her swimming clothes into a backpack. Thrusting it over her shoulder, she clutched the railing and hobbled down the stairs. *I wasn't planning to go to the pool, but after last night…I really have to see her.* She took the stairs slowly, one by one. *No matter what.*

"What the heck?" She gasped when she reached the kitchen. On the floor was her photo, smothered with bits of eggshell. *How did this get off the fridge?* Her hand went to her head, which was now spinning as if it were on a wild circus ride. She struggled to keep her nausea at bay after ingesting so much alcohol the night before. With great effort, she squinted at dozens of sketches of Chaussette, stretched out in various poses, scattered over the floor, covered in broken eggs. Clearly, Marc had taken out the rest of his frustrations with his artistic creations.

Chaussette rubbed her face against her ankle. A bit of egg stuck to her nose.

"Seems like you had a good time while Maman was gone, *bébé*." Hélène plopped down on the cold tiles next to her slimy, eggshell garnished photo. *Tiens, where is that jerk anyway?*

In response, loud snores erupted from the living room. "Ah, of course," she whispered, donning her florescent cycling vest. *No more excuses for him.* On all fours, she crawled toward the living room.

Crawling as quietly as she could past the snores, she snatched her helmet from behind the sofa. When she fastened it, the buckle made a loud "click."

Darn! Inching past the sofa on all fours, she made a beeline for the front door.

Marc sat straight up and grabbed her florescent vest as she wiggled past. "*Alors*, that's how your teacher taught you to do the *crawl*, eh?" He smiled callously. "What a loser…Speaking of swimming, where are you headed, Little Miss Sunshine?"

Hélène kept trying to crawl away.

"If you think I'm gonna let you see that idiot again, you're dreaming." Marc pulled hard on her vest. "You're staying right here with me, and we're goin' to the market just like every Saturday. Understand?" He gave the vest a quick jerk.

The material ripped, causing Chaussette to spring for cover.

Velcro saves the day! thought Hélène, breaking free from Marc's grip and burning her knees on the carpet, scrambling toward the entrance. Before he could intercept her dash for the door, she ran outside. "Crap!" Her ears heard the smacking of two bodies—

hers and someone else's—which caused a pair of jaybirds, formerly pecking at seedlings in the grass, to fly away in fright.

Hélène stood staring at Cecile's long eyelashes fluttering from the shock. *What's she doing here?* Her pulse was pounding as she tried to get away. But Cecile, eyes wide and pupils dilated, was blocking her escape. Hélène tried to get around her, but Cecile remained planted on the doorstep, clutching her paper bag and lacy pink umbrella, swaying from side to side. A glossy, red-nailed finger went to her sensuous lips—most likely to ease the sting. Hélène stepped back to examine her best friend, whose lips had just smacked hers for the very first time.

"*Bonjour* to you too, *ma chérie*. That's what I call a real kisseroo…" Cecile laughed wholeheartedly as she stepped back to take in the cycling helmet and fluorescent vest draped around Hélène's neck. "Sweet outfit. Goin' somewhere?"

Before Hélène could reply, Marc dragged her into the house. "Over my dead body, she is! That wench has—"

"*Vite*, come with me!" whispered Hélène, grabbing her best friend.

"Who are you calling a wench, *eh?*" Cecile poked her lacy umbrella at Marc as Hélène yanked her forward. Marc opened his mouth to speak but emitted a yelp instead when the tip of the umbrella stabbed at his groin. He let go of Hélène, and she pushed past him. Cecile raced after her into the kitchen.

Once she had safely locked them inside, Hélène wedged a chair under the doorknob. "Whew, that was close!" Yet before she could wipe the sweat off her face, Marc was banging on the kitchen door.

"Let me in, Hélène. Or I'll ring both of your necks!" he shouted with a noticeably higher pitch to his voice, likely thanks to Cecile's swift umbrella move.

Leaning her full body against the door, Hélène felt the pounding wood thump against her helmet. *Hardly the best remedy for a hangover*, she mused, wincing. This time, humor wasn't going to cut it. Her usual sense of denial wasn't working. With her heart pounding as hard as Marc's incessant thumping, she tried to control her raging fear as she pressed hard against the door. Deep from within, her intuition was calling. *This situation is worse than usual!* She tried to breathe calmly as she racked her mind to find a solution to save herself and Cecile. *We've got to get out of here before he breaks down the door!* Cecile, on the other hand, didn't seem at all fazed by the imminent danger. Leaning against the counter, she plucked a fresh croissant from her paper bag. "Now's as good a time as ever." She bit into the buttery pastry. "Mmm. These critters are amazing. Want one, honey?"

Hélène nearly screamed with frustration. She jumped out of the way. "Watch out, he's breaking down the door!"

"Someone's gotta teach that man how to use a skillet," said Cecile, just as the door flew off its hinges, crashing to the floor.

Marc lunged at Hélène, who tried to block him, but he thrust her aside. Just as she started to go after him again, Cecile smacked him in the skull with a skillet.

Mon Dieu! Hélène watched in shock as Marc stumbled under the blow. He slid over the scattered egg shells before his body crashed to the floor. To her horror, his head hit the tiles with a hollow thud.

Hélène's mouth dropped open. "Ceci, what have you done?" She took a step toward her motionless husband. But then she stopped abruptly. "Wait a minute." She checked her watch. "I'll just check to make sure he's breathing." As soon as she was certain he was still alive, she announced, "*Désolée*, I've gotta run. Besides, I don't owe him a damn thing after what he just did to us." She raced out the back door. "I'll explain later!" Suddenly, there was a loud rip as her cycling vest caught on the handle. Like a slingshot, her body propelled forward as the vest ripped off.

"*Merde!*" she swore under her breath as it fell to the ground. "Too bad. I can ride without it…It can't hurt, just this once—"

Cecile shooed her away. "Go on, *chérie!* I'll take care of Monsieur Jerk here."

"*Merci,* Ceci. Call an ambulance, *d'accord*? And then get the heck out of here!" replied Hélène as she hopped on her bike.

She pedaled swiftly through the rain, ignoring the menacing

clouds suspended like waterlogged nuggets in the sky. Sounds of thunder crackled in her ears while cold rain streamed under her helmet, pasting her hair against her brow.

Faster! She pushed her legs harder than ever. Deep down, she knew she had to get away from him—in order to reach *her*. It was all so clear now. *I need her. She makes me feel safe. Why didn't I realize this before?* She was pedaling so quickly through the rain that she could no longer feel her thighs. And her head felt numb; her only reminder that it was still attached to her neck were the wet drops crashing into her cheeks, licking diagonal lines over her glasses. As her tires skimmed over the slick roads, Hélène tuned everything out. She was on a mission, yet her tears were messing with her vision as much as the rain. And she wasn't wearing her fluorescent safety vest. In her haste to reach the pool to meet Sylvie, she was taking more risks than usual, but she didn't care. The only thing that mattered was getting to the pool. *Please let her be there.*

Even though Hélène's legs were exhausted, she pressed down on the pedals with all her might, propelling her bike through the rain. When she reached the last roundabout, she slowed down just enough to glance at her wrist: *7:59 a.m. Not a minute to lose.*

Resisting the urge to stop, she swallowed a breath of fresh air, glanced over her shoulder, and entered the roundabout. But just as her bike turned right, toward the pool, she saw a flash of white heading straight at her.

"*Attention!*" Hélène screamed at the car. But it was too late. There was a loud crash. Hélène's screams resonated in her head until something hard hit her body.

❖

Even though Hélène's bike took most of the impact, her forehead hit the car's front fender before her body flew into the air. Like a discarded rag doll, she landed beside the moving car, which finally skidded to a stop. Gradually, the screams in her head gave way to complete silence. What seemed like hours later—though she knew it was probably only a few minutes—she opened her eyes to discover her mangled bike lying on its side, a few feet from her head.

She tried to touch her forehead, to calm a sharp pain over her eye, but her right arm was numb. After several futile attempts, she gave up and shut her eyes.

Non, don't give up... Each time she was about to surrender, a voice in her head kept bringing her back. Ever so slowly, she turned her head until her cheek grazed the rough, wet ground. When she opened her eyes again, she gasped.

"*Au secours!*" she screamed for help in French, realizing with horror that her right arm was pinned under a car's front tire. She couldn't tell for sure—since her glasses were missing, and her right arm was numb—but that pale thing next to her face sure looked like a limb... Which made her scream again.

"*Au secours!*" To her distress, there was only silence. She hollered again. Still no answer. Hélène's heart was pounding. Waving her left hand frantically, she pointed to the offending tire. "Somebody, get this *car* off my arm!"

Unable to understand why nobody got out of the vehicle despite her desperate cries, Hélène imagined the worst. With her arm literally stapled to the pavement, she panicked. If the person driving the car went into reverse instead of driving forward, the tire parked on her arm, only inches from her head, would run over her neck. *I don't want a crushed windpipe—or a neck as flat as a crepe on a skillet. I'm not ready for my life to end. I'm supposed to be swimming with Sylvie right now.* Feeling an increased sense of panic, she yelled louder, to no avail.

At last, the driver got out of the car. Hélène observed him as he squinted at her through his thick lenses. Despite her cries for help, he just stood and stared. She yelled even louder. *Is he blind or deaf or what?* At last, the man reacted. He shrugged and gave her an awkward smile. This made Hélène livid. Just when she was about to scream, he leaned into the car and murmured something in a foreign language. *What's he doing? Get this thing off me!* Hélène formed a fist with her left hand since her right one, still pinched under the car tire, was useless. *I'm gonna smack the daylights out of this jerk when I get out from under here*, she decided as her eyes focused on his calf—nearly within biting distance. Her head ached terribly, and her vision went blurry. Then she heard someone reply from inside the car. *What language is that?* The voice was gruff. The driver standing next to her pinned body shrugged again. Hélène let out a frustrated groan. *Maybe I should switch to English?*

Before she could react further, she felt a warm trickle of liquid—under the cold, pelting rain—slide down her temple. Then everything went dark.

CHAPTER SEVENTEEN

Sylvie sat on the bench, tapping her feet on the tiles. To pass the time, she counted up to a hundred in Greek. Then she counted backward in French. This was her third round. But when she got to forty-eight, she stopped. *C'est ridicule.* She shifted from one stiff buttock to the other. *I'm wasting my time. She's not coming.*

Sylvie rubbed her hands together to keep warm. Under the goose bumps on her forearms, she admired her smooth skin, which had bronzed heavily from soaking up Santorini's sunshine and salty seawater. She tried not to think of Yaya and the sad moments she had just passed with her family. Her native island seemed so far away now. She had gotten up early this morning—a Saturday—just for her. *And to do what? Sit on this cold bench in my bathing suit for nothing!* She frowned. *I was looking forward to seeing her again, though I'm not sure what will come of it. The nerve. She doesn't even care enough to show up. I should've stayed with Mama in Santorini instead of coming back for a woman—married at that—who only causes me heartache. When will I ever learn?*

It had only been a few days since she left Brussels for Santorini, but so much had happened. She shook her head. *Non. I'm not going to think about that.* Her heart sank as her thoughts—despite her strongest intentions—returned to Mama and to her beloved Yaya, who had just left this world.

Through the damp morning chill, Sylvie contemplated her surroundings: the indoor pool's bare walls, the cold cement floor, the lofty ceiling with solid beams and florescent lamps, the rain-streamed windows. A knot formed in her throat. *My life is as empty as this wretched pool.* Gazing at the water, she tucked the edges of her bathrobe to her chest and shivered. For the umpteenth time, she checked the wall clock. It now read 8:21.

That's it. She's really not coming. Trying to drown out the pitter-patter of her flip-flops, she plodded back to the locker room. She threw on her jeans and faded T-shirt, then her yellow raincoat. *Her loss.* She hoisted her backpack onto her shoulder. *I've got way better things to do with my time. I'll find a woman who wants me for me. One I don't have to chase.* Jogging from the building temporarily jostled the adverse thoughts from her mind. Instead, they metamorphosed into immediate physical preoccupations in the form of a violent rain shower.

Sylvie ran through the silvery, gushing sheets to her VW Bug. Her face was drenched by the time she hopped into the driver's seat. As always, she stuck a CD into the stereo system. This was her medicine. And today, the rain slamming into the windshield meshed perfectly with the CD's upbeat Greek tunes.

Now that Sylvie's toes had thawed, she tapped her soaked sneakers against the car floor, creating squishy, gushing sounds. The resulting vibrations—a compilation of rain, music, and squeaky wet sneakers—filled the interior of Sylvie's car and her soul. She understood this bizarre concert was in fact a healing performance, created in part by nature's instruments. As powerful emotions gripped her body, her ears felt full—as if in an airplane—ready to explode. She wrapped her arms around the steering wheel and held on tight. Like a dejected lover, she pressed her soggy face to its hard, cracked surface. Now, with free rein to roam, her nerves simply collapsed. As hot tears poured out of Sylvie's eyes, her chest heaved to the steady beat of the rainstorm mixed with the soothing music from her homeland.

That is, until the CD stopped playing. To her surprise, Sylvie heard Yaya's voice in the car.

"Hush, Sylvie. This is important. You never know if I'll get another chance to tell you this. So, listen carefully..."

Sylvie sat straight up and stared at her speakers. Then she

swiveled around, searching the car. *Nobody's in here but me.* The realization that she was alone with Yaya's voice—her beloved Yaya, who had just passed away—made her shiver all over.

The voice continued.

"If you want something bad enough, child, don't let anything stop you. Just go for it. And I promise, you'll get it."

Sylvie quickly pushed a button on the car stereo. As soon as the CD's upbeat music began playing, her muscles relaxed. *Good. Now let's try the radio.* She pushed another button and held her breath. But instead of the radio, once again, Yaya's voice came on, even louder:

"If you want something bad enough, child, don't let anything stop you. Just go for it."

Sylvie's eyes began to water as Yaya's words hit her. *How could this be happening?* She felt goose bumps on her thighs. *Never mind.* She'd figure that out later. Now, as Yaya's message entered her consciousness, she knew what she needed to do. She grabbed her screwdriver, revved up the car, and sped away.

When a love song from the seventies started playing on the radio, Sylvie smiled with recognition. *Life is truly a gift.* Tears lined the corners of her eyes, waiting their turn to tumble down her cheeks. Simultaneously, thick fingers of rain slid down Sylvie's windshield, testing her skill in navigating Brussels's slippery streets.

Just as she reached the roundabout, Sylvie noticed dozens of people crowding around something in the street. Her heartbeat sped up as she took her foot off the accelerator. Maneuvering past the throng of onlookers, she caught her breath.

There lay Hélène's blue mountain bike—completely mangled— next to a white Toyota. The crowd huddled together like an anxious group of sheep. Slamming on her brakes, Sylvie leaped out of her VW Bug and sprinted over puddles toward the curious herd.

"Excusez-moi!" Sylvie forced her way through the crowd, knelt beside Hélène, placed her head on her chest, and listened for signs of breathing. There were none. *She needs CPR.* Thankful that her job required frequent first-aid training, she choked back the emotions swelling in her throat. *Keep calm!* She quickly checked the scene

for safety and ordered bystanders to call an ambulance and fetch a defibrillator. Then, as skillfully as an emergency medic, Sylvie performed cardiopulmonary resuscitation, vigorously pumping Hélène's chest. *Please. Please, Hélène.*

Even though the downpour was at last subsiding, Sylvie had to clamp her fingers together to keep them from slipping. *Focus.* She aimed steadily at her target. When it was time to stop pumping and give Hélène some air, she checked for signs of breathing again. *Still none.* Knowing that every second counted, she placed her lips over Hélène's. Expertly sealing the space between their lips, she transferred the air from her own lungs into Hélène's. Inexplicably, the urgency of the situation made time seem to freeze. Meanwhile, Sylvie couldn't help noticing how cold Hélène's lips were. As Sylvie breathed again into her mouth, she pleaded silently, *Vas-y, Hélène. Breathe!*

Today's lifesaving event was real—not at all like Sylvie's lazy weekends years before, when a certain girlfriend-of-the-moment would beg her to practice mouth-to-mouth resuscitation on her. In those days, they would rehearse the "lifeguard-victim" scenario in bed, imagining vivid scenes where Sylvie would bravely rescue a drowning swimmer—clad in a loose paréo or sparse loincloth, if dressed at all—on some faraway island beach. Fiji was Sylvie's favorite fantasy location. Lowering her voice to a raspy, sexy tone, she would pretend to speak Fijian. Each time she whispered *"Hoolahooliee"* or *"Baalagaai Lalaai"* into her girlfriend's ears, mouth, or navel, even though it meant complete nonsense, her girlfriend went nuts.

But today, Sylvie wasn't pretending to be a hero. And Hélène wasn't feigning to be her victim. As the crowd watched, Sylvie threw all her efforts into reviving Hélène. Her mind kept repeating *Vas-y, breathe!* It became her mantra. Never mind her weary arms, the splitting pain in her back and shoulders, and her spinning head from rapid breathing. Like a fully charged, battery-operated toy, Sylvie's body performed with extrahuman effort to resuscitate the victim.

Sylvie paused to listen for signs of recovery, until, miraculously, when she next put her hands on Hélène's chest, it moved on its own. *Oui!* Sylvie placed her ear close to Hélène's lips. The sounds of a weak exhale, bringing warm air to her cheek, made Sylvie dizzy with joy. She lifted her head to see Hélène's eyelids flutter in slow motion, like wings on a drowsy butterfly.

❖

As Hélène's eyelids quivered, she thought she saw someone's lips hovering over hers. The image was a blur until she blinked a few times. Then she recognized the nose. *I must be dreaming. What's she doing here?* She gazed at Sylvie's flushed cheeks, the droplets of water sliding off her hair, and her dark, gentle eyes brimming with concern.

Just as Sylvie pulled away, Hélène extended her uninjured arm and grasped her raincoat collar. *Attends. We're not done yet.* She drew her head toward hers, and before Hélène could think it through, she was kissing her.

Sylvie's lips felt good, incredibly good. They tasted delicious. Just like at the beach and in all Hélène's dreams…

The siren wailed like a shrieking baby. The ambulance cut through the early-morning traffic—lighter on Saturdays, but still hectic—and misty clouds settling over Brussels.

Hélène wasn't in the habit of playing the role of ambulatory patient, nor was she used to being the star of the show. Rather than try to justify—or even comprehend—what had just happened, she shut her eyes; it was preferable to pretend she was asleep—or, better yet, dead. That way, she could mull over what to do next. Despite her exhausted state, however, adrenaline raced through her system. She could feel the blood pumping in her veins. She forced her eyelids closed to calm her nerves—in vain, for each time the ambulance hit a rut in the street, a jolt went through her right arm. Even though it was in an inflatable cast, it was throbbing like mad. *There goes my idea of playing dead*, she mused, wincing.

Then she remembered Sylvie. She had asked her to ride with her to the hospital. *What is she thinking right now?* She felt a soft caress on her good shoulder. Despite the intense pain she was feeling, the light, caring touch made her feel better. She could almost smell the sweet warmth of Sylvie next to her in the jostling ambulance. With her eyes still closed, she settled back on the stretcher, letting her muscles relax as best they could. Deep down, somehow, she knew Sylvie would take care of her no matter what. It was all so clear now. The way she touched her, kissed her, and cared for her was more than comforting—it was loving and unconditional.

Can she read my thoughts? Hélène struggled to open her eyes to look at Sylvie, who was kneeling next to a paramedic in the ambulance, softly caressing Hélène's shoulder. She jumped as soon as Hélène's eyelids fluttered and slowly opened. She turned her head toward Sylvie and smiled feebly. As soon as she saw her beautiful eyes, Sylvie's heart soared. Tenderly, she swept Hélène's damp hair from her face. Then she placed her broken glasses over her nose.

"How are you?" she whispered, her eyes glossy with emotion.

Hélène smiled weakly.

❖

For an instant, their eyes locked. Sylvie sent her a silent message of comfort. She gave her a broad smile and gently squeezed Hélène's fingers. *Oh no. They're cold. She must still be in shock.* She held her uninjured hand until she felt the coolness of Hélène's skin lessen. *Now it's time to warm up the atmosphere...*

"Great idea, racing in the rain." Sylvie glanced at Hélène's inflatable cast, chuckling nervously. "Who do you think you are, Eddy Merckx? Or Lance Armstrong?" She whispered into her ear, "Seriously, Hélène. Next time, just call me, and I'll pick you up. *D'accord?*"

Hélène nodded as a tear rolled down her cheek. "I was on my way to you. I'm so sorry—"

Just then, the ambulance swerved. In addition to screeching tires, Hélène screamed as splinters of pain seemingly shot down her arm. The paramedic swiftly gave her a shot of painkiller.

Sylvie felt sick as a muffled cry erupted from Hélène's pillow.

She watched as her body twitched, then twitched again. *I wish there was something else I could do to help.* To her relief, when the drug kicked in, Hélène rolled back, and a sleepy grin spread over her face. *She looks so peaceful now. I never want to be separated from her again. I love her.* The realization made Sylvie's skin tingle. Like a knight who had just saved his princess from danger, she swept a few strands of wet hair from Hélène's face. *But what will happen to her now?* The question made her insides churn. *I hope she's not too injured.* And then there was Hélène's husband she needed to deal with.

As soon as they had entered the ambulance, Hélène had given her her cell phone. She had insisted she call Cecile, who explained that the couple had had a fight that morning, which had left Marc in a terrible state. Sylvie wasn't sure how that could've happened, but she'd get the details later from Cecile, who was meeting them in the emergency room. For now, she needed to make sure Hélène had the best medical care possible. If it was Marc's fault that she was in this state... She clenched her jaw. *Non. I can't think of him right now. I have to think of Hélène.* She knew she wanted to take care of her for the rest of her life. If only she could be sure she'd be okay.

Sylvie hardly ever prayed, but she squeezed her eyes shut and asked the heavens to protect Hélène. When she opened them, she was relieved to see Hélène's eyelids descend at last, forming a pair of droopy clamshells.

CHAPTER EIGHTEEN

L ike most emergency rooms on Saturday mornings, the place
was full of people. Patients spilled into the hallway, waiting for
nurses to call their names. Some merely sat in the stiff plastic chairs,
staring at the sterile linoleum floor, while others held their limbs,
groaning in agony.

Marc and Cecile stood on one side of Hélène; Sylvie stood on
the other. While waiting for Dr. Duprès, Sylvie gripped the bed's
metallic bars like a life raft at sea. She tried to block out the annoying
sounds of Marc tapping his foot impatiently on the linoleum floor.
Her eyes darted from Hélène's pale cheeks to Cecile's anxious
face, to all the others in the waiting room. As she listened to the
tongues clicking in French, Dutch, Russian, Arabic, Polish, Spanish,
Chinese, and other exotic languages, Sylvie's mind wandered.

Most likely, it was her subconscious mind protecting her from
the painful, yet real, moments she was experiencing right now. She
couldn't believe she was standing next to Hélène, who was lying
on a rolling bed, comatose after her latest round of painkillers. Her
mud-streaked face had been washed, and a gauze bandage covered
her eyebrow. And right next to her stood Hélène's abusive husband
and her best friend. *Non.* Sylvie didn't want to be feeling what she
was feeling right now, and she certainly didn't want to ruminate
about the stressful events leading up to this moment.

Despite her frazzled nerves, Sylvie smiled inwardly at the
diversity surrounding her. Each patient, local or foreign, had a unique
story to tell. This was one of the reasons why she had emigrated

to Belgium. Not only was Brussels the capital of Europe, but tiny, humble Belgium represented a cultural melting pot, notorious for its generosity to foreigners. Moreover, its medical professionals, highly trained yet exceedingly underpaid, were considered to be among the best in Europe.

Sylvie discreetly looked at the folks around them. Like her— in a yellow raincoat and weekend athletic clothes—they wore a mishmash of garments. Some dressed as Belgians, in layers, given the country's unpredictable weather. Others remained in their traditional dress. She admired the colorful fabric worn by the Congolese women, contrasting with the heavy makeup and platinum-streaked hair garnishing the young Central and Eastern European women and the small, imitation-leather shoes worn by an elderly couple from China.

Sylvie also studied their facial expressions. How she wished she had her camera. She would have loved to capture the painful, yet tender, emotions lurking in that sterile room. All enthusiasm vanished, however, as soon as her eyes returned to Hélène— bandaged and unconscious—at her side. And when she glanced at Marc and Cecile, her throat tightened.

She hadn't wanted to call Hélène's best friend, whom she had never met, and she certainly hadn't wanted to call Marc. But she knew she didn't have a choice—Hélène had asked her to. Without knowing the details about what had happened that morning at their house, she sensed it had been something serious. Her heart raced each time she thought about it. She couldn't help disliking Marc and the way he treated Hélène. *If that idiot caused her accident, I'll make him pay for it in more ways than one.* She hadn't had time to learn more from Cecile once she showed up at the hospital. They were all too worried about Hélène. Then again, maybe Marc wasn't worried. He didn't seem like the worrying type. Nor the caring type. But she and Cecile certainly cared. They were her real friends, and Sylvie knew deep down she was much more than a friend to Hélène. At least, she hoped so.

❖

Hélène was as groggy as could be. Lying on her back, she tried to concentrate on a spider slowly crossing the ceiling. Its legs hesitated with each step forward. But each time Hélène blinked, the spider was back in the same place, next to the myriad of fine cracks above her head.

Gotta get these new lenses checked, thought Hélène, mentally adjusting her glasses. She tried to reach up but couldn't lift her hand. Her entire arm felt numb. *What's going on?*

She blinked in distress.

Now she saw only half a spider. She blinked again. *What kind of warped dream is this?*

"*Ca va?*" came a familiar voice. It was a female voice. Before Hélène could react, Dr. Duprès entered the room and cleared her throat. Her gray eyes settled on her patient. "You're a very lucky woman."

Hélène heard her doctor's voice, but it sounded like mush, as if her ears were plugged with cotton. Finally, the thought resonated in her mind: *I'm a lucky woman. Oui, a very lucky woman.* She frowned, trying to figure things out. *I wonder why?*

Someone squeezed her hand. "*C'est vrai.* She's got her own room, and not everybody—" began Cecile.

"*S'il vous plaît*," snapped the doctor. "I've a very tight schedule." She directed her attention back to Hélène. "Despite your forceful impact with the car, you've only got a concussion and a bruised arm. Nothing's broken, and there's no nerve damage."

Cecile burst out, "*Mais c'est incroyable!* A car parked on your arm, and you escaped with just a few bruises!"

Hélène knit her eyebrows, confused. *Whose room am I in? Whose bed is this? Whose nightie is this?*

"How long did they park on you, anyway?" Cecile asked while smacking her gum.

"How would she know, she passed out, remember?" whispered Sylvie with an annoyed look.

"*En tout cas*, you could've fared much worse." Dr. Duprès smiled. "All that swimming must have strengthened your arm muscles."

When Hélène heard the word "swimming," her mind cleared. Through her crushed lenses, she finally recognized Marc, then Cecile. *I must be dreaming.*

At last, she squinted at the face hovering over her. She saw a nose. A most prominent nose. One that she very much admired.

When Hélène realized it was Sylvie, she held her breath. She had no idea how she got where she was—wherever it was—or what was going on, but she didn't care. Her eyes strained to see through her broken lenses. They followed the muscles down Sylvie's arm to her strong, tan fingers, which were clasping hers. *I'm beginning to like this dream*, she decided, exhaling softly.

Sylvie whispered in Hélène's ear, "*Tu vois,* I told you swimming would make you muscular. Looks like it saved your life."

"That's a relief," said Marc. "Thank you for your help, *Docteur.*"

Hélène felt like a baby in a crib. Completely helpless. She peered at her husband, then Sylvie, and then back at Marc and Cecile. *This one seems so real,* she told herself. *Just in case it's not a dream, I'd better be polite.*

"*Merci, Docteur.*" She smiled at Dr. Duprès, even though she wasn't exactly sure why she was thanking her.

"Just one more thing," added the doctor. "Apparently, you took my advice to the T. Your last blood test was *extraordinary*. Strange that they tested for so many illnesses, though."

Hélène suppressed a giggle, recalling how she herself had ticked off dozens of items on the list.

"Anyway, everything came out just fine." Dr. Duprès nodded. "You're as healthy as can be, *ma chérie*. Exercise seems to suit you, so whatever you've been doing, keep it up!"

Marc cleared his throat loudly while glaring at Sylvie.

Ignoring his manly grunt, Hélène beamed. "I will, *Docteur*. I've never felt better in my life."

"Except for one minor detail." Cecile pointed to her best friend's arm. "Not only is it as flat as a coin, but it's a great car advertisement...Full of tread marks."

Both Marc and Sylvie winced.

"I wouldn't worry about that, Hélène. Judging from the way your body is functioning now, your arm shall soon be as good as new."

Hélène watched Dr. Duprès's eyes zero in on Sylvie, who was holding her hand. She seemed puzzled, especially when her gaze fell on Cecile, who was standing near Marc. The doctor looked from Sylvie to Cecile. "Are you also family?"

Hélène wondered how they would respond during the uncomfortable silence that ensued. She glanced inquisitively at Sylvie, beaming down at her. *How I love those adorable dimples. How I love her.*

Cecile broke the silence. "Sort of." She sent a discreet wink of solidarity to Hélène and Sylvie.

❖

Sylvie shifted her legs self-consciously as she felt the intensity of Dr. Duprès's stare. *Her eyes are boring into me. Probably because I'm holding Hélène's hand instead of Marc.* But she didn't care what the doctor thought. She wasn't about to let go of Hélène's hand, not if she didn't have to.

Sylvie shifted her legs again. *What should I say?* She smiled down at Hélène. *I'm just relieved you're all right. It's a miracle.* The warmth beaming back from Hélène's azure eyes hit her straight in the heart. *It's true. I love you. I wish we could be family...* She did her best to force all negative feelings about Marc out of her mind. But the fact was, *he* was her husband—her family—and he was standing uncomfortably close to Hélène.

She had no idea what they were going to do about Marc, and the way Cecile had winked at them made her think that perhaps Hélène had told her best friend about Sylvie after all. That thought gave rise to hope; maybe Hélène was ready to be with her too. She avoided Marc's inquisitive glare and concentrated on Hélène. She was all that mattered.

Before she could figure out what to say, an extremely well-dressed African woman sauntered into the hospital room with an immense bouquet of flowers. She rushed over to Hélène's side, shoved her bouquet in Sylvie's face, and kissed her friend's forehead with a loud smack. Startled, Sylvie caught her breath. *Who is she?*

"*Salut,* pumpkin. Got here quick as I could. What terrible news!" the woman announced while staring at Hélène's bandaged eyebrow. To Sylvie's horror, she tapped the bedspread until she located Hélène's right arm, hidden under the blankets. She held it up. "*Mince.* I wanted to see the tread marks," she added, dropping the bandage-covered limb. As Hélène winced in pain, Sylvie grew livid. *What does she think she's doing?*

As if she had heard her thoughts, the woman turned to face Sylvie. Lowering her long lashes, she parted her sensuous lips and flashed her a toothy smile.

"So delightful to finally meet you, Sylvie," the elegantly dressed woman gushed, wrapping her arms around Sylvie. "*Je suis Mathilde,* if you haven't already guessed." She smacked her with a kiss on both cheeks.

"Right," stammered Sylvie. *Who the heck is she? Hélène's never mentioned her before.* "Nice to meet you too, I'm Hélène's—"

Mathilde smiled broadly. "Swimming instructor. *Je sais.* I think it's wonderful too."

Sylvie paused. Then she grinned. *Hélène told someone else about me. About us.* The thought warmed her heart. "It is," she replied. "In fact, she's become quite a good—"

"You don't say?" Mathilde's black eyebrows shot up. She flashed Hélène a devious grin. "*Alors,* Hélène, aren't you just a beehive of secrets? I'll give it to you, *ma fille,* you're sure talented at concealing things from your friends!" She let out a whistle. "Never would've guessed this in a million years!" She raised her hand, laden with a half dozen clanging golden bracelets, and smacked her friend's injured arm, provoking a wail from Hélène.

Sylvie was struggling to force Mathilde's five dozen flowers into a narrow vase. But when she heard the shriek erupting from Hélène's bed, she turned to Mathilde. "*Attention!* You're forgetting she's injured. We're in the hospital because of her accident, remember?" Sylvie sent Hélène a silent kiss of comfort. "But you're right about her talent at concealing things. When I first met Hélène, how could I have guessed she'd turn into such an athlete? And so quickly."

"*Wacht!*" said Mathilde in Flemish, calling a time-out with her hands. "Things are getting hot around here." She wiped the sweat from her neck with a handkerchief. "I need a drink." Reaching over Hélène, she grabbed a plastic goblet from her tray and inserted its straw into her mouth.

While Mathilde was busy slurping, Hélène added, "Believe it or not, it came to me quite naturally."

Mathilde's lips quivered around her straw. "That's what they all say, *ma fille*."

Sylvie observed Hélène's reaction with interest. She looked perplexed.

"*Ah bon?* Could've fooled me. I'm just a beginner." Hélène smiled broadly. "And I got a late start, as you know. But the doctor says I should keep it up. Apparently, it's really healthy. At least for me. She says it makes me more muscular, which—"

"Stop!" Mathilde put her hand up. "Pumpkin, I'm so happy for you. But keep the gory details to yourself, *d'accord*? I'm open-minded and all, but…" Sylvie watched her eyes dart from Hélène to herself. Now, they were lingering on her muscular biceps. Mathilde's voice rose a notch. "Until proven otherwise, I'm still a hard-core, one hundred percent heterosexual woman."

Hélène's eyes bulged. "Mattie, what's wrong with you? I was talking about swimming."

"*Ah bon?*" Mathilde brought her fingers to her lips. "Sorry… It's just that…" She chuckled. Her chuckle was infectious. Sylvie put her hand over her mouth to keep from giggling. "Cecile already filled me in. On *everything*." She touched Hélène's bandaged arm again.

She's more fun than I thought, mused Sylvie, relieved to see that Mathilde touched Hélène's arm very gently and even added a perceptive wink. "Not exactly what I imagined, but hey, why not?" Mathilde smiled. "If you're happy, *ma petite*, I'm happy."

Sylvie felt Mathilde's gaze swim over her shoulders until it landed on her face. She could feel the intensity of her dark eyes caressing her own. *This is awkward. She certainly isn't shy.*

"Hmm." Mathilde licked her generous lips, slowly and deliberately, as if licking a spoonful of honey. "You don't happen to have a studly brother on that Greek island of yours who teaches swimming and might be single, *non?* I wouldn't mind relocating to some exotic…"

Sylvie jumped when a thud from the other side of the bed interrupted Mathilde's discourse.

"*Mon Dieu!*" exclaimed Sylvie when she saw Marc lying on the floor, clutching his stomach. She had been so focused on Hélène and Mathilde that she hadn't even noticed him, and come to think of it, he'd been strangely silent, even though he'd been glaring at everyone. Her ears grew hot with rage as she recalled how badly he had been treating Hélène. *He's probably the reason she had this accident. At last, he's getting what he deserves.* She put her hands on her hips, contemplating her next move. Her job as a swimming instructor was to take on different roles, even challenging ones, swiftly adapting to unanticipated circumstances.

But today, the situation was different. She wasn't in a swimming pool saving some kid from potential harm. She was in the hospital with Hélène and her well-intentioned, seemingly close friends. Marc was the outsider, the person who should've known better. Marc was the one who was making Hélène suffer so much. He had hurt her, and now, *she* could make a difference.

She felt the positive energy flowing from Hélène, Mathilde, Cecile, and herself. Together, their strength, their female power, was exactly what she needed. Her eyes bored into Marc, lying on the floor like a dying dog—mere centimeters from her feet.

"*Nom de Dieu.*" Marc's face was pale; he spoke to Sylvie in a feeble, almost haunted, voice. "You're the swimming instructor. You're the one she's been seeing." He shook his head like a sick cat, his eyes wide. "My wife's been cheating on me with a woman?"

Hélène responded from her hospital bed. "Not cheating. Not exactly…" She looked up at Sylvie, who grinned down at her. Then Sylvie stared back at Marc, who was still clutching his stomach. *He must be finally realizing what a jerk he's been to her all these years. He deserves what he's getting, and it's making him sick. So what if he's in pain? Make him suffer. Make him pay.*

❖

Sylvie flipped her thick hair gingerly, like an actress. Her voice, usually strong and sexy with its slight Greek accent, grew flat. And fake.

"*Ah, bonjour Marc*," she said, shimmying her shoulders. "How's it goin'?" She flashed him a nasty grin. "Aren't these fluorescent lights just the worst? From up here, your face looks surprisingly green."

Hélène watched Sylvie heave her husband by the loops of his pants and escort him out of the room. Marc's obscenities resonated down the hospital corridor until a door slammed. All went quiet until Mathilde launched a loud, one-sided phone conversation with her assistant, who was arranging the interpreter's flight arrangements to Berlin the following morning. Hélène ducked under the covers to block out the noise. Until someone knocked on the door.

Hélène poked her head from the covers and glanced at Mathilde, who was gesticulating wildly and shouting orders into her cell phone.

Hélène sat up in bed. "*Ca va, ma chérie?*" she said. "He didn't try to punch you on the way out, did he?"

Sylvie moved to her bedside and took her hand gently. "*Non, ma chérie.* He's cooling off in the waiting room, but I have a feeling he's going to leave. Are you okay with that?"

Hélène could see the worry in Sylvie's eyes. "More than okay with it. I don't want to see him again if I don't have to." She paused when Sylvie held up a finger and turned to steer Mathilde from the room. With a grin, Cecile gave her a little wave as she followed them into the hall.

Sylvie came back in and took her hand once more. "Sorry, I couldn't hear you over that racket. Go on."

Hélène continued before she lost her nerve. "He was different when we got married. Now…it doesn't matter." She raised Sylvie's hand and kissed her knuckles. "I love you. And I want to be with you." A flutter of fear made her freeze. "Is that what you want?"

Sylvie leaned down and kissed her gently, sweetly. "I couldn't want anything more."

CHAPTER NINETEEN

Hélène and Sylvie left the hospital loaded with get-well gifts: huge bouquets of flowers and sumptuous Belgian chocolates. While waiting for their taxi, Hélène glanced at the late-afternoon sun and its reflection bouncing off the puddles at their feet. Instantly, a new poem emerged:

The pale sun melted, slathering its surface over the clouds, like lemon yellow frosting. Feeling like a blossoming flower, she looked at Sylvie. *I think I've found my muse.*

Once their taxi arrived at the scene of the accident, Sylvie went straight to Hélène's mangled bike. "Pretty sure we can salvage it."

Hélène rolled down her window. "Just leave it. It brought me bad luck."

"*Mais non,*" replied Sylvie, shaking her head. "Without that bike, you wouldn't have had the accident. And if you hadn't had the accident, I wouldn't have performed mouth-to-mouth—"

"*D'accord,* you win." Hélène licked her lips, recalling the moment she'd woken to find Sylvie's mouth on hers. The taxi driver made an indiscreet "humph" noise, but both women ignored him.

Sylvie tossed the bike in her car. "I'll get it fixed in no time."

Once the taxi was gone, Hélène caressed Sylvie's muscular forearm. "*Eh bien,* aren't you just the…" She gave Sylvie's bicep a slight pinch. "Butchiest little thing. And so *sexy.*"

"I resent that." Smirking, Sylvie flexed her muscle. "I'm not *little.*"

Hélène caught her breath as the bicep hardened in her hand. "*Ah non?* You're amazing!"

"Talking about sexy..." whispered Sylvie in low, raspy voice. Leaning against her yellow VW Bug, she pulled Hélène close and pressed her moist lips to Hélène's. At last, their mouths merged for an unforgettable, passionate kiss.

Consumed by desire, Hélène became oblivious to everything else, including vehicles whizzing by. For icing on the cake, another rainbow materialized; Hélène watched as its brilliant arc caressed Sylvie's face with multicolored prisms.

Soon, however, a car in the roundabout honked at the couple. Then a few more cars honked.

"Humph!" exclaimed Sylvie. "We get the message, you jerks. Some things are better in private anyway." Reluctantly, she detached her body from Hélène's—but not for long. As soon as they entered her car, she pulled Hélène close.

Sylvie's lips were trembling. The color had drained from her cheeks, and she was gazing at the rainbow, which was now disintegrating.

What's wrong? Before Hélène could ask, Sylvie's lips parted, and her soft voice seeped out. "Thank you, Yaya. You were right, as always."

Hélène was more confused than ever. She stared at Sylvie's features—usually so fresh, prominent, and bold. They now seemed so pale. The goddess from within, instead of radiating energy and beauty, seemed to have cracked the stalwart Greek statue that Hélène so admired. Hélène's eyes caressed traces of sadness on Sylvie's motionless face. *We're together. Why is she acting like the world's ending? Is she having second thoughts?*

Unable to stand it any longer, Hélène blurted, "What's this all about?"

Sylvie drew in a deep breath. "I'll explain in a minute. Just hold this for me, *d'accord*?" She handed Hélène the keychain and bent down to search the floorboard.

As Hélène fondled the silver fish, she whispered, "You know, if it weren't for this little sliver of metal here, I probably wouldn't be here with you right now. I love this beat-up, yellow VW Bug that won't start without a screwdriver. Just like I—"

"*Je sais.* It's really special." Sylvie sat up and wiggled the yellow tool. "Just like my keychain. I'll never let it out of my sight again." She took the silver keychain from Hélène and held its shiny, worn surface to her cheek. "It's the only thing I have left…"

Sylvie's voice cracked, and tears cascaded down her cheeks. Hélène took her hand and kissed her softly.

"Hey, *ça va*," she whispered gently into Sylvie's ear. "That's not the only thing you've got." She peered into Sylvie's eyes. "Now you've got me."

Sylvie sniffled like a small child as Hélène brushed her tears away.

"I know," she began. "It's just that…*Enfin*…" She took a deep breath. "It's all I have left to remind me of my grandparents."

Hélène blinked.

"She…She…" Sylvie burst into tears again. "You know." Her dark eyes scanned the wet road outside.

Hélène felt her chest tighten. She placed her uninjured arm around Sylvie's neck and peered into her glistening eyes. Usually so fresh and inviting, they were now red and swollen. *She does look tired. Exhausted even. And thinner.* Ever so gently, she asked, "She what?"

"She died on Wednesday."

"I'm *so* sorry!" Hélène felt terrible that Sylvie had been suffering such a loss, and she hadn't even known about it. "But why on earth didn't you tell me?"

Then another thought occurred to her. She couldn't contain it even though it was selfish. "Does this mean you have to go to Greece?"

Sylvie frowned. "Why would I go again? I just got back last night."

"*Quoi?* You went to Greece?"

The pain in Sylvie's expression put a dent in Hélène's heart. Sylvie narrowed her eyes. "I explained it all on the phone, remember? About Yaya being sick, about how I had to go to Greece to—"

Hélène's face turned crimson. "How could I have been so...
stupide?" She hit her fist on the dashboard.

"What do you mean?"

Hélène gave a little cough. "I thought you were..." Her voice
trailed off.

"You thought I was what?" prodded Sylvie, lifting an eyebrow.

"This is embarrassing. I thought you were moving in with
that..." Hélène made a face. "That..." She shook her head to force
the words out. "That Greek woman."

"What Greek woman?"

At Sylvie's obvious confusion, Hélène lost control. The words
spilled out of her mouth like salt from a broken shaker. "The *one*
you were with that day when you left the Greek restaurant. The *one*
in your apartment late at night, eating fruit salad with you. Feeding
you cherries. *My* cherries. The *one* plastered all over your fridge,
who you're hugging so tightly in that stupid, skimpy bathing suit.
The *one* who took Goldie. The *one* who drives a fancy car—"

"Shh..." Sylvie brought her finger to her lips. "*Calme-toi, ma
chérie.* You're worrying me. And you're talking about my cousin,
Aphrodite. Not a girlfriend. Family."

"I'm worrying *you?*" Hélène spat. "It's *me* who should be
worried. You know exactly who I'm talking about! You spend enough
time with her and—" Hélène stopped as Sylvie's words finally
penetrated her cloak of anxiety. *Cousin. Did she just say cousin?*
Holy shit. "*C'est juste que...*I'm not sure how to tell you this, *mais
je suis vraiment désolée.* I didn't listen to all your messages."

Sylvie's dark eyes widened. "You didn't? Which ones didn't
you get?"

"*Eh bien...*" Hélène looked down at her knees. "Um...All of
them. I really blew it. I sort of lost my head that night I came to your
place for dinner and later, I saw you with someone else. It made me
crazy."

"Who did you think I was with?" Sylvie lifted an eyebrow.
"Never mind."

Hélène couldn't tell if Sylvie was angry or just making fun of
her. "I got jealous. I thought you were seeing someone else, and even

though I didn't have any right, I couldn't help myself. So…I erased them. *Quelle idiote!*" She smacked her forehead, then squealed in pain.

Sylvie grabbed Hélène's sling. "*Arrête!* You're so hardheaded, you'll break your arm." Their sudden burst of laughter lightened the mood in the car. Then Sylvie whispered, "So, all this time, you had no idea I was in Greece? Where did you think I was?"

Hélène averted her eyes sheepishly. "Moving in with someone."

"*M'enfin,* Hélène. I know you're a poet, but your imagination's gone way too far. *Alors…*" Sylvie rubbed her hands together in anticipation. "You thought I was shacking up with Aphrodite!"

Hélène stammered, "I…I saw you with a young, dark, sexy Greek woman. You left the Greek restaurant with her last Saturday, and she was at your apartment on Sunday night." She looked straight at Sylvie. "I saw you. She was feeding you cherries. You were hugging and kissing her. She took Goldie. She certainly didn't look like family." She grabbed the door handle.

With an amused look, Sylvie pointed at Hélène's nose. "Didn't anyone ever teach you not to spy on folks?"

"I wasn't spying on you, I swear. It was just a coincidence." Hélène released her grip on the handle. *All I want right now is to disappear.* She squeezed her eyes in a vain effort to fight off an onslaught of tears.

Sylvie cupped her face and gave her a long, slow kiss.

Despite the intense pleasure she was feeling, Hélène tried to remain lucid—and keep the bandage on her forehead intact. "*C'est pas vrai,*" she sputtered, pulling away. "Her name's really Aphrodite?"

Sylvie's moist, full lips formed a dazzling smile. "Sure is."

"And you swear she's your cousin?"

"I swear." Sylvie pulled out her Greek keychain. "I swear over my grandma's—"

But before she could finish, Hélène lunged forward, silencing Sylvie's lips with her own. Then she abruptly pulled back. "First cousin?"

"*Oui, Madame.* She's my first cousin and my closest friend."

Sylvie traced the contour of Hélène's breasts with her keychain. "I swear."

Hélène shuddered at the cool metal sliding over her breasts. *What a waste*, she thought. *Why haven't I been living? Truly living? I've been dead to the touch. And wasting time thinking Sylvie was with someone else.* Her mind zoomed in on the intense sensations she was feeling. The tender skin of her breasts—like the underbelly of a bottom fish—had scarcely been touched, let alone caressed, for decades.

Tears of relief were streaming down Hélène's face as she passionately kissed Sylvie back. She was floating in a world lighter than dreams, with no past or future—only this present, blissful moment. They remained in their intimate bubble until the car windows fully fogged, the rainbow dissolved, and darkness draped over them like a shroud.

Sylvie pulled away. "My stomach's rumbling." She cracked a smile. "You should be resting that banged-up head of yours, and we haven't eaten all day."

Hélène stared at Sylvie's dimples in the darkness. *So sexy.* She nodded. "How could we?"

"*C'est vrai.*" Sylvie caressed Hélène's sling. "With one exciting event after the other…Unforgettable." She placed her hand gently over Hélène's.

"Speaking of unforgettable, I almost forgot to tell you…I think I have a brother. And I think you know him." Hélène smiled sheepishly. "I'm not really sure yet. Maybe you can help me figure it out."

Sylvie's pupils widened. "You *think* you have a brother? That's amazing. I can't wait to hear about this. But first, *chérie*, I'm about to pass out from hunger. Can you tell me about it over dinner?"

Dinner. Hunger. Frank. Dinner… Thoughts of an empty refrigerator popped into Hélène's head. *What am I doing? It's already dark, and I haven't prepared Marc's dinner.* She ignored the bandage sticking to her forehead. *I didn't do the shopping, and he'll be wondering where…* Then reality hit. *My marriage is over.*

I don't have to go back. I'm free... Hélène's soul was glowing. Not only was she safe from Marc's terrible tantrums, she could be with Sylvie, the love of her life, every day, from now on. Her cheeks grew flushed with heat. They would start their new life tonight with an intimate dinner, then they would kiss, then they would...

"*Ca va?*" asked Sylvie.

"Must be the shock." Hélène traced the bandage on her forehead. She might be wounded on the outside, but inside, her heart was bursting with joy. "After the accident."

"*Je suis désolée*, Hélène. Of course, you're in shock. And all I can think of is my stomach. I'm so—"

"How about your place?" interrupted Hélène, realizing that she was trembling with desire to get to know Sylvie—all of Sylvie—every way possible. Starting with this very minute.

"Sounds good." Sylvie licked her lips.

Then Hélène recalled her lack of culinary skills. "Wait. Got any food in your fridge?"

Sylvie's dimples resurfaced. "Not really, unless you consider cereal—"

"Chinese take-out would be great. My treat. Since you saved my life and all."

"*D'accord.*" Sylvie grabbed her screwdriver. "But why Chinese? What's wrong with Greek?" Just then, an orange cat sprang over a puddle in front of the car. Its bushy tail disappeared into the bushes.

At the same time, they faced each other and shrieked, "The cats!"

"They must be starving," said Sylvie, gunning the engine. The old yellow VW Bug raced through the slick streets of Brussels.

As they headed to Sylvie's place, Hélène asked, "Can we see if Marc's car is at the house? If it isn't, I can get Chausette and bring her to your apartment. *Ca va?*" Hélène couldn't imagine leaving her furry little *bébé* alone with Marc, who had despised the kitty even before he'd found out his wife was leaving him for a woman.

Sylvie turned the car toward Hélène's. "*Bien sûr.* Tell me where the cat carrier is, and I'll go get it." When Hélène started to protest, Sylvie shook her head. "*Non*. You shouldn't be moving around right now, and I can go faster."

Hélène gave in and told her where the carrier was. When they pulled up, the house was dark, and Marc's car wasn't there. Sylvie took Hélène's keys and was back with Chaussette within ten minutes. The whole time she was gone Hélène felt as if she couldn't breathe, but the moment she returned and they left for Sylvie's, a feeling of relief swept over her. Mingled with this relief was a strong feeling of rightness. Beaming inwardly, she kept her hand on Sylvie's hard thigh muscle as she drove; she knew her life was finally headed in the right direction.

CHAPTER TWENTY

A month later, a shrill cry filled the air. Immediately, Sylvie leapt from the sofa. Grabbing her shrieking kettle, she poured its contents into a plump yellow teapot.

Hélène wandered in, cradling Goldie in her arms. She was feeling more relaxed than she had in years, except for one practical issue. She looked at Sylvie. "I can't get her to stop meowing."

Sylvie kissed Goldie's head. "*Bien sûr*, it's four o'clock."

"*Ah*, that's funny. She can tell time?"

"When it's mealtime. And four o'clock, *bien sûr*, is tea time."

Hélène shook her head. "You've got to be kidding."

"Absolutely not. Seven o'clock is breakfast, one o'clock is lunch, four o'clock is tea time, and—"

"What happens if you're not here?"

"She meows until I get home and feed her." Sylvie rubbed Goldie's chin. "*N'est-ce pas*, my spoiled little princess?" The kitty purred loudly.

"She's got you wrapped around her little paw." Hélène shook her head. "What if she wants you to read her a bedtime story?"

"You'll have to stick around more to find out." Sylvie swept a lock of hair from Hélène's eyes. Then she leaned in and nibbled Hélène's ear.

"*D'accord*," agreed Hélène, feeling the heat. "If you keep this up, my glasses will fog up again." Discreetly, she peeked at the photos on Sylvie's fridge. For the hundredth time, she stared at the one featuring Sylvie and Aphrodite on a secluded Greek island.

They were both so tan, they looked more Indian than Greek. And Sylvie was so attractive in her bikini—with her smooth stomach and wild, wind-blown hair—smiling eagerly while posing with Aphrodite. *They seem so intimate.*

"How long are you going to stare at it this time?" tittered Sylvie, pulling away.

Hélène frowned. "About ten years. Maybe more."

"What's so intriguing? I already told you, she's my cousin… Ahem. My *first* cousin."

"*Je sais.* It's just that…You're so different now," replied Hélène, cuddling Goldie.

"*Merci.* I'll take that as a compliment." Sylvie laced her strong arms around her waist.

"Of course it is." Hélène set Goldie down. "It's just that…" She raked her fingers through Sylvie's luscious, dark hair. "You look so young in the picture."

"*M'enfin,* I *was* young!" Sylvie gave Hélène's hips a squeeze.

"Speaking of young, we should invite your cousin too."

"Excellent idea. I already did," replied Sylvie, fishing the tea bag from the bottom of the pot. "*En fait*, they're both coming."

Hélène's eyebrows shot up. She stammered, "What do you mean? You've got another cousin?"

"*Bien sûr!* Loads of them. But they're all in Santorini, except for two."

Hélène paled. She focused on the liquid oozing out of the used tea bag. "Is your other cousin as gorgeous as Aphrodite?"

"*Ouais.* Just hairier." Sylvie dropped the tea bag on a yellow plate. "Remember Vassilios, the waiter? He took our picture when I took you to—"

"*Je me rappelle,*" Hélène interrupted. *How could I forget?*

"*Eh bien*, Vassilios happens to be Aphrodite's brother, and since we're having the party at his restaurant, he'll be there."

Hélène flushed. *I'm such an idiot. I wonder if I'll ever be less insecure or jealous.* She ripped open a package of whole-wheat biscuits. "*Ma chérie*, we'd better speed up with these Greek lessons.

I don't get half of what's going on around here!" She popped a biscuit into her mouth.

❖

Under a string of rainbow-colored paper lanterns, a lively crowd inhabited Dionysos Taverna's quaint garden. By ten o'clock, a constant buzz of French and Greek—peppered with back-slapping, gusty laughs, and cocktail clinking—poured out of the garden's brick walls and into the night air. The Saturday-night party guests were having a marvelous time. Animated couples danced in circles to loud Greek music. Others devoured plates of homemade Greek delicacies and guzzled ouzo cocktails concocted by Vassilios, which were so strong, Hélène was sure a single drop could bore a hole in the grass.

Every few minutes, Hélène jumped at the unexpected crash of plates soaring to the ground. *For good luck*, Hélène quickly learned, cringing each time a pile shattered at her feet. But it made the party all that more exciting—and so very Greek. Halfway through the night, Sylvie led Hélène mid-garden for her private Syrtaki lessons. Sylvie clearly tried to focus purely on dance moves; instead, her eyes remained glued to Hélène's low-cut blouse and tight black pants. Hélène had worn her most attractive outfit tonight to reveal her new, slim figure after months of nutritious eating and daily workouts with Sylvie.

Fully aware that Sylvie's eyes were on her, Hélène drank up the attention. In fact, after several celebratory cocktails, she forgot all about her arm sling. She kicked her legs and slapped her thighs so fast, Sylvie struggled to keep up with her.

Hélène laughed freely. The feeling of loneliness she'd been living with for so many years was completely gone. She was a new woman, with an entirely fresh view of the future. Instead of berating herself for wasting so much time in her old life, in her unhappy marriage with Marc, she planned to make every moment count. A huge burden had been lifted from her; she now saw positive choices in how she wanted to lead her life. She squealed like a teenager as she watched her best friends, Cecile and Mathilde, tear up the dance floor. As usual, Mathilde had jetlag. In the past two weeks, she had flown back and forth to Tokyo, Milan, Buenos Aires, Rio, and Manila. Not surprisingly, an exotic mélange of foreign words streamed from her mouth as she performed the samba and bump-and-grind with Cecile.

Hélène took in this blissful moment. *Every moment is precious, starting right now.* The lightness she felt now that she was with Sylvie propelled her forward, lifting her off her feet, as she partied with her friends. She was happy that people were watching her—seeing her—for once. She finally accepted herself, and that was a huge blessing.

The festivities went on all night. In the early-morning hours, once all the guests had left, Vassilios opened the door and Sylvie, Hélène, Paul, Ramon, Jimmy, Mathilde, and Cecile stumbled onto the sidewalk. After partying all night, they hardly noticed the sun rising behind the restaurant.

"Anyone see Aphrodite?" asked Sylvie casually.

Vassilios nodded. "After spending all evening watching all of you…straight, gay, lesbian, whatever…madly in love, she decided to improve her chances." He grazed his fingers through his wavy hair. "She went upstairs to get her beauty sleep."

Hélène frowned. *"Quoi?* If that girl gets one more milligram of beauty, she'll—"

"Shh, *chérie*, she can hear you," whispered Sylvie, pointing at the window above them. "Tell her good-bye for us, Vassili, and thanks again for everything." Leaning over the massive basket of homemade Greek food he had thrust into her hands, she kissed her cousin's cheek. Then she added in Greek, "We had an incredible time," and Hélène nodded, repeating in Greek, "Yes, Vassili, we had an incredible time," and kissed his prickly cheek.

"Welcome to the family, Hélène!" He kissed her three times before pulling her into a bear hug, flattening the bouquet perched between her breasts.

"Regardez. Pressed flowers!" blurted Hélène with a snort.

Then her attention turned to Ramon, who had moved next to Vassilios and proclaimed, "Next in line..." But as soon as he pressed his face against the waiter's, he shrieked, "*Aiie!*" His fingers flew to his cheek. "That's some serious stubble you're sproutin'," he blurted, looking at Paul's peach-fuzz face.

"Can't help it. I'm Greek. And so's Sylvie, so you'd better watch out, Hélène." Vassilios chuckled. "Stubble runs in the family."

"You're such a jerk sometimes." Sylvie elbowed her cousin in the ribs.

"I'll just avoid the danger zone," announced Ramon, smacking Vassilios on the lips.

"What the?" blurted the waiter, pushing Ramon away with a scowl. "*Eeew.*"

"Just protecting my tender skin," said Ramon with his adorable Spanish accent. "And guess what, *mon pote?* Your thick, perfectly molded Greek lips are as soft as a baby's—"

"That's enough, Ramon." Paul positioned his wheelchair between his lover and Vassilios. "*Désolé.*" He extended his hand.

"No problem." Vassilios grinned broadly.

Next, Mathilde and Cecile gave everyone plenty of kisses before heading down the street, arm in arm, and singing some indistinguishable song.

Holding Sylvie's hand, Hélène watched them go and felt deep gratitude for the gift of friendship and love in her life.

Then she felt a light tug from Sylvie.

"Shall we go?" Sylvie flashed her an expectant, almost urgent look. The connection between them was sizzling.

Hélène felt the heat rush to her cheeks. It felt good to be wanted, to be loved, by her. She was the Greek goddess she had met at the market. The woman she had taken private swimming lessons with each morning in the pool. The person she most admired in this world. *Sylvie.* And she was going to spend the rest of her life with her. Starting now.

Hélène turned toward Sylvie and gave her a soft kiss on the cheek. Her skin, soft as silk, smelled as sweet as honeysuckle in spring.

"Let's go," she replied, gazing into Sylvie's eyes. "I can't wait another minute to be alone with you at last."

Sylvie wrapped her strong arms around Hélène and whisked her down the sidewalk. As Hélène's feet fell in step with Sylvie's, she thought about what lay ahead for the two of them. *We're a couple now. A real couple.* A shiver ran down her spine. She couldn't keep herself from beaming at how happy she was right now.

But what if it's just another daydream?

To make sure it wasn't, she pinched her own arm. *Ouch!* The tender skin confirmed that, for once, she wasn't in one of her habitual daydreams. This time, she would no longer wake up and realize she had escaped reality. *This is the real thing, so I'd better make the best of it.*

Sylvie seemed to know what she was thinking. Hélène loved how she graciously held the passenger door open for her. *She treats me like a queen.* And how she swept her in her muscular arms to take her to her bedroom. She could hardly breathe when Sylvie finally touched her with her lips. She started kissing her, softly and tenderly. Hélène returned her kiss, feeling a jolt of electricity pass between them. She loved how Sylvie's firm body felt on hers. As they lay on Sylvie's spacious bed, their tongues mingled. Hélène felt chills all over her body. The feelings intensified when Sylvie began kissing her cheeks, then she brought her soft lips to her ear.

"*Je t'aime*, Hélène," she whispered.

Sylvie's warm breath on her ear made Hélène shudder. But the words in her native tongue, pronounced with Sylvie's sexy Greek accent, excited her even more. The meaning of this intimate message went deeper than she could've ever imagined. The delicate skin on her neck was tingling as she took it all in.

She loves me.

Hélène cupped Sylvie's face and peered into her dark eyes. They were glowing with the heat of passion. *I love you too.*

"*Je t'aime*, Sylvie." As if to seal their promise of eternal love, Hélène planted a deep kiss on Sylvie's beautifully carved lips. *She's my lover. We'll be together forever.* It felt as if they were living out a fairy tale. She was the sleeping princess, and all she'd needed was Sylvie's honeyed touch to awaken her. Hélène's new life was waiting for her—for them. They were a couple now. She couldn't imagine living any other way. She felt such a strong bond with Sylvie, she wanted to purr like a blissful cat.

"I'm so much happier with you in my life, *ma chérie*."

Sylvie hugged her tightly to her bare chest. "Me too. I don't know how I managed without you all these years. I'm so glad we found each other, at last."

Hélène felt chills running down her body as she stroked her shoulder, and then her breasts, which led to more stroking and kissing. With each strategic move under the rumpled bed covers, they felt a deepening of their passion for each other. And as their passion reached ecstasy, they seemed to be joined as one. Then they fell silent in a moment of peace and satisfaction. Full of gratitude. Hélène was a poet, but she was at a loss for words. For words could never capture the sweetness of their embrace, nor the love and passion they felt for each other at that very moment.

CHAPTER TWENTY-ONE

Hélène sniffed at the exquisite aroma emanating from her basket of Greek delicacies. Every few steps, she dipped her nose into one of the cellophane-wrapped packages. This triggered a rush of pleasure that traveled from her nostrils to her stomach to her good arm, which was wrapped snugly around Sylvie's waist. They had just come from another scrumptious dinner at Dionysos Taverna. Vassilios had spoiled them rotten, once again. He had sent them each home with a huge basket of goodies.

Now that she was living with Sylvie, he seemed to be doing everything possible to help her feel more comfortable with Greek culture, starting with his taverna's delicious, yet nutritious, cuisine. She nearly skipped over the cobblestones, she was so delighted at how things had changed in the past few weeks for her and Sylvie. She was touched by how Vassilios and Aphrodite were making tremendous efforts to make her feel at home in the Greek community. *Of course, they know they're making Sylvie happy too. After all these years, they've figured out the best way to her heart is through her stomach. And mine too.*

To relish the cool, refreshing air, Hélène leaned into Sylvie. Now that they were a couple, she loved walking together through the streets of Brussels at this time of night. She felt so safe with her. They were laughing at their dancing shadows on the sidewalk, when suddenly, Hélène looked up and saw a dark, hunched silhouette.

"Look who's here," Sylvie whispered, grinning as they approached the man cradling a bottle between his knees.

"*Bonjour Frank, comment ça va?*" Sylvie reached out to shake the man's hand.

Frank slowly lifted his head. "Okay, I guess," he answered groggily.

"This is for you." Sylvie handed the man without a home her savory basket of Greek leftovers.

Hélène snuggled into Sylvie's strong arm around her shoulders. She still experienced dizzy spells after her concussion, and celebrating like they had just done at Dionysos Taverna, with carafes of retsina, made her weak in the knees. As she observed Frank's expression of surprise, a bitter taste filled her mouth. The bitter taste of guilt. *What if he was my brother? Why haven't I done anything about this?* She wished she'd tried to contact him ever since she learned from Hilde that she had a brother living in Brussels who was homeless. But she had been so caught up with Sylvie, trying to find her, then getting hit by a car, etc., she had pushed the idea out of her mind. She gulped nervously.

"They're a little squished, but *voilà*," she said, handing Frank her bouquet. She had picked it up at the market earlier that day before going to the taverna. The deep lines on Frank's face softened as he grasped the tender green stems.

Hélène tried not to look at his long, soiled fingernails. She wanted to warm up to him, to let him know that she cared about him. She'd always wanted an older brother, and now she knew she had one. Even if it wasn't him, and even if he wasn't exactly how she had hoped so long ago, when she was a kid playing with her dolls and wishing she had a brother. She had always had a vivid imagination, ever since she was a toddler. She smiled at Frank, half hoping that he was her sibling. *I won't be alone anymore. He will be part of our family.*

She turned to Sylvie, who was still smiling at Frank. They exchanged a knowing look, since she had told Sylvie about the psychic and her long-lost brother. To her horror, despite her good intentions, her mind started cranking out a new poem: *Encrusted with dirt, blended with oily scalp secretions, the homeless man's nails trapped...*

Then the unexpected occurred. Hélène's eyes moistened. Instead of disgust, a sensation of warmth spread through her body. This warmth emanated from an intense feeling embedded in her chest, which was now ready to blossom—compassion. She remembered how Frank had brought her home that evening on her bike. She had been in a sorry state, plastered with endless beers, belting out off-key, meaningless songs. Yet even though he had nowhere to live himself, he had shown compassion for her—a complete stranger—gently guiding her through the streets. And Marc had slammed the door in his face as if he were a monster. *La honte.* She cringed with embarrassment. Then she looked at him again, peering deep into his eyes. Now, they were soft and compassionate—like puppy eyes.

Hélène had another troubling thought, which made her feel even more guilty. *Does he know I might be his sister? Has he been trying to protect me all along?* Hilde had said she was supposed to protect her older brother, but maybe it was the other way around. *Psychics can make mistakes, can't they?* She looked at Frank, then at Sylvie. They seemed to be getting on fine, but she was utterly confused. Her disadvantage was that she had been raised in a matter-of-fact manner, where respect was granted to individuals utilizing logical thinking processes. Her mother had raised her to be pragmatic, reasonable—a straightforward thinker. Quite logically, she had learned to fully develop the left side of her brain, governing languages, mathematics, and science. Creativity, on the contrary, was a right-brain domain, regarded as an exception rather than the rule. Like dessert after a tedious, flavorless meal.

This is why when flowery poems about nature's effervescence first erupted in Hélène's adolescent mind, she wondered if something was wrong with her. It all seemed so foreign. But in the end, she realized she didn't care. Years later, her respectable, yet boring, scientific translation work provided a steady income while her poems, sprouting like seasonal mushrooms, evolved into a clandestine pastime.

Throughout Hélène's forty years, during a constant struggle between logic versus creativity, not once had she contemplated the significance of compassion. She had felt it instinctively when she cared for plants and animals, but for humans, it simply had never occurred to her—until she met Sylvie. Up to then, she would give a few coins to people living in the street, like Frank, without lingering to see if her meager generosity made a difference. And touching them was unthinkable.

Hélène peered at Frank through tender eyes as he dipped his nose into her flowers. Sure, she had cared, but not enough to make a difference—in his life or hers. As she realized her error, her head began spinning. *Must have had too much retsina.* She took a step back as a powerful, soothing voice claimed her thoughts:

Material gifts are like plastic. They cannot last. They yellow, they tarnish, they crack. They are neither resistant nor permanent. They touch the surface of things but fail to dig deep into the meat of the matter.

Material things are like Band-Aids plastered on a wound: convenient but temporary. They patch our hurts, help us heal, fulfill our needs for a limited time, but they never reach the source of injury.

Time seemed to stop. Leaning on Sylvie, she shut her eyes. *Where did those words come from?* All her life, Hélène had been taught to avoid people like Frank. The marginal ones were the ones who—either by choice or circumstance—ended up on the sidelines. These people lurked on dirty streets, their odors offended civilized people's nostrils, and their presence represented all that was unknown, thus scary. Like most Belgians she knew, she had been taught to play it safe in life. She shook her head. *I was so wrong.* When she opened her eyes, the real message hit her. *I'm marginal too.* But instead of worrying about other people's reactions, Hélène simply squeezed Sylvie's arm with a silly grin. Since her mother's passing, she finally felt safe with someone. It was time to begin life all over again. And perhaps Frank would be part of their lives as well. Especially if he was her brother.

As if watching a movie, Hélène studied Sylvie's strong features as she explained each Greek delicacy to Frank before he popped them into his mouth. *I'm fulfilled at last,* she realized. *Emotionally, intellectually, physically, spiritually. Completely fulfilled. I don't* need material things to make me happy. I'm not lonely anymore. I've finally found myself, and that's enough. And the person I love: Sylvie. Along with Chaussette, and Frank... With this realization, Hélène's dizziness evaporated. Her feet become heavier. Her toes seemed to spread in her shoes as her legs bore down on the sidewalk. She had never felt more grounded, more firmly rooted to the earth, and more invigorated. She relaxed as the early-morning breeze caressed her face.

She closed her eyes again to savor the warmth of Sylvie's body pressed close to hers. Here was a woman whose athletic—yet feminine—body was stronger and sturdier than most men's. Especially on the inside. A tingle of anticipation ran up Hélène's spine.

"Frank, would you like to have breakfast with us?" She wasn't sure what else to say, but if being with Sylvie had taught her anything, it was that sharing food with people you cared for opened the door to their hearts.

Frank nodded, his gaze shifting between the two of them as he stood, as though he wasn't sure what the catch might be.

They stood before Café Hom@lone, scrutinizing an oversized, rainbow-colored poster. Hélène tried to hide her embarrassment at the illustration of two erect croissants shooting butter out their tips. She glanced at Sylvie, then at Frank. He was staring at the drawing, which had a yellow liquid oozing from a phallic honey bottle into a hefty mug. Hélène shifted her feet nervously on the cobblestones. The mug was in the form of a muscular, naked man. She read the words printed on the poster: *Café Hom@lone's early-bird special: two crispy croissants bursting with butter, high-powered honey, and an exploding espresso for only €3.30.*

She turned to Frank. "What do you think? It's the only café around serving breakfast this early."

The corners of his eyes crinkled as his lips formed a slow smile. "Why not?"

"*Super*. Let's go." Sylvie opened the door for Frank, then took Hélène's hand and whisked her inside. "My treat." As soon as they were settled in a booth and had ordered three early-bird specials,

Hélène knew she should be the first to speak. But she didn't know what to say. *This is awkward. I'm not used to having meals with homeless people. How should I begin?* She cast a sideways glance at Sylvie, who was sitting beside her.

As if Sylvie could read her mind, she put her arm around Hélène and smiled at Frank. Her voice was gentle and soothing, as if she were speaking to a child who had just fallen and skinned his knee. "We wanted to invite you to breakfast to get to know you a bit better."

Frank looked briefly into her eyes before glancing away. He shifted in his seat.

He's more nervous than I am, thought Hélène, watching him fiddle with his napkin. *He probably isn't invited out for meals very often. Especially by lesbian couples.* Yet he seemed like a nice guy. A genuine guy. She dared a peek in his direction again. Those eyes. They seemed as if they could go on forever, as if connected to a limitless shoreline of fine sand. Despite the rugged wrinkles on his sunbaked skin, she noticed a concealed tenderness and purity—a rare deepness—connecting his soul to all of humanity and to her. This gave her a warm sensation. *He's my brother.* At that very moment, she knew. She felt tingles all over her body. *We're of the same blood. He's my family.* She looked at Sylvie and her gorgeous Greek face. *And she's my family.*

With this realization, Hélène relaxed. She knew somehow that everything would be right again. She wasn't going to have to live a life of loneliness or denial like she had been enduring with Marc for so many years. She exhaled, leaning her neck into Sylvie's arm, which was still around her shoulder. She loved how she felt so protected and safe. And how she adored the sweet smell of Sylvie's skin. Even in this popular café, which still presented lingering odors from last night's celebrations—beer, disinfectant, fries, and day-old smoke—she could smell hints of peaches on Sylvie's skin and honeydew shampoo in her hair.

Frank, however, carried a persisting odor that came from living in the streets—indescribable. *I can't let that ruin this blissful moment.* Making a conscious effort to concentrate on all the positive things surrounding her, Hélène mentally shut off her olfactory functions as the three of them polished off their buttery croissants and "exploding espressos." She leaned back, relieved to see Frank enjoying his breakfast. Without even asking, Sylvie promptly ordered him two more croissants.

As Frank ate in silence, Hélène toyed with the tiny pastry flakes and unsalted butter lingering on her plate. *I've got to ask him. But how?* She hated how she was fidgeting with her food. Her nervousness had returned. Or was it sadness? As the three of them sat together in their booth, she noticed his gnarled knuckles around his tiny espresso cup. Did he have the same knuckles as Papa? She couldn't remember her father at all; she had been too young. Yet somehow, she had the feeling that Frank's soul seemed tortured. Perhaps it wasn't now but in the past. Her heart sank. *What happened to him? How did he become homeless?* She wanted to ask him these questions but couldn't find the right words. The last thing she wanted was for him to run away. She wanted to keep him in her life now that she had found him again.

Sylvie seemed to notice Hélène's agitation. She spoke gently and looked Frank straight in the eyes. "We want to get to know you better because we think you might be related to Hélène. Do you happen to know a woman named Hilde? She's a psychic."

Hélène watched Frank's Adam's apple rise and fall as he gulped. His eyes registered surprise. "I don't know any Hilde or any psychic," he said gruffly, shaking his head. A wave of disappointment, as chilling as ice water, washed over Hélène. She had had her hopes up, but now they were crushed. She looked at Sylvie dejectedly.

Sylvie squeezed her hand to comfort her.

Then Frank continued. "But I do know who Hélène is." He looked straight at her and smiled with genuine kindness.

To Hélène, it seemed like ages before he formed the words she would never forget. Despite his gruff exterior, his tone sounded so gentle, like soft butter.

"You're my little sister."

Hélène felt her cheeks flush. She looked at Sylvie, who beamed at her with her gorgeous dimples, then back to Frank. His cracked lips spread into an even wider grin. She couldn't help noticing that his teeth were irregular and discolored, and some were missing, but his delight at having her for a sister shone through. Her heart leapt with excitement.

"*Comment?*" she asked, stammering. "How…how do you know this?"

Frank seemed to find his words all of a sudden. Before, they had come out slowly, almost staggering. But now, they tumbled off his lips. With a renewed sense of eagerness, he explained that he had always known he had a sister. He had been two years old when their father had taken him away from her and their maman, never to return. Hélène had probably been too young to remember him, but he remembered her. He had lived with their father on a remote island, and for years, they hadn't returned to Belgium. Their papa had never wanted to give him the address where they had lived. After they had left Brussels, their papa had always been very bitter about their maman and never wanted to talk about her or his little sister.

When Frank had finally moved back to Brussels a few years before, he didn't know where his maman and Hélène were living, but he did all he could to find them. When he learned that their maman had passed away, he had been very sad. He had wished he could have come back sooner to be reunited with her and Hélène before she died. Once he finally located Hélène, he had observed her from a distance. He didn't like how Marc had treated her. He realized how Marc was a terrible person—very self-absorbed and abusive toward Hélène and everyone else he encountered. Frank had seen them often at the market on Saturdays. He kept at a distance, but even from afar, he could see how unhappy his sister was. It made him feel so bad. He wanted to help her, protect her…keep Marc away from her.

To his relief, when Hélène met Sylvie and started swimming lessons at the pool and biking to work, she seemed much happier. Then Frank had wanted to tell Hélène that he was her brother, but he was too embarrassed. These past few years—ever since he moved back to Belgium—had been hard on him. His wife had divorced him, and he had lost custody of their two kids. It was all because of his drinking problem. He couldn't keep a job, and due to mounting debts, he finally ended up on the streets. He knew he could never tell Hélène about his situation. He could hardly face himself. And for all he knew, she hadn't even known she had an older brother. He stewed about all these things as he wandered the streets. If she ever found out, how would she take the news? How would she treat him? He was homeless, penniless, and grimy. He rarely had a chance to bathe.

Even though he smelled like rubbish, he knew Sylvie would be wonderful and accepting. She always was. But his sister? He doubted it. So it was easier to just stay away and keep an eye on her from a distance. Until that evening when he found her drunk and stumbling out of a bar, and he had taken her home on her bike. Marc had slammed the door in his face, and he became even more worried about her safety. Luckily, she was with Sylvie now, and Marc was out of the picture.

"That's the gist of it. I hope you can forgive me for not telling you. But I always looked out for you, even if it was from afar." His eagerness seemed to wane as he fiddled with a napkin on the table, not making eye contact with them.

Once Frank had finished explaining everything, even where their father lived, Hélène felt a profound sense of ease. It was as if there had been a huge piece missing from the puzzle of her life, and he was the missing piece. At this point, she didn't want to think about her father. Later, if she wished, she could ask him for his address. Right now, she just wanted to help Frank, her brother, and she promised herself she would do everything in her power to help get him bathed, clothed, fed, and sheltered. Her heart beat quickly as blood raced through her veins. She had a new sense of urgency to make everything that had been going wrong for Frank right.

She and Sylvie shared a look that said, *We've got to help him.* They would find him a job, a safe place to live, help him with his drinking problem…and he would be as happy as could be. Hélène was sure of it. Inviting Frank for breakfast had been a great idea.

There they were, sitting in the same booth in the Café Hom@lone where she had sat with Ramon and Paul. She had been so afraid not too long ago, when Frank had walked by the window and seen her, and then she had spotted Sylvie with Aphrodite and thought they were lovers...and gotten sick in the bathroom because of it. How horrible that day had been.

Hélène smiled inwardly, realizing how much she had changed. Now, not only was she living with Sylvie, the love of her life, and their two adorable kitties, but she had a new family member whom she hadn't even known about. *Sacré Hilde. Sacré Maman!* All those feelings of loneliness and fear that had filled her in her former life with Marc were gone. She was a new person. Glowing with pride, she ran her fingers over her thighs, now firm from daily biking and swimming; inside and out, she was stronger, more independent, and couldn't imagine being happier than she was right now. Reaching across the table, she took Frank's knobby fingers in hers, and nudged Sylvie playfully. "I've got a brother."

CHAPTER TWENTY-TWO

Eight months later, behind a fresh bunch of yellow daisies, Sylvie watched her two goldfish swim together in their fishbowl. Goldie and Chaussette sat behind the bowl with their furry faces pressed side by side. Their bulging eyes were alert as they followed the shiny pair sliding so effortlessly through the water.

Kneeling on the floor, Sylvie pried her nose between the two kitties. The fishbowl created a distorted effect by greatly enlarging the threesome's eyes. Their bloated irises—like a six-pack of hard-boiled eggs—chased after Yin and Yang as they swam in circles to the rhythm of Greek gypsy music and water bubbles.

All of a sudden, Hélène's exuberant voice interrupted their amusement, "*J'ai fini, ma chérie!* I'm *finally* done!"

Like a trio of synchronized swimmers, Sylvie and the cats twisted their heads in unison. The kitties sat serenely while Sylvie hoisted her body to an erect position. She laughed as she looked in the mirror. Her enormous belly—hovering like a blimp between the cat's tiny heads—seemed to swell even more through the glass fishbowl. *I'm enormous. Just like a cow.* She pointed her blimp in Hélène's direction and waddled over to the sofa, where Hélène was sitting with a huge grin on her face.

"That's fantastic, my love!" exclaimed Sylvie in Greek. She draped her arms around Hélène's shoulders and planted a kiss on her neck.

"Take a look." Hélène handed her a thick stack of papers. "Hot off the press."

Sylvie couldn't contain her excitement. *She's finally done it. After all these months!* She read the title page out loud: "*Broad Awakening*, a novel by Hélène Du—" Clutching her belly, she gasped, "*Oh ma chérie!* It's ki...kicking! I think our baby likes the title!" She chuckled as Hélène pressed her ear against her bloated belly.

"*C'est vrai.*" Hélène nodded. "Sounds like someone's playing football in there!"

"Or karate!" Sylvie clutched the manuscript to her chest as Hélène eased her to the sofa. She couldn't contain her happiness as her lover propped her head with pillows, like a princess, then snuggled her body against hers. She loved having Hélène next to her. Cuddling had turned into one of her favorite pastimes. It was something Lydia and her other ex-girlfriends had hated, but she and Hélène could cuddle together for hours, whispering sweet nothings into each other's ear after making love.

"Good thing I lost all that weight." Hélène slung her arm around Sylvie's belly. "Otherwise, we wouldn't both fit on the sofa, *n'est-ce pas?* Little Miss Blimp—"

Sylvie grimaced. This sweet nothing wasn't so sweet. "That's so unfair. Having a baby wasn't only *my* idea, remember?" She poked Hélène playfully on the cheek. "I just happen to be younger, healthier, fitter, stronger—"

"And cuter." Hélène silenced Sylvie's lips with a soft kiss.

Giggling, Sylvie gasped for air. "*Ouais*, cuter. And—"

"Humbler, *non?*" Hélène tickled Sylvie's prominent nose.

"Precisely. All Greeks are humble. You should know that by now," replied Sylvie in Greek while puffing out her chest.

She laughed when Hélène frowned and said, "*Mince.* What have I gotten myself into?"

"Trouble, if you don't sit up this instant. I can't breathe." Sylvie prompted Hélène to climb off her. But she kept her close by. She had never felt as warm and loved as she did right now. She gazed into Hélène's eyes and, ever the expert swimmer, dove deeply into their midst. *Your eyes are as blue as the beautiful water of Santorini, my precious island.* To show Hélène how much she truly cared, she hugged her as tightly as she could without denting the tender bubble of flesh lodged between them. *I love you, and I love our baby. Our precious baby.*

Like an airplane, she dug her nose into Hélène's soft hair. After a moment of deep tenderness, she held up the manuscript before pecking Hélène's cheek. "I'm so impressed. *Tu sais*, you've come a long way since those silly poems you used to churn out—"

"*Attends!* Those were great poems." Hélène made a face. "I even stuck a few in the manuscript."

"I bet you did, *chérie. Voyons.*" Sylvie licked her finger and turned to page one. But she couldn't read the first line. Her eyes were tearing up. What had sparked these emotions? Okay, they joked around a lot, but didn't most couples tease each other? She shifted uncomfortably while dabbing at her tears with her shirt sleeve. *I'd do anything for you, Hélène. I love you so much.*

She cleared her throat and looked up. "*Désolée.* It's just…I'm sort of nervous. It's your first novel and all."

"*You're* nervous?" Hélène set her jaw. "What about *me*? You might hate it. You might want—"

"*Ah non.* Of course I won't, *chérie.*" Sylvie gave her one of her sly looks. "By the way, am I in it?"

Hélène snorted. "*Ne sois pas ridicule.* Of course you are!"

"How about Goldie?"

Sylvie forced herself to stay calm as Hélène tickled her ribs.

"Don't be silly; we're all in it!"

"*Super.*" Sylvie tried to contain spontaneous tickle giggles. "I've got an idea. Why don't you read it to me? I'm exhausted, with the baby and all." She pointed to her swollen belly.

"Happy to oblige, *mon amour.*" With a joyous voice, Hélène started reading her novel out loud.

Sylvie listened attentively while brushing strands of Hélène's hair from her beautiful blue eyes. How she loved the scent of her. She smelled as pure as fresh powder on a snowy mountain. As their love story unfolded, she looked at the pictures lining the wall behind them. Her favorite one was an enlarged photo of the two of them, together with Cecile and Mathilde. They were standing in their bathing suits on the beach, with their arms around each other's shoulders. The two suntanned couples were wearing diving masks, fins and snorkels. Behind their smiles fluttered a large Greek flag, with another flag next to it, declaring *Welcome to Santorini*.

Sylvie had had the best time of her life during that vacation. She wondered if Hélène had put it in her novel. She listened carefully as her lover started on the next page. As her ears absorbed Hélène's story, her eyes gravitated toward another photo.

Frank, previously without a home—freshly bathed, shaved, and coiffed by Jimmy's team of stylists—was wearing brand-new blue jeans and a stylish, beige cotton sweater. He had a relaxed demeanor in the photo as he sat, legs crossed, in his garden chair. He was conversing with the other dinner guests at Dionysos Taverna— at Hélène and Sylvie's most recent celebration of love. Sylvie had examined this photo many times. It was one of her favorites. In fact, she was planning to ask Frank if she could do a photo shoot with him soon, since this one had come out so well. She loved the discreet smile on his suntanned lips as his taste buds investigated the exquisite Greek dishes. He couldn't stop talking about how delicious they were. Of course, they were delicious. They were Greek. She knew each bite would be even more flavorful than the last.

It had warmed her heart that Vassilios had taken Frank in under the condition that he join Alcoholics Anonymous and quit drinking. After all these months, he was sticking to his promise of sobriety. And not only was he doing household tasks to contribute to their monthly rent, but Vassilios was training him to be a waiter at Dionysos Taverna. Like Hélène, he was a natural linguist and quickly learning Greek. After tasting the mouth-watering delicacies from his new place of employment, his ultimate goal was to become an expert chef.

She took another look at the recent photo of Frank, freshly coiffed and handsome in his beige sweater, relaxing in his lawn chair. *What a joy that we could help him get off the streets and into our lives. Our lives...* These two words brought her back to the novel. As Hélène turned each page, her excited voice filled the air, and Sylvie smiled inside. *It's our story. Our love story. And we're living it right now.* She knew deep down she had finally found the woman she wanted. Her heart told her so. She was so glad she had taken Yaya's advice. She had been courageous and followed her intuition instead of giving in to her doubts about chasing the wrong woman. She and Hélène were meant to be together. So were their kitties, who were getting along like angels. Thrilled to be an expectant mother, she caressed her huge belly. *We're a family.* Knowing this, Sylvie felt more complete and satisfied than she'd ever been in her life.

About the Author

Mickey Brent is a multicultural author and creative writing teacher who lives in Southern California with her partner. As an active member of the LGBTQ community, Mickey relishes the opportunity to share her ideas about the craft of writing, multiculturalism, LGBTQ issues, and her books with avid readers at local and international events, bookstores, libraries, and book clubs. Mickey spent nearly two decades living in Europe and loves writing quirky stories about Europeans, their diverse cultures, languages, and lifestyles. Mickey has written numerous travel articles, book chapters, poems, and screenplays, publishing various genres of fiction and nonfiction under other noms de plume. Mickey's objective is to offer readers a more fun, lighthearted, and romantic view of life. She has created this vivid reality with *Underwater Vibes*, a well-crafted, contemporary lesbian romance showcasing a unique cast of characters thriving in the multicultural city of Brussels, Belgium, the capital of Europe. In this exciting sequel, *Broad Awakening*, the memorable characters from *Underwater Vibes* continue their zany adventures in Brussels, Belgium, and Santorini, Greece.

For more information about Mickey and her speaking events, please visit www.mickeybrent.com.

Books Available From Bold Strokes Books

Against All Odds by Kris Bryant, Maggie Cummings, and M. Ullrich. Peyton and Tory escaped death once, but will they survive when Bradley's determined to make his kill rate 100 percent? (978-1-163555-193-8)

Autumn's Light by Aurora Rey. Casual hookups aren't supposed to include romantic dinners and meeting the family. Can Mat Pero see beyond the heartbreak that led her to keep her worlds so separate, and will Graham Connor be waiting if she does? (978-1-163555-272-0)

Breaking the Rules by Larkin Rose. When Virginia and Carmen are thrown together by an embarrassing mistake, they find out their stubborn determination isn't so heroic after all. (978-1-163555-261-4)

Broad Awakening by Mickey Brent. In the sequel to *Underwater Vibes*, Hélène and Sylvie find ruts in their road to eternal bliss. (978-1-163555-270-6)

Broken Vows by MJ Williamz. Sister Mary Margaret must reconcile her divided heart or risk losing a love that just might be heaven sent. (978-1-163555-022-1)

Flesh and Gold by Ann Aptaker. Havana, 1952, where art thief and smuggler Cantor Gold dodges gangland bullets and mobsters' schemes while she searches Havana's steamy red light district for her kidnapped love. (978-1-163555-153-2)

Isle of Broken Years by Jane Fletcher. Spanish noblewoman Catalina de Valasco is in peril, even before the pirates holding her for ransom sail into seas destined to become known as the Bermuda Triangle. (978-1-163555-175-4)

Love Like This by Melissa Brayden. Hadley Cooper and Spencer Adair set out to take the fashion world by storm. If only they knew their hearts were about to be taken. (978-1-163555-018-4)

Secrets On the Clock by Nicole Disney. Jenna and Danielle love their jobs helping endangered children, but that might not be enough to stop them from breaking the rules by falling in love. (978-1-163555-292-8)

Unexpected Partners by Michelle Larkin. Dr. Chloe Maddox tries desperately to deny her attraction for Detective Dana Blake as they flee from a serial killer who's hunting them both. (978-1-163555-203-4)

A Fighting Chance by T. L. Hayes. Will Lou be able to come to terms with her past to give love a fighting chance? (978-1-163555-257-7)

Chosen by Brey Willows. When the choice is adapt or die, can love save us all? (978-1-163555-110-5)

Gnarled Hollow by Charlotte Greene. After they are invited to study a secluded nineteenth-century estate, a former English professor and a group of historians discover that they will have to fight against the unknown if they have any hope of staying alive. (978-1-163555-235-5)

Jacob's Grace by C.P. Rowlands. Captain Tag Becket wants to keep her head down and her past behind her, but her feelings for AJ's second-in-command, Grace Fields, makes keeping secrets next to impossible. (978-1-163555-187-7)

On the Fly by PJ Trebelhorn. Hockey player Courtney Abbott is content with her solitary life until visiting concert violinist Lana Caruso makes her second-guess everything she always thought she wanted. (978-1-163555-255-3)

Passionate Rivals by Radclyffe. Professional rivalry and long-simmering passions create a combustible combination when Emmet McCabe and Sydney Stevens are forced to work together, especially when past attractions won't stay buried. (978-1-63555-231-7)

Proxima Five by Missouri Vaun. When geologist Leah Warren crash-lands on a preindustrial planet and is claimed by its tyrant, Tiago, will clan warrior Keegan's love for Leah give her the strength to defeat him? (978-1-163555-122-8)

Shadowboxer by Jessica L. Webb. Jordan McAddie is prepared to keep her street kids safe from a dangerous underground protest group, but she isn't prepared for her first love to walk back into her life. (978-1-163555-267-6)

9 781635 552706